LIVE
WIRE

JAY
MACLARTY

POCKET BOOKS
New York   London   Toronto   Sydney

The sale of this book without its cover is unauthorized. If you purchased this book without a cover, you should be aware that it was reported to the publisher as "unsold and destroyed." Neither the author nor the publisher has received payment for the sale of this "stripped book."

An *Original* Publication of POCKET BOOKS

POCKET BOOKS, a division of Simon & Schuster, Inc.
1230 Avenue of the Americas, New York, NY 10020

This book is a work of fiction. Names, characters, places and incidents are products of the author's imagination or are used fictitiously. Any resemblance to actual events or locales or persons, living or dead, is entirely coincidental.

Copyright © 2006 by Jay MacLarty

All rights reserved, including the right to reproduce this book or portions thereof in any form whatsoever. For information address Pocket Books, 1230 Avenue of the Americas, New York, NY 10020

ISBN-13: 978-1-4165-0347-7
ISBN-10:   1-4165-0347-1

This Pocket Books paperback edition April 2006

10 9 8 7 6 5 4 3 2 1

POCKET and colophon are registered trademarks of Simon & Schuster, Inc.

Cover design by Carlos Beltran

Manufactured in the United States of America

For information regarding special discounts for bulk purchases, please contact Simon & Schuster Special Sales at 1-800-456-6798 or business@simonandschuster.com.

Simon Leonidovich delivers the goods in Jay MacLarty's international thrillers

THE COURIER

"A perfect thriller. There is no putting this book down once it's opened."

—Bookreporter.com

"An edgy debut. . . . Leonidovich is a fascinating character. . . . A taut, enjoyable ride."

—*Publishers Weekly*

BAGMAN

"Razor sharp. . . . Equal parts Dashiell Hammett and James Patterson. . . . Heart-pounding, brilliantly paced. . . . An unmatchable, edge-of-your-seat thriller."

—Brad Thor

"MacLarty's writing is crisp and colorful. All of his characters, especially Simon, are carefully drawn with depth and complexity."

—*The Oakland Press*

"Well-rounded and compelling. [*Bagman*] has all the elements of a great thriller—and MacLarty balances these components expertly. . . . Simon [is] a character worth following."

—*Publishers Weekly*

Live Wire is also available as an eBook

Also by Jay MacLarty:

Bagman
The Courier

Steph
this one's for you, with love

Acknowledgments

Sometimes, even after you've done it a few times, writing a novel can be likened to rolling a very large boulder uphill. This book was very much like that, and I owe special thanks to those who helped push.

First and foremost, to my agent, Jane Dystel, and her partner, Miriam Goderich, who plucked *The Courier* from the pile, for which I'll always be thankful.

To my editor, Kevin Smith, for his unflagging encouragement and for giving me the time and space to work it out.

Anne Mazzulla, for her assistance with research.

Carole McKinnis and Elaine Nelson, for their suggestions and corrections of the manuscript.

Holly McKinnis, for being a good cheerleader, an underrated but important contribution.

To my friends and writing colleagues, who week by week, chapter by chapter, work so hard to make me better:

In Sacramento: Louise Crawford, Elizabeth Crain, and Gene Munger.

In Las Vegas: Marie Diane Gerace, Mark and Sunny Nelsen.

And finally, to the honorable and honorary president of my mythical fan club, Jackie Nugent, who with enthusiasm and generosity has purchased and sent copies of my previous books to so many "Texas boys" serving in Iraq.

LIVE
WIRE

CHAPTER ONE

The White House, Washington, DC

Friday, 21 May 17:18:59 GMT –0500

The two Marine guards snapped open the side-by-side doors, allowing Tucker to enter the West Wing without breaking stride. It was one of those little perks he would miss, all the bowing and scraping to his position. *Tucker Stark, Director of Central Intelligence,* he would miss that too. The job, the title—everything.

Christ Almighty, how did it come to this? What if the President hadn't made that one slip of the tongue—his acute interest in oil leases off the coast of Alaska—and what if Tucker hadn't started to investigate? What if he hadn't found the offshore corporations, the hidden accounts, the bearer bonds, and the foreign depositories the President used to hide his ownership and illegal profiteering? Accounts buried so deep, hidden behind so many shell corporations and false names that no official investigation—one that would need to abide by international regulations of confidentiality—would ever uncover.

The young woman behind the reception desk, a uniformed Secret Service agent, grinned with chirpy enthusiasm. "Good afternoon, Mr. Director."

Tucker forced his thoughts back to the here and

now and somehow managed to conjure up a smile. "Good afternoon." If only it was.

"You're looking very good today."

He knew better. Beneath his easy-fitting, summer-weight Armani suit, his six-foot, four-inch athletic body had started to go soft, a consequence of too many take-out meals since the death of his wife and children. For the first time since puberty, he looked older than his age—fifty-six—his hair having gone from black to steel gray in less than two years. "Thank you."

He scratched his name into the logbook and started down the hall, still questioning what he was about to do. But how could he not? Like it or not, he knew too much. And now that he understood the pattern, he could see how the President made financial decisions based on legislation he would either sign or veto. And worse, how he pushed for legislation simply to benefit his portfolio, even when it hurt the country. That was too much. *Way too much!* The man was a menace and had to be stopped.

Bette Ann Collins flashed an irritated scowl, just enough to let Tucker know this unscheduled late-afternoon visit was not appreciated. Though her title—Personal Secretary to the President of the United States—came with no special powers, Bette Ann was guard dog to the most powerful man in the world and wasn't shy about expressing her feelings, not even to the Director of Central Intelligence. "He's waiting."

Tucker didn't bother to respond—if he had his way the old bitch would be working for an ex-President soon enough—and pushed open the door to the Oval Office. John Paul Estes, the President's Chief of Staff, an unattractive man with more nervous tics and twitches than a hyperactive two-year-old, was pacing impatiently back and forth in front of the desk. The President was slumped in his chair, looking bored and anxious to escape his gilded cage. Tucker purposely ignored Estes—it was a game they played, one of mutual disrespect—and focused on the President. "Mr. President, thank you for seeing me on such short notice."

The President—tall and urbane in a perfectly tailored bluish-gray worsted suit—stood and extended his hand across the desk, a rosewood showpiece containing a stylish array of mementoes and photographs, and not a single file or scrap of paper. Just like the man, Tucker thought, all flash and facade. "No problem," the President said, showing his perfect and freshly whitened teeth. "No problem at all. The people's work must be done."

"I hope this is important," Estes said, "I've got a shit pile of reports I need to get through."

That Tucker believed. For all practical purposes, John Paul Estes ran the Executive branch of the government while the President campaigned, something he did sixteen hours a day, 365 days a year, election year or not. "When I call, Mr. Estes, you should pray it *isn't* important."

Estes smiled without humor and motioned toward one of the chairs facing the President's desk. "What's so critical it couldn't wait until morning?"

Tucker ignored the question and kept his eyes focused on the President. "I'm afraid it's a Red Issue, sir. Your ears only."

The President nodded with great solemnity—the perfect visage of Presidential concern and attention—and turned to his Chief of Staff. "I'm sorry, JP, you'll have to excuse us."

Estes expelled a long breath, letting Tucker know exactly how he felt about private conversations with the President. No one understood the man's intellectual limitations better than John Paul Estes, a secret he had diligently tried to protect for more than twenty-five years. "Is this really necessary?"

"I don't make the rules," Tucker answered. "If the President wants to share the information, that's up to him."

Estes recognized the trap immediately. If the President made such a decision before hearing the information he would look stupid, and if Estes insisted on sitting in, it would make the President look weak. "I'll be in my office." He gave the President a look, a secret exchange only the two of them understood. "Please call me when you're done." Despite the "please," it sounded more like an order than a request.

Tucker waited until the door closed before speaking. "I think we should move to your private office, sir."

"Oh?" A momentary look of confusion spread across the President's face, the time it took for him to grasp the implication, that this was not an Oval Office discussion, where conversations were routinely recorded. "Of course." For the first time he looked half interested, as if he expected Tucker to expose some juicy bit of political scandal. "Excellent idea."

That the President would assume it was "an excellent idea" only confirmed what Tucker now knew to be true: in addition to being an avaricious profiteer, the man had a room-temperature IQ—and the sooner he was gone, the safer the country would be.

Though Tucker had been Director for nearly two years, it was his first visit to the small room where Clinton had his infamous tryst with Monica Lewinsky. That history and the voyeuristic image it conjured up was more interesting than the room itself, which was rather plain and unimpressive, the walls decorated with photographs of the President and world dignitaries.

The President circled around behind his desk—a mahogany Chippendale style partners desk with drawers on both sides—and settled into his chair, a tufted leather wingback. "Okay, Tuck, what's up?"

"It's bad news, Mr. President." Tucker opened his laptop, wanting to check his countersurveillance scanner before saying too much. "Very bad."

The President frowned, apparently realizing that when the Director of Central Intelligence said "very bad" he wasn't referring to some innocuous bit of political scandal. "I'm listening."

Satisfied there were no active listening devices, Tucker activated the recorder and positioned the laptop on the edge of the desk, where the microphone could easily pick up their conversation. "It's North Korea."

"Again! I thought we settled all that."

"Yessir, but I'm afraid we dramatically misjudged the situation."

The furrow between the President's perfectly plucked eyebrows deepened significantly. "We?"

Exactly the response Tucker expected—the political response—the only language the President understood. Not *how* or *why,* but an immediate attempt to distance himself from the epicenter of any problem. "The Agency, Mr. President. Contrary to all the assurances we've received, and what we believed—" Tucker paused and took a deep breath. "We've now confirmed their nuclear program is not only active, but is much further along than we ever anticipated."

The wrinkles tightened around the President's eyes. "Define 'further along.'"

"Their efforts at miniaturization have been successful."

It was obvious from the President's expression he understood the ramifications. Without miniaturization America was relatively safe; a nuclear weapon was useless to any country without the missiles to deliver it, but once a bomb was miniaturized, it could be hidden and moved without limitation. "You're absolutely sure about this?"

"Yessir, we should have caught it earlier." Tucker tried his best to look appropriately contrite. "Much earlier."

"This is very bad news, Director. Very bad."

Tucker noted the shift from Tuck to Director, but that too was expected. "It gets worse."

The President rolled his hand impatiently. "Continue."

"It's on the street."

"On the street? You mean they're actually trying to sell the damn thing?"

"To anyone with money. And I mean anyone. Al-Qaeda, Hamas, Hezbollah—"

"They wouldn't dare."

They both knew that wasn't true; North Korea was one of the biggest arms dealers in the world, and they didn't get that way by judging the moral standards or intentions of their clients. "Yessir, I'm afraid they would."

The President shook his head angrily. "Christ Almighty, I guess we all knew it would come to this eventually."

"Yessir."

"You're absolutely sure?" he asked again, clearly hoping for a different answer.

"Yessir. One hundred percent."

"That's what you said about Iraq and WMD."

"That wasn't on my watch, sir."

"A distinction I doubt the UN will find convincing."

"The UN, sir?"

"Of course the UN," the President answered without any hesitation or doubt. "They're the ones who will have to handle this thing."

Tucker nodded, being careful to show only the slightest disapproval. "Yessir."

The President opened his mouth, then hesitated, a look of uncertainty creeping into his eyes. "You don't agree?"

"You said it yourself," Tucker answered, trying to make his disagreement sound like agreement. "Our track record is not so great. I doubt the UN would act on our information unless we can verify its credibility."

"You said it was solid."

"Yessir, absolute bedrock, but disclosing the information would mean exposing our most valuable intelligence-gathering asset."

"For God's sake, Director, we develop intelligence to protect ourselves from exactly this type of thing. Now you're suggesting we sit on our hands because it might compromise an asset? Don't you think that's just a bit ass backwards?"

"That's not—"

"And don't think for a minute that damn bomb wouldn't end up here in DC. You know better. Ever since Iraq we've been number one on everyone's hit list. No siree, I'm not letting some crazy-ass extremist group get their hands on a nuclear weapon just so you spy boys can protect an asset." The way he said *asset*, he might as well have said *dog shit*. "Not on *my* watch."

"This is no ordinary asset, sir. It's offensive as well as defensive."

"Are you saying it's a weapon?"

"No, sir, not exactly, not in the traditional sense, but it's certainly as dangerous as the bomb."

"As dangerous as the bomb," the President repeated, a look of confusion spreading across his face. "You're talking in riddles, Mr. Director."

Now it was *Mr. Director.* "Yessir, I guess I am. Sorry, it's just that . . . it's just that you're not going to like this."

"Meaning I should have been told about this *asset* earlier?"

Tucker nodded, trying again to look appropriately contrite. "It's the very latest in surveillance technology. Code name Live Wire."

The President nodded slowly, thinking. "So this is some kind of . . . what? Listening device?"

"Yessir," Tucker answered, surprised the man had connected the dots so quickly. "A satellite-deployed, wireless electronic ear combining the latest in laser, digital, and audio engineering, capable of isolating sound to an area as small as six square meters. Once we have a lock, we can follow that sound anywhere on the surface of the earth."

"When you say sound, are you talking about human conversation?"

"Yessir, that's exactly what I'm talking about. And with a voice print, which of course we have for virtually every public figure in the world—" To emphasize his point, he purposely let his gaze wander toward the photographic array of world leaders. "—we now have the ability to identify and track their movements."

"And listen to every word they say?"

"Yessir, every grunt, grumble, and fart."

"Jesus H. Christ!" The President slumped back in his chair. "Big brother is truly here."

"Yessir."

"And it's us."

Despite all his preparation and cerebral role-playing, Tucker could barely maintain his somber expression. "Yessir."

The President expelled a deep breath, a sigh of resignation. "So if I understand this correctly, if you've got a bird sitting over Washington with this technology you can hear every word that's spoken?"

"Not quite. Not yet anyway. At this point it's target specific."

"And if the Oval Office were that target?"

"Yessir, we could hear any conversation and identify any speaker."

"In other words—" The President turned and stared pointedly toward his wall of dignitaries. "I can forget about ever having a private conversation."

Tucker scowled, just a little, as if he found the idea offensive. "Believe me, sir, we would never target the White House."

"I'm sorry, Mr. Director, but this is Washington, where people trade secrets for power. I don't have a lot of confidence in *never*."

"I understand your concern, Mr. President, but think of the possibilities. Once we have someone in the crosshairs of Live Wire, they're ours. If we had this technology in 2003 we could have gotten Saddam without ever planting a boot in Iraq."

"That sounds great, and I'm sure many people would see it exactly that way."

"But you don't?"

"I've read *1984*. It's not an appealing picture."

Tucker could barely contain his skepticism; the President was a legendary nonreader and was rumored to ignore even his PDBs—the Presidential Daily Briefing memos—that summarized the important issues of the day. "I understand your concern, Mr. President. At least we're the only ones who have the capability."

"At this point," the President said, throwing Tucker's words back at him. "Technology has a way of advancing and spreading without regard to political borders or ideology."

"Yessir, I'm afraid you're right, there's no way to contain the evolution. Our only defense is a good offense, to stay ahead of the pack."

"And if we go to the UN with this bomb thing, it would open the doors to the pack?"

"All we have are recorded conversations," Tucker answered. "The words are conclusive, but unless we could prove their legitimacy, which we can't do without exposing Live Wire, the Security Council would never accept or act on the information."

The President slumped lower in his chair. "I'm afraid you're right. So if we don't go to the UN, how do we handle this thing? What's your recommendation?"

Tucker smiled to himself—they both knew it wasn't his job to recommend, it was his job to lay out the options—but he had the hook set and could now yank the President in exactly the right direction. "We have a number of choices, sir. The decision, of course, is yours." Tucker knew that was the last thing the President wanted to hear. The man didn't like choices. Didn't like making decisions. He wanted consensus and the denial of responsibility. Tucker raised a hand, one finger extended. "We could send in the Army." Something he knew would never happen, not after the military quagmire in Iraq.

The President took a deep breath, visibly trying to reenergize. "No, we'd end up fighting the Chinese. Besides, the American public would never buy it. I even whisper WMD and they'd be storming the gates."

Tucker nodded and extended a second finger. "Full economic sanctions."

The President shook his head. "Too slow. We have to stop this thing before it happens."

Third finger. "Naval blockade."

"A lot of good that would do," the President snapped back. "If I remember correctly, they share a border with China. How do we close that?"

Tucker ignored the question—it wasn't meant to be answered—and extended a fourth finger. "We could buy the bomb ourselves. Through a surrogate, of course."

"And what exactly would that accomplish?"

"It would give us time to work on the problem."

The President hesitated, thinking about it. "That's

assuming they only have one of the damn things to sell. Do we know that?"

Tucker shook his head, admitting the weakness of such a plan. It wasn't, of course, a serious proposal—none of them were—he was simply working the President toward the deep water.

"What else?"

"After that—" Tucker hesitated, trying to appear reluctant. "—after that the ideas get a little weird, sir."

"Like what?"

"Like a terrible nuclear accident. The bomb exploding on their soil."

"We could do that?" the President asked, his tone a mixture of interest and indignation.

"No, but we could lay down one of our own and claim that's what happened."

"And we could sell that?"

"To the American public," Tucker answered, "no problem. They believe anything their President repeats often enough." He smiled, acknowledging the President's power to *tell and sell*, the mantra of his political career. "To the Russians and Chinese—no. They would know immediately what we did. As would the Brits, but we could control that."

The President shook his head. "Too risky, we could end up in a nuclear war. What else?"

The hook was set, time to start reeling the man in. "We could overthrow the government."

The President stared back across the desk, his expression fixed and rigid, the polite half-smile of someone not quite sure what was being suggested. "I assume that's the government of Kim Jong-il you're talking about, Director."

Tucker barked a laugh, as if that was the funniest damn thing. "Yessir, of course."

The President nodded, then rocked back in his chair and stared at the ceiling, the image of a man struggling with a great moral dilemma. Tucker knew better. A politician struggling with morality was like a professional wrestler contemplating his next move: how to make the phoniness look real. This display of ethical contemplation continued for a good three minutes before the President finally rocked forward and asked the question Tucker had been waiting to hear. "Could that be accomplished?"

"Yessir, I believe it could."

"Lay it out."

"As you know—" Tucker seriously doubted if the President could find North Korea on a map. "—there's widespread opposition within the country to Kim's government. Most of this resistance is disorganized and ineffective, a bunch of hungry wolves howling at the moon, but there is one anti-Kim faction, the KUP, who could pull it off—given the proper financial and logistical support."

"The KUP?" A bewildered frown slowly creased the President's forehead. "I don't recall hearing that name."

"They're a small group, but well organized."

"What's their agenda?"

"Reunification with the South. That's what KUP stands for, the Korean Unification Party."

"Unify as what? What's their political ideology?"

"As a democracy," Tucker answered without hesitation, knowing that's what it would take to get the President's support. "They've seen it work in the South. They want to be part of it."

"But you said they were small. Who would do the fighting? And don't tell me mercenaries, Director. The last thing we need is another Bay of Pigs."

"No, sir, absolutely not. The group has good leadership. If we gave them the plan and the money, they could do it themselves."

"It doesn't sound like there's enough time to get something like that organized. We can't let that bomb slip through our fingers . . ."

"It could be done, sir. It's not like they need to take over the country. They get rid of Kim and the government will collapse."

"But how can you be sure this group ends up in control?" the President asked, his tone doubtful.

"That shouldn't be hard," Tucker answered, trying to make it sound simple. "The media is owned and controlled by the government. Whoever controls the media controls the people. We'll make sure our boys—" He used the words *our boys* purposefully, trying to give the proposal a proprietary feel. "—have the only voice."

"Even so, with all the planning and—"

"Already done, sir. The operational plan was one of a dozen what-if contingency plans we developed

with the military last year. And now that we have
Live Wire, we'll know exactly where Kim is—" He
paused, just long enough to make the point. "—and
how to deal with him." A euphemism for *assassinate,*
which was illegal under current law.

The President nodded slowly, the wheels turning
as he tried to anticipate every possible outcome and
how he could spin it to the press and sell it to the
public. "We couldn't afford another debacle like
Iraq," he warned, "where we lost control after the
battle was over."

"No, sir, we can't have that," Tucker answered, as
if the decision had already been made. "And we
won't."

"You sound very sure about this, Tuck. That's not
like you."

Good, back to Tuck. "Yessir, I'm sure it's the right
thing. That doesn't mean I don't have concerns."

"Such as?"

"Containment," Tucker answered. "If word gets
out, we're dead."

The President rolled his eyes heavenward. "Literally, if we don't get that bomb."

Tucker nodded, showing a bit of reluctance, as if
he were the one who needed convincing.

"Who knows about all this?"

"Only one analyst," Tucker answered. "I'm trying
to keep the lid on Live Wire. All the reports come
to me."

"That's good," the President said, assuming the

tone of command. "And how many people would it take to pull off this operation?"

"If you give me the go-ahead I could do everything outside The Company. All contact with the KUP could be handled through independent contractors. They wouldn't even know who they were working for. I'm sure I can handle containment on my end—" He paused, trying to ascertain whether the President had picked up the challenge, couldn't be sure, and hammered it home. "It's the White House I'm worried about."

"I don't see the problem," the President responded. "I'd prefer not to involve anyone at this end."

"Of course." But it wasn't the White House in general that Tucker worried about; it was one man, John Paul Estes, who never let the President do anything before the idea was vetted and tested before a focus group to be sure the President could *sell it,* whatever it was. "What about Mr. Estes? I suppose you'll need to run it by him." Tucker purposely used the word *need,* subtly implying the President couldn't make the decision on his own.

The President hesitated a moment, then shook his head. "JP's got enough on his plate. We'll keep this between us."

Tucker tried to hide his relief behind another question. "What about the National Intelligence Director?"

"Does he know about Live Wire?"

"No, sir."

"Let's keep it that way. It's hard enough to keep a secret in this town." The President leaned forward, an expression of deep concern, one he usually reserved for victims of natural disasters. "Tuck, you understand, if something goes wrong I won't be able to cover your back?"

"Yessir, I do understand. That's the way it should be."

"We're talking about the presidency here, not me, you understand, *the institution.*" He made it sound like the pearly gates to heaven. "This country doesn't need another Watergate."

"I understand, sir."

"This is not a political thing," the President continued, his tone shifting from concern to cheerleader. "We're not nation-building here."

"No, sir, absolutely not."

The President began counting off the objectives, as if he needed to justify his position. "We're overthrowing a dictatorial regime more interested in selling bombs than feeding their citizens. We're clearing the Korean peninsula of nuclear weapons. We're reunifying North and South Korea as a democracy."

"Those are all righteous causes, sir."

"The people deserve it, Tuck."

Tucker wasn't sure what *people* the President meant—the people starving in North Korea, the people who might be incinerated by a nuclear explosion, or just the people of the world—but he wasn't about to start questioning Presidential grandiosity. "Yessir, they do. And if we pull this off—" Tucker nodded his head deliberately, as if he actually believed the words coming out of his mouth. "This, sir, will be your legacy."

The President smiled, clueless as to the legacy Tucker had in mind.

CHAPTER TWO

Las Vegas

Simon glanced at his watch—*Ugh*, eighteen minutes to go—and immediately reduced his pedal rate. The problem with a stationary bike, he decided, was the stationary. The same repetitive motion, the same view, the same pain in the ass. Not that the eighth fairway on the TPC Canyons offered a bad view—a plush river of grass surrounded by rocks and sand and a dozen varieties of cactus—but it was hard to enjoy the landscape when the temperature, even in the shade of the awning, exceeded a hundred degrees and you were pumping away in one spot for thirty minutes.

Caitlin stepped onto the porch, a tray of fruit and cheese in one hand, a glass of white wine in the other. She had shed her work attire in favor of a sleeveless cotton blouse and white drawstring shorts that made her slender legs look even longer and tanner than normal. "Want something to drink?" she asked, sliding the tray onto a small teakwood table next to one of the swivel lounges.

"Sounds great." Twelve minutes and his T-shirt was already soaked with sweat. "How about a Corona?"

She cocked her head, a kind of half-teasing, half-admonishing expression. "Now that makes a lot of sense, Leonidovich, drink beer while you exercise."

"I exercise so I *can* drink beer. It's a vicious cycle."

"Don't give me that bull, you're back on that machine because you're trying to lose weight again—"

He glanced down at the sweat dripping off his legs—the only really toned part of his body—and grunted a denial. But of course he was trying to lose weight. He was always trying to lose weight.

"Because you think that's what I want."

Not true. After six months together he actually believed she liked his oil-tanker body—weird as that seemed—but that didn't mean he did. What man wanted to feel like Frumpy the Frog standing next to Cinderella? No, not Cinderella. Caitlin Wells was not some virginal fantasy. Caitlin Wells was a woman, a real woman—from the top of her taffy-blond hair all the way down to her firm breasts, down to her flat stomach and narrow hips, down, down, down those long, slender legs to the very bottom of her bare feet—seventy-one perfect inches of beauty and brains. *Oh mama!*—how did you get so lucky, Leonidovich? "Why should I care what you think, Wells? Las Vegas is full of beautiful women with long legs."

"And plastic boobs bigger than my head," she fired back.

"I love plastic."

"No, you love me and my real ones, small as they are."

He couldn't deny that, not unless he wanted to sleep on the couch. "Maybe a little."

She narrowed her eyes. "Just a little?"

"But lots of lust, Wells. Significant lust."

"Lust!" She feigned a look of outrage. "That's all I am to you, Leonidovich, your Sin City hottie?"

"Don't marginalize my feelings, Wells. I'm deeply committed to this lust."

She groaned and laughed at the same time. "Okay, commitment is good. It's one of the twelve key words in the female handbook."

Number two—right after *marriage*—he would have bet the family marbles on that.

She started toward the door. "You want a lime in that beer?"

"Please." He leaned into the pedals, determined to stay at least even in his war against calories and bad cholesterol. Domesticity, he decided, was not bad. Not bad at all. Good, actually. *Very good.* But not simple: dividing his time between New York and Las Vegas, between two offices, between Caitlin's townhouse in the desert and his hotel apartment overlooking Central Park, between bachelorhood and . . . ? What? Where was this going? What did she expect? Unlike most women, Caitlin never mentioned marriage, never indicated she even thought about it. He couldn't ask, not without some hint, not if there was any chance she might turn him down; things like that had a way of ending relationships. What about children? If her forty-two-year-old biological clock was doing any nervous ticking, he hadn't heard it. And what did he want? For the relationship not to end, he was sure of that.

She was back in less than a minute with a cold beer and an equally cold hand towel, which she draped over his shoulders. "Don't go having a heart attack, Leonidovich, you're not so young anymore."

"Younger than you, Wells." Only thirty days, but he liked to remind her frequently of her *senior* status.

"Older and wiser," she shot back. "You don't see me out here gasping for air in the heat."

"No—" He took a quick breath, trying not to sound winded. "—you're out here at five in the morning—" Quick breath. "—a sure sign of senility if I ever saw one."

She retreated to her chair and glass of wine. "No better way to start the day—the sun coming over the mountains, a nice cool breeze rippling over your bare skin."

"Bare?"

"Of course, I always ride in the raw."

Ride in the raw, now that conjured up an enticing image. "Simon says"—quick breath—"big sweaty man know when to change mind."

"Ha! Big sweaty man think with little head."

Before he could defend himself from this scurrilous attack—true as it was—his cellular began to vibrate. He reached down, unclipped the tiny unit from his workout shorts—a new smartphone with lots of cool features and an incomprehensible manual—read the number on the display, then whispered loudly into the receiver, "I told you never to call me here."

Of course he knew it was Lara, his sister, the other bookend in his female-dominated life. "I think she's getting suspicious."

Caitlin rolled her blue-gray eyes, not fooled for a second.

"Is she there?" Lara asked.

"Uh-huh."

"Tell her she could do better."

"Thanks, Sis." He pressed the MUTE button. "Lara says you're one lucky woman, Wells. That you could never do better."

"You tell her, *better* is a *relative* term."

He released the button. "Caitlin says when it comes to *relatives,* I could do better."

"Ha! You tell her . . . hey, what's all that huffing and puffing? Don't tell me you're—"

"Don't you even go there, Sissie. The only thing I'm riding is a bike. What's up?"

"Just got a call," Lara answered, switching to her all-business voice. "Some guy from the State Department. John Clayton. *Insists* on speaking to you."

"Regarding?"

"Refused to say. In his words, 'the matter is urgent and private.' I explained that I was the brains behind this outfit, but he didn't seem impressed."

"I understand, I've never been impressed with your brains either." Nothing, of course, could have been further from the truth; Lara was like a super-computer when it came to speed and efficiency.

"I'll get you for that one, Boris."

And he knew she would—any excuse to embarrass

her older brother with the story of how Boris Leonidovich Pasternak Simon became Simon Leonidovich—but that was just part of their relationship, all the good-natured jabbing and poking. "You sure he didn't think we were FedEx?"

"No, he didn't think we were FedEx." She made a little spitting sound. "May their name be written on the buttocks of Satan."

"Be nice, Sissie, they're not our competition and you know it. They do their thing, we do ours."

"I tried to lay out our fee structure—that always scares away the idiots—but he wasn't interested."

"Wasn't interested?"

"That's right. Said cost wasn't a concern."

Wasn't a concern—no wonder the government couldn't balance their checkbook. "So how did you leave it?"

"He's waiting for your call. I just sent you a text message with the number. You should have it."

Simon glanced at the phone's display. The envelope icon was open and blinking, indicating he had a text message waiting. "You sure this guy's legitimate? Did the call come through the State Department switchboard?"

"No, I tried to back-trace the number but couldn't get a thing. Zip. Even my guy at the phone company couldn't tell me anything."

Lara had dozens of *guys*—a generic term that included women as well as men, all technocrats who loved to show and share their hacking skills—but she hadn't dated seriously in six years, not since her husband died, and not at all since her traumatic experience with Eth Jäger. "Couldn't or wouldn't?"

"Couldn't. According to the phone company, the number is unassigned."

Though it sounded odd, he realized the State Department probably had scores of unregistered numbers for things they considered *urgent and private.* "Okay, Sis, I'll give the man a call. And you give the kids a kiss from their uncle Simon."

"Good night, Boris."

"And don't call me—" But as usual she had gotten in the last word and was already gone. "Damned woman."

Caitlin gave him a puzzled look. "She called you a damned woman?"

"No, that was me striking back at the female race."

Her puzzlement dissolved into a look of amusement. "Good luck with that."

Right—all the luck in the world wouldn't change anything—he was outnumbered and surrounded. He snapped the phone into its clip, checked his watch—twenty-nine minutes—and immediately began to ease off on the pedals. "I need to make a call, want me to go inside?"

She shook her head. "I'll keep my mouth shut."

He slid into the chair beside her, attached his earplug to the phone, pulled the stylus, highlighted the number in Lara's text message, and tapped CONNECT. Despite the lousy manual, the phone was intuitive and easy to use. More important, it included full PDA and MP3 functionality, thus eliminating two electronic gadgets from his travel bag. A soft click interrupted the first ring, followed immediately by a computer-generated voice: *Please identify yourself, your company, and the party to whom you wish to speak.*

"This is Simon Leonidovich—" He made a point to pronounce his name slowly—Le-on-o-vich—letting them know the *d* was silent. "—with WorldWide SD, returning Mr. Clayton's call."

Instantly, another soft click echoed back over the line. "This is John Clayton." His voice was flat and without resonance—not that different from the synthesized recording—as if his words were being run through a computer and washed of any distinctive markers. "I appreciate you getting back to me so promptly."

"What can I do for you, Mr. Clayton?"

"We have some documents we need delivered overseas. Pretty routine stuff for you, I'm sure."

Too routine. Why would the government spend ten thousand dollars—his minimum fee—for *pretty routine* when they had their own team of couriers operating under the auspices of diplomatic immunity? "Who's we?"

"I explained that to your secretary. I'm with the State Department."

Secretary, Lara would love that. Among her many self-anointed titles—Office Manager, Executive Administrative Assistant, Irreplaceable One—secretary was most decidedly *not* on her list. "Oh, she failed to mention that." He gave Caitlin a little wink. "You know women, they're so scatterbrained." He managed to absorb a poke in the ribs without yelping into the man's ear. "Just some documents, you say?"

"Yes."

Either the man was an automaton or purposely holding back. "Then you sure have come to the right place," Simon said, easing into his Simple Simon act, hoping the man might be encouraged to open up. "WorldWide Special Delivery, that's our name, that's our game."

"How soon could you be in Washington?"

"Well, let me see now." He tapped the phone's CALENDAR icon, though he already knew he had nothing scheduled for the next few days. "We could have someone there tomorrow."

"Not someone," Clayton said, the words, if not the tone, finally revealing a bit of emotion. "We want you to deliver the documents personally."

Simon had already assumed that—the man did *insist* on a personal conversation—but it didn't explain *why*. "I assure you, all our agents are bonded and—"

"No," Clayton interrupted, the soft lash of admonishment in his tone. "We don't want some off-duty casino guard handling State Department documents."

Simon nodded to himself; someone had obviously done their homework if they knew he now used Sand Castle security officers to handle some of his routine assignments. It also told him the job was anything but *routine*. "Okay, I'll need a few details." He tapped the phone's RECORD icon. "Let's start with destination." Then the ON button. "Where are the documents to be delivered?"

"I don't feel comfortable discussing this over the phone," Clayton answered. "We can review the details when you get here."

Hardly routine, and though it was against his self-imposed rules to accept any assignment without the details, he couldn't blame the State Department for being cautious. "Okay, where exactly is *here?*" As Clayton dictated, his voice as monotonous and irritating as a running toilet, Simon entered the address in the phone's NOTEPAD program—just to be on the safe side—even though the conversation was being recorded. "What time?"

"10 A.M."

Ugh, another long and sleepless night at thirty thousand feet. "Okay, see you then."

"Ask for Uncle Sam."

Uncle Sam, was the guy trying to be funny or . . . ? There was a soft click and the line went silent. "Yeah, nice talking to you too." *Jackass.* He pressed the END button, terminating both the recording and the call. "A swell guy."

Caitlin nodded knowingly. "Meaning you're ditching me for him."

"I wouldn't put it exactly like that."

"How would you put it?"

"It's a family thing. Uncle Sam needs me."

"The government?"

"State Department."

"Since when did the State Department start using private couriers?"

"Good question."

"Can they afford you?"

"Apparently so, I paid a lot of taxes last year."

"Thanks to my boss."

"Speaking of Big Jake, when's he getting back?"

"Now there's a question—" She snorted with amusement. "If Billie has her way, this is one honeymoon that's never going to end."

"Weird honeymoon, taking their daughter and grandson along."

"It's apparently working, they've been gone four months. So when are you leaving, Leonidovich?"

He hated to tell her—he'd been back less than forty-eight hours—but as hard as it was, he believed his frequent absences actually strengthened their relationship; they never had a chance to become *comfortable*, the bane of lust and passion. "In about four hours. I need to catch the red-eye to DC."

She nodded in an understanding way, though failed to keep the disappointment out of her voice. "How long this time?"

"Not long. The guy said it was just a routine document drop." Even as he said it, he didn't believe it. "But I'll probably spend a day or two in New York on the return leg."

Her eyes narrowed. "If the job's so routine, why don't you have one of the other guys do it?"

He shrugged, pretending to have no idea. "For some reason they want me to handle it personally."

"See—" She poked the word at him, as if that was exactly what she suspected. "—that's what happens when you become famous." She held up her hands, painting the words in the air. "Simon Leonidovich, the man who can deliver anything, anywhere."

"Don't you start with that, Wells, people are going to start believing that crap."

"Of course they believe it. Why do you think Uncle Sam called?"

That was exactly why. And that's what bothered him.

CHAPTER THREE

Washington, DC

Friday, 4 June 21:35:06 GMT –0500

Tucker Stark glanced at his watch—9:35—then turned back to the double row of high-definition, twelve-inch surveillance monitors located on the soundproof wall separating the driver from the van's rear compartment. They were heading south on North Capitol, toward Union Station, the evening traffic unusually heavy. Tucker swiveled toward the audio console and toggled the communication switch marked DRIVER. "How we doing?"

The woman—who looked no more imposing than a middle-aged librarian, but was in fact a well-trained and highly skilled former East German double agent who owed her life and loyalty to Stark—glanced toward the pinhole camera hidden in the sun visor. "I think we'll make it."

"It's important." He didn't want to be late—the general was a stickler about punctuality—but realized there was little the woman could do without drawing attention, and that was the last thing Tucker wanted. The problem with Washington—post 9–11 Washington—were all the damn cameras. The city had become a fishbowl—you couldn't diddle your

secretary without someone recording the event. It
was, in his opinion, a contributing factor in the erosion of American society, in the erosion of government, and more specifically in the erosion of those
elected to run it. No one with a modicum of common
sense would subject themselves to the unrelenting
scrutiny of the press, the attack ads, and the unblink-
ing eye of the camera. Certainly not the people who
made things happen, who pushed society forward in
business and culture and science, and who, as a result of their achievements, created controversy and
enemies. No, the doers were too smart to run for
public office, they left it to others: the mediocrists,
the failed lawyers, and the political pretty boys,
whose sole talent lay in their ability to avoid controversy and do nothing. Make no waves. *Disgusting!*

As the van turned onto Massachusetts Avenue,
Tucker kept his eyes fixed on the monitor marked
5–7—indicating the camera's visual scope in relation
to clock hours—watching carefully for any sign of a
tail. The possibility seemed highly remote—the van
was registered to a well-respected delivery service,
painted to match their fleet, and displayed no outward signs of its electronic gadgetry—but you could
never be too careful, not when it came to overthrowing the government. He toggled the communication
switch. "Clear."

The woman nodded, knowing her head and shoulders were visible on at least one of the eight monitors, and turned into the Union Station lot. She
circled around—just someone looking for a good

place to park—while Tucker continued to monitor the entrance. "Clear."

The woman nodded again and continued to circle until she found two available spots side-by-side. She pulled into the left slot and turned off her lights, letting the engine idle. Tucker glanced at his watch—9:45—smiled to himself and punched the slot number into a text message on his cellular and pressed SEND. No other information was necessary, the numbers meaningless to anyone who hijacked the signal. Five minutes later a nondescript Ford Freestar with sliding doors on both sides and dark privacy glass pulled into the vacant spot. Tucker flipped the INTERNAL RECORD switch to OFF, which in fact activated the recorder and twenty-eight microphones hidden throughout the van—an insurance policy he hoped never to use—then killed the lights and slid open the door. The side of the Freestar was no more than two inches away, the doors perfectly aligned. He reached out, tapped the dark window, and stepped aside. The door slid open and two figures stepped across the narrow opening between the two vehicles. Tucker barely had time to close the door and snap on the lights before the van started to move. The entire exercise, from the time the Freestar pulled in until the van pulled away, took less than fifteen seconds.

Captain "Buddy" Baggett settled into his usual spot at the control console, his gaze already fixed on the eight surveillance monitors. Though dressed in civvies, his shirt and slacks were dead-on army green; the same color, Tucker suspected, that ran through the man's veins. Even sitting, Baggett seemed to be at attention, erect and alert, ready to explode into action at the first sign of trouble, his forty-year-old, hard-ass body honed by years of military training. With his clean-shaven head and sun-beaten skin, he had the intense, get-out-of-my-way-or-die look of an army Ranger, which he had been prior to becoming the general's military attaché. Where he acquired the nickname "Buddy," Tucker couldn't imagine; the man was less congenial than a rattlesnake, and the two of them never spoke unless absolutely necessary. In fact, Captain Buddy Baggett was about the only man on earth Tucker Stark actually feared.

The general lowered himself into one of the two remaining chairs at the back of the van and waited for Tucker to sit before speaking. "Corporal."

Tucker nodded. It had been that way for over thirty years, since their time together in Vietnam, when Tucker had been a lowly corporal and the general a second louie fresh out of West Point. When the war ended, Tucker left his military career behind, his rank forever frozen in the general's mind. "Good evening, General." Though his crewcut had gone from dark to gray and his uniform from camouflage fatigues to a black tuxedo, the man looked no less imposing than when he first arrived in Vietnam. "You're looking especially dapper this evening."

The general gave a scornful chuckle. "Just another damn fund raiser. Democracy for sale."

"Yessir, we need to change that." And there wasn't a doubt in Tucker's mind that this was the man to do it, the man who could lead America back to greatness. A man who had proven himself in battle as well as peacetime. A man with respect for the past and a vision for the future. A man with brains as well as balls. Everything but the vanilla personality and good looks so necessary for political success in the land of red, white and blue. No, despite all his talents and achievements, the general was too outspoken, too honest, and too independent to be elected dogcatcher, let alone President.

The general swiveled his chair toward Baggett. "Captain, are we good to go?"

Baggett momentarily diverted his attention from the video monitors to a cluster of dials and switches that controlled the van's antisurveillance equipment. "Yessir, all systems GTG."

Obsessively careful, the general pulled a tiny cellular from beneath his cummerbund and checked the display, which showed a flat-line signal despite the fact that they were now rolling west on Pennsylvania Avenue—literally at the epicenter of microwave heaven—halfway between the Capitol and the White House. He nodded, satisfied that no one could tap into their conversation, and turned back to Tucker. "Okay, Corporal, what's our status?"

"GTG," Tucker answered. "The facility is ready. Everyone is in place."

"All freelance?"

"Yessir, all foreign born, all holding foreign passports."

"Anyone asking questions?"

"No, sir. No one has any idea who they're working for or what the mission is about."

"The courier?"

"Contacted," Tucker answered. "He'll be here in the morning."

"Our liaison with the KUP?"

"Standing by."

"Timetable?"

"On schedule."

The general leaned back in his chair, his fingers entwined over his chest, his gold-embossed "US Army" cuff links glinting from his sleeves. "You still think a trial run is necessary?"

Tucker hesitated, the question enough to indicate the general had doubts, but if they skipped the trial and something went bad, some unanticipated glitch, they would never get a second chance. "Yessir, I do."

"Why?"

Tucker wasn't used to being questioned in such a manner—as if he *really was* a lowly army corporal rather than Director of Central Intelligence—but was careful not to show his irritation. "We have time. The festival is still two weeks off."

"You think it's that important?"

"Yessir, we need the crowd and the cameras." Tucker could see the general was unconvinced, so he bolstered the point with a military argument. "Even more important, if I was running the KUP, I'd be planning on, if not expecting, some kind of double-cross. That's how they've managed to survive for so long in a police state, by anticipating the worst. We need to suck them in with enough money and good information to validate our intentions."

The general didn't reply for a long moment, thinking it through. "Right. Advance misdirection. Okay, I'll buy that. And what about the President? Any chance he'll open up to Estes?"

Any chance. Another question with no right answer. Tucker glanced toward the monitors. They were just passing the White House, most of the lights still burning. "There's always a chance, but it hasn't happened yet."

"You're sure."

"Yessir. One peep out of the President and Estes would light up the phones with questions about Live Wire." Tucker could barely contain a smile of satisfaction. "And since the weapon only exists in my mind, no one could tell him anything. He would have to call me."

"Yes. Right." The great man nodded thoughtfully. "That was a very clever idea, Corporal."

Tucker tipped his head, surprised at the compliment; not something the general handed out with abandon. "Thank you, sir."

"And you don't think that will happen?"

"No, sir. The President is more concerned about his portfolio than he is about the country. As long as Rome isn't burning, he's not going to raise any alarms."

"He's that consumed?"

"Yessir. At the present rate he's going to rake in over two hundred million this year alone. You can hardly blame the man for wanting to be reelected. Another term and he'll come out of office a billion-aire twice over."

The general made a sour face. "The man has no shame." He shook his head, a look of deep regret. "Even so, I hate doing this."

"Yessir, we all do."

"There's just no other way."

Tucker might have mentioned that the Constitution prescribed another way—a little something called elections—but he knew better than to say that, even in jest. One more election, one more do-nothing avaricious President, and there wouldn't be any country to save.

CHAPTER FOUR

Washington, DC

Saturday, 5 June 09:50:12 GMT –0500

Simon stared up at the building, then down at his notes, making sure he had the right address. Located near Capitol Hill, one of the city's more desirable commercial areas, the ten-story building of green glass and gray steel was not exactly what he expected when he thought of the State Department.

The cabbie swiveled around in his seat. "Twenty-two fifty."

Satisfied he had the right address, Simon slipped a twenty and two fives into the plexi money slot and stepped onto the curb. Though not yet hot, in comparison to Vegas the air was suffocating, heavy with moisture and sticky as taffy. With his travel bag in one hand and his security case in the other, he shouldered his way through the heavy glass door and into the lobby. The area was large and empty, green marble from floor to ceiling, without adornment or directory, and utterly silent, not even the obligatory Muzak to fill the void. The far wall contained a bank of three elevators, no buttons, and a flat telephone panel with instructions.

ENTER SUITE NUMBER

Simon punched in the number, realized he was staring directly into the fish-eye lens of a security camera, and offered a congenial smile.

A female voice, polite and distinctly Asian, echoed through the tiny speaker. "May I help you, please?"

"This is Simon Leonidovich, with WorldWide SD. I'm here to pick up a package."

"Yes, thank you." The door to the nearest elevator began to slide open. "We are here expecting you."

Here, Simon quickly discovered, was a door on the eighth floor marked North Korean Trade Legation. Considering the current embargo against all North Korean imports, he had a feeling the office might be an unofficial and unrecognized front for the DPRK— the Democratic People's Republic of Korea—which, despite the presumption of its name, was not *democratic,* was not a *republic,* and did not represent *the people.* The door opened into a pristine and rather austere waiting area with a circular reception counter, home to an extremely attractive young woman dressed in a traditional Korean hanbok. Some things were the same everywhere, Simon thought, East or West, Communist or capitalist: the receptionist was always chosen for her physical attributes. By the time he reached the counter, the woman was standing and smiling, one of those wickedly demure little smiles that Asian women did so well. "You would be Mr. Leonidovich, no?" Though heavily accented—the *v* in his name pronounced as a *w*—her words were clear, her voice soft and soothing.

"In the flesh."

"Mr. Sam will be with you in a few minutes only." Her smiled expanded, just a little, as if she recognized some humor in this *Sam* business—then extended her arm toward a stylized arrangement of very uncomfortable-looking hard-backed chairs surrounding a low, Tansu-style table. "Would you mind to wait, please?"

Yes, he did mind; after eight long and boring and sleepless hours on a plane he couldn't think of anything less appealing, but such was the life of moving objects from point A to point B. "Sure, no problem."

"I would be pleased to offer you tea."

What he needed was a double espresso, but felt certain the decadence of five-dollar coffee had yet to penetrate the communist psyche. "No, thanks, I'm fine."

He dropped his travel bag and security case next to one of the chairs and settled in to wait. The place seemed more like a showroom than a working office, everything perfect and precise, from the neatly arranged fan of magazines to the plaintive whisper of lute music that emanated from speakers hidden in the ceiling. Not quite so hidden, he noticed, were the tiny surveillance cameras located around the perimeter of the room. Exactly what kind of trade required so much security, he had no idea, but had a feeling he was about to find out. One thing he was sure of, this job would not be *routine*.

Before his butt had a chance to atrophy in the brick-like chair, a very tall, very Caucasian gentleman emerged from one of the doors along the back wall.

Dressed in a well-tailored navy suit, he projected an enthusiastic if somewhat exaggerated congeniality as he came striding across the room, hand outstretched. "Mr. Leonidovich, sorry to keep you waiting. I'm Stanley Powers."

He pronounced *Leonidovich* perfectly—always a surprise—and though he didn't sound like the voice on the phone, there was something familiar in the cadence, enough to consider that John Clayton's voice had been altered electronically and that both men were one and the same. "Not Uncle Sam?"

The man laughed and engulfed Simon's hand in one of those two-handed, double-pump political handshakes. "Close enough, Mr. Leonidovich. Close enough."

"Call me Simon."

"And I'm Stan. Please follow me."

Simon reached for his security case. "Okay if I leave my travel bag here?"

"Leave them both," Powers answered. "No one will touch them."

The statement struck Simon as odd—as if he thought someone would—and though he assumed he would eventually need his case, he decided not to argue the point. Partly out of habit, but with an added sense that everything was not as it seemed, he reached into his pocket and activated the case's antitheft measures as he followed Powers down a short hall and into a small boardroom. Like the lobby, the room had no windows and was decorated in a rather austere, Asian fashion, with muted paintings that looked like blown-up postage stamps. The eight hard-backed chairs that surrounded the glass table looked seriously hard, as hard and serious as the two people sitting next to each other at the far end of the table, a distinguished-looking man in his mid-fifties and a younger woman, not more than thirty, both Korean. At least Simon assumed that—they had the wide face, upward curving eyes and square-at-the-jaw features he associated with Koreans—though he knew the physical distinctions between the various Asian cultures were subtle and unreliable.

They stood up as Powers began the introductions. "Mr. Leonidovich, this is Ms. Jin Pak."

Dressed in tan slacks and a brown mustard-colored blazer over a white blouse, the woman stepped forward and extended her hand. "Mr. Leonidovich."

"Ms. Pak." Short and stocky, with a crushing handshake and a voice two octaves lower than most men, the woman was not exactly the image of East Asian femininity.

"And—" Powers turned to the man. "Mr. Ang Lee Han."

Han, dressed in a dark business suit, stepped forward, his handshake a perfunctory single pump. Powers motioned Simon toward a chair at the head of the table, opposite where Pak and Han had been sitting. "Please, make yourself comfortable."

The situation felt staged and uncomfortable, especially when Powers joined the other two at their end of the table. It was possible, Simon realized, that his sleep-deprived brain might be trying to turn some innocent cultural protocol into something more nefarious, but his cautionary antennas were humming.

"I'm sure you're wondering," Powers began, "why you're meeting someone from the State Department in the offices of the North Korean Trade Legation."

Simon hesitated, choosing his words carefully, conscious of at least two security cameras aimed in his direction. "Actually, I was wondering if you really *are* with the State Department."

Powers smiled, plucked a laminated identification badge from his breast pocket and casually skipped it across the glass surface of the table.

The badge looked authentic, though Simon realized it could have been a well-made forgery and he wouldn't have known the difference. He tried to memorize as many details as possible before sliding it back. "And what about Ms. Pak and Mr. Han?"

Powers glanced at Han, received a slight nod, then turned back to Simon. "Ms. Pak and Mr. Han are with the DPRK."

Surprise! "The what?"

"The Democratic People's Republic of Korea."

"Oh." He offered an embarrassed smile, considered asking whether that was North or South, but decided that might be taking Simple Simon to an implausible level.

"Before I proceed—" Powers plucked a document off a stack of papers. "I'll need you to sign this."

Simon scanned through the four-page document— a hybrid nondisclosure agreement—something he had signed in various forms at least a hundred times, though never one that referred generally to the Constitution of the United States or specifically to Article II, Section 4 regarding "Treason, Bribery, or other High Crimes and Misdemeanors." *Hardly routine.* "I have no problem signing this." He paused, just enough to make sure Powers understood the terms. "As long as you acknowledge my right to refuse the assignment once you've disclosed the details."

"Of course," Powers answered. "As long as *you* understand, you may never disclose the details of this assignment *whether or not* you accept it."

In the back of his mind Simon could hear the theme music from *Mission Impossible.* "Understood." He scratched his name on the signature line and slid the document back down the table. "Okay, so what can I do for the State Department?"

"As I'm sure you know, the United States does not maintain diplomatic ties with North Korea. But, *unofficially,* our government is, and has been for some time, involved in sensitive and confidential discussions with their government. Unfortunately, some countries would be less than pleased to learn of these discussions."

Not inclined to expose what he knew or understood, Simon maintained a passive expression, though it didn't take a genius to figure out that neither China nor South Korea would be happy to discover the US was dealing directly and secretly with the DPRK.

"And would," Powers continued, "do almost anything to sabotage our efforts."

Han, who had yet to speak, leaned forward, his

voice soft and confidential, with only the slightest hint of an accent. "We have reached now a critical stage in our talks, which could, if exposed, lead to a *serious* interruption in our work." He hit the word *serious* hard enough to make it reverberate, a kind of warning echo.

"The stakes are very high," Powers added with that special inflection that made it sound catastrophic. "The global ramifications immense."

Simon felt like the target of a tag-team pair of salesmen. Why the hard sell? What did they want him to do?

Han seemed to anticipate the question. "We no longer feel comfortable with the passing of documentation using government emissaries."

"We need an independent," Powers continued. "A person outside the political arena. Someone whose international movements do not draw attention. Someone discreet and above reproach. You have such a reputation."

Simon nodded, acknowledging the compliment, though he had the feeling his freshly buttered backside was about to hit the fire. "Exactly what is it you want me to do?"

Both men turned to Jin Pak, the silent one whose dark eyes seemed to miss nothing. "Very simple," she said, "no problem." There was nothing pleasant about her voice, her accent brittle and harsh, though easy to understand. "You take documents Pyongyang. You bring documents here."

"Sounds easy enough." *Too easy.*

"Not here," Powers clarified. "Not this office."

Jin Pak nodded. "Eyes everywhere. Watch everything."

That Simon believed; he could feel a couple of electronic ones drilling holes in his forehead at that very moment. "Okay, where?"

"Change every time," she answered. "New York. Boston." She delivered each word with a distinct punch, serious as ice picks. "Always East Coast."

"Always a public place with lots of tourists," Powers added. "Where you can make the transfer without being noticed or photographed."

"How many trips are we talking about?" Just the thought—knowing there were no direct flights between the US and North Korea—was enough to make his sphincter clench.

"Three," Powers answered. "Four at the most."

Ugh, three or four too many. "Sounds like fun."

"So you'll accept the assignment?"

Simon hesitated, the warning line from *Mission Impossible* echoing through his cranium— *"Should you or any member of your I.M. Force be captured or killed, the Secretary will disavow any knowledge of your existence"*—but the thought of turning his back on his country, a country that had welcomed his immigrant parents, made him feel a bit like Crockett running from the Alamo. "Of course. I'll even give you my special government rate." Which didn't exist until that moment. "Expenses only."

Powers tried his best at a humble smile but he couldn't hide the relief, like a bad poker player who had just filled an inside straight. "That's excellent, but we absolutely insist on paying your normal fee. It's policy."

Simon knew better than to argue; once the government established a policy—even one as idiotic as a spend-more policy—there was no way to fight the system.

"Ms. Pak is a trained security officer and will brief you on the particulars."

Jin Pak took this as her signal to take over, and the men as their excuse to withdraw from the room. As the woman started through her list of instructions, Simon felt the vibration of his security alarm, but before he could reach into his pocket it stopped, indicating his case had moved, but only slightly, as if someone in the waiting room had shoved his bags to the side. He ignored it—the case was empty except for his laptop—and if anyone tried to open it they would be in for a surprise: a loud, though harmless explosion, with lots of glow-in-the-dark pink dye.

Pak laid what looked like an old and somewhat bulky satellite phone on the table, along with an extra battery, a charger, and a full set of international adapters. "Use this phone only. Never turn off."

"Use for what?"

She shrugged, which seemed her only expression of animation. "Should you have problem. Need to change schedule. Such as that."

That's what worried him—*such as that*. "And what's special about this phone?"

"Safe to talk. Everything scrambled. No GPS identifier."

"And who do I call if there's a problem?"

"You call Jin Pak. My number pre-set one. Easy to remember." She proceeded to lay out a complete set of travel documents—a double-entry visa between China and North Korea; a round-trip airline ticket, New York to Beijing, Beijing to Pyongyang; a city-only travel permit; a hotel reservation for one night; and nearly a thousand dollars in euros—everything signed, stamped, and ready to go. She placed a large briefcase on the table, the brown leather scarred from use. "You carry this."

"Which contains the documents?"

She nodded. "Contact in Pyongyang have identical case. You switch, you walk away. Very easy. Everything very well arranged."

"What about customs?"

She shrugged and snapped open the case, showing him the contents, which appeared to be nothing more than a collection of manuals relating to hydroponic farming. "Nothing look important. No problem."

Right, *no problem*. So why did everything feel wrong?

CHAPTER FIVE

Washington, DC

"Any problems?" Tucker asked as soon as the van started to move.

The general checked his cellular, confirming that the antisurveillance system had been activated before answering. "No, but let's keep it short. Too many awkward questions if anyone notices I'm gone."

Tucker nodded. It was hard enough for him, but he couldn't imagine living in the general's twenty-four-hour-a-day fishbowl. "Yessir. Thirty minutes max."

The general glanced toward his omnipresent shadow, Captain Buddy Baggett. "Captain, you've got the clock."

Baggett gave a thumbs-up, never taking his eyes off the double row of monitors.

"So, how are you doing with the tapes?" the general asked. "We're running out of time."

Tucker pulled a summary of his recordings from the side pocket of his briefcase. "Got everything I need. It's just a matter of combining the pieces."

The general slipped on a pair of half-lens readers and began to scan down the double-column list of phrases. "Can I hear a sample?"

"Yessir. It won't be perfect on my laptop, but you'll get the idea. What would you like to hear?"

"Let me see." The general ran his finger down the TS column, the recordings Tucker had made of his own voice. "How about A-19—" He moved his finger over to the POTUS column, the recordings Tucker had made of the President. "—B-11, B-3, and B-14? That order."

Tucker leaned forward, selected voice-file A-19, added a 3.6 second pause to the end, dropped the file ahead of B-11, added a 1.4 second inhale—the President's normal hesitation between sentences—attached the combined file to the front of B-3, added another hesitation, then dropped the entire file in front of B-14 and hit PLAY. Instantly his own voice reverberated from the tiny speaker: "Mr. President, I strongly recommend you bring the congressional leadership and the Committee on Foreign Relations into the loop on this." Then a pause followed by the President's voice: "Are you kidding? Those idiots would fumble away pussy if you handed it to them on a platter. They can't be trusted with anything."

The general smiled over the rim of his glasses, clearly impressed. "Very nice, Corporal. The next time some politician screams 'out of context,' I might just believe them."

"Trust me, General, by the time my audio tech finishes splicing, filtering, and over-recording, not even the First Lady is going to believe the President when he claims the tapes were manufactured."

"How the hell did you get him to say all that?"

In truth it hadn't been that hard; the President almost never deviated from his political-speak syntax—short, uncomplicated sentences, rarely more than seven or eight words. "The 'are you kidding' was easy. He says that kind of thing all the time. 'They can't be trusted with anything' was about his Labrador puppies, and the 'pussy' remark was in response to my question about what he thought of the Redskins this year."

The general hooted, a rare show of exuberance, and even the enigmatic Captain Baggett, whose attention never strayed from the surveillance monitors, cracked a smile. After a year of planning, of sleepless nights and clandestine meetings, it was so good to see the general laugh, Tucker couldn't resist extending the moment. "You'll love this." He selected another file—a draft recording he had spliced together that afternoon—and hit PLAY. The familiar voice of the President echoed from the laptop's speaker: "I can't emphasize enough how important this is. Can you help us out?" There was a momentary pause followed by a second voice: "Yessir, of course. Exactly what is it you want me to do, Mr. President?"

The general stared back over his glasses, his eyebrows arcing upward like squirrel tails. "I didn't recognize the second voice."

"That's Simon Leonidovich, the courier we hired to deliver the documents."

"What?" The general yanked off his readers, making no attempt to hide his displeasure. "You put a delivery boy in the same room with the President?"

Leonidovich wasn't exactly a boy, Tucker thought, but that wasn't the issue. "Of course not, that would have been completely unrealistic. Not to mention there's a log and video record of everyone who enters and leaves the White House. This recording will turn up on the courier's laptop—" Tucker paused to emphasize his point. "—as a phone call that *he recorded*. Something he does as a matter of practice whenever he accepts an assignment by phone. It all fits within his normal routine. The investigation will reveal the call went directly from the President's private office to the courier's phone. The length of the call will, of course, match the length of the recording, tying the President and the courier together from two divergent sources."

The general nodded slowly, thinking about it. "What about this guy? The courier. You sure he bought your story?"

Tucker leaned forward, selected another voice file, scrolled down to one of his preselected markers and hit PLAY. "So you'll accept the assignment?" There was a momentary pause followed by the voice of Leonidovich: "Of course. I'll even give you my special government rate, expenses only."

The furrow between the general's eyebrows deepened. "What's that? He offered to donate his services?"

"What can I say? The guy's a patriot. Bought the story hook, line, and noose."

"But what about the money? We need something besides the recordings that lead back to the White House."

"No problem, our man insisted he accept payment. We've already made the transfer."

"Which will lead?"

The question was completely out of character—the general normally avoided such details, as any commander should—and Tucker didn't appreciate the sudden and unexpected excursion into his area of responsibility. This was no time for second-guessing, but he couldn't think of any reasonable way to dodge the question. "Directly back to a slush account the White House keeps for—" He threw up some quotation marks with his fingers. "—*special projects*. It's buried pretty deep, but not too deep. I'll make sure of that."

The general smiled, obviously satisfied. "Okay. Good work. Sounds like we're set and ready."

Tucker nodded, the plan as perfect as he could make it. Not that he could take credit for the opportunity, that was serendipitous, just one of those rare moments in history when the right circumstances presented themselves. If the President hadn't been so arrogant and stubborn in choosing a running mate—a man with a history of heart disease—and if the VP hadn't dropped dead two months after being sworn in, there would have been no opportunity. But it happened, and now the President would pay for his mistake. *Poetic justice.* The time was right, the stage set, the actors in place—all they needed was someone to snap on the lights and scream "action"—a service Tucker felt honored to provide. The production would be embarrassing and messy and filled with great drama, but there would be no blood in the streets, no troops storming the White House, and before it was over the political pundits would be pontificating about how well the system worked. Yes, it was perfect, a bloodless coup no one would ever realize took place. "Yessir, set and ready. I've got layers over switchbacks, and switchbacks over layers. No one really knows what the exercise is about or who's involved."

"All contingencies covered?"

"Yessir." *All but one.*

"It sounds like you're having fun, Corporal. You sure you're not going to miss the action once this thing is over?"

That was a question Tucker had asked himself numerous times over the past year, but he knew that once the scandal broke there would be no way to avoid the fallout or save his job. And that was okay—he had known the circumstances going in and had no regrets about his decision. *For God and country.* "No, sir. I'll do my duty and retire gracefully." He glanced toward the surveillance monitors. They were on Seventeenth, heading directly toward the Tidal Basin, one of his favorite spots, especially at night when the monuments rose up out of the darkness. It wasn't as spectacular on the small screens—the Jefferson Memorial straight ahead, the Lincoln Memorial on the right, the Washington Monument on the left—but still inspiring. "But I will miss the city."

"You don't have to leave."

Tucker knew better. "The press would never stop

asking questions. I'm thinking about Costa Rica. Find myself a nice quiet little place on the beach, drink Corona and watch the sun set."

"That does sound pretty nice," the general admitted. "With four million in cash you might even find someone to apply the sunscreen."

Though it was never about the money, Tucker couldn't deny it would make retirement easier. Easier to escape, easier to hide from the press, and easier to find a companion, something he hadn't really thought about in the sixteen months since a drunken trucker had squashed the life of his wife and children. "Yessir, might even find that."

"Captain Baggett has everything arranged," the general added, as if Tucker had doubts.

Despite the general's intention, *Captain Baggett* and *everything arranged* were not congenial terms in Tucker's mind. Once the job was done, his position on the balance sheet would shift from asset to liability; and though Tucker didn't think the general would ever order his elimination, it was the type of thing Captain Buddy Baggett would do to protect his commander. Tucker had his own idea about the way things should end. *The last contingency.*

CHAPTER SIX

New York City

Feeling a bit like Johnny the Juggler on Thorazine, Simon shuffled his bags awkwardly from one hand to the next, slipped his keycard through the reader and shouldered his way into the lobby. He started toward the stairs—after five brain-numbing days at thirty thousand feet, he needed the exercise—then realized he would never make it the three flights to his office and detoured into the elevator. *Tomorrow.*

Lara, who was dictating into her computer using a wireless head-mike while simultaneously pumping out an aggressive eighty strides per minute on her elliptical cross-trainer, nearly levitated off the machine when Simon unexpectedly pushed open the door. "Damn you, Boris! You could have given me a little warning!"

Before he could respond, she was off the machine and had him in a sisterly hug. "You look like shit."

"Thanks, it's good to see you too."

She stepped back and wriggled her nose. "Don't smell so good either."

"The woman next to me got airsick." He dropped his bags and collapsed into a chair. "It wasn't pretty."

"Ewww!"

"No, they served *ewww* on the flight over. This looked more like green eggs and ham."

"Thank you, Dr. Seuss. I get the picture. The life of an international courier is not all glim and glamour."

"Definitely not glamour. What's *glim*, anyway?"

"Good question." She swung the tiny head-mike up from under her chin and toggled the three-way switch on her belt. "Dictionary, define glim: G-L-I-M."

The computer answered back instantly, the synthesized voice remarkably lifelike: *Glim. A source of light, as a candle. Short for glimmer.*

Lara smiled, clearly pleased with herself. "And now we know."

Simon pointed to the brown briefcase lying next to his security case. "While you're playing Star Wars, put that in the safe, will you?"

She eyed the scarred leather case. "That's a package?"

"It is."

"Why bring it here?"

He shrugged nonchalantly, though the last-minute text-message instruction from Jin Pak bothered him as well. "I haven't been told where to deliver it yet."

Lara picked up the case and started across the room, dictating as she went. "Lara says—2, 7, Y, 7, 2—open sesame." The grid beneath the under-counter refrigerator slid silently to one side. She toggled her microphone switch to MUTE. "What's in this thing?"

"Not a clue."

"Don't bullshit me, Boris. You went through customs."

"Documents, that's all I know."

She placed the briefcase in the safe, stepped back and re-toggled the switch on her belt. "Lara says—2, 7, Y, 7, 2—clam up." The heavy steel grid moved silently back to its locked position. "Aren't you curious?"

"No." A lie of course, but an acceptable lie, because she knew he was lying and because she also knew it was none of her damn business.

Typically, she ignored the hint. "Why would the State Department hire you to transport documents in and out of North Korea? It doesn't make sense."

He wasn't surprised she had tracked his movements; anyone with a modicum of computer skills could have done that, and Lara had more snoopy-dog skills than a bloodhound. "I don't know what you're talking about."

She shook her head, the flop of coppery hair, and feigned a look of disappointment. "They called me first, remember?"

"Listen, I had to sign a very nasty and life-threatening nondisclosure, so unless you want to see your brother on bread and water, don't ask."

She was clearly undeterred by any vision of brotherly incarceration. "If it's so important, why not use a diplomatic pouch?"

"Interesting question," he answered, as if considering it for the first time. "But I don't believe we have diplomatic relations with North Korea."

Her eyes narrowed thoughtfully. "Still, it seems to me—"

"Bread and water, Sissie. Bread and water."

She emitted a sound, a little eruption of disbelief. "So? You could stand to lose a few pounds."

"Thanks a heap. You try sitting on a plane for fifty-three hours and see what happens to your skinny ass."

She twisted around, making an exaggerated inspection of her Lycra-encased backside. "Not bad for an old broad with two kids, uh?"

He could have pointed out that thirty-four wasn't exactly ancient, but being eight years her senior and about to expire from fatigue, he really didn't want to explore the subject of *old*, and he certainly didn't want to discuss the subject of his sister's ass. "Whatever you say."

"So what's it like?"

He hoped the question had nothing to do with her gluteus maximus. "What's what like?"

"North Korea, you idiot. Is it as bad as they say? Is everyone starving?"

"Not in Pyongyang, but that doesn't mean much. The capital is strictly a showcase city, designed to impress the world. It's got lots of parks and trees, with huge buildings and titanic monuments. Very clean and very few cars."

"Sound's like Washington DC about 1900."

He nodded, almost too tired to answer.

"What about the people?"

"Polite, but not friendly. Kind of closed-off, like the

capital itself. No one can travel in or out of the city without a special travel permit—" He paused to emphasize the point. "Visitors or citizens. And no one can live there without a residency permit. It's pretty damn restrictive, and the people reflect that." He pushed himself out of the chair. "I'll tell you more tomorrow. Right now I'm going—" He almost said *home*, a word that never failed to elicit an attack against his hotel-suite lifestyle. "—to my place, take a shower, and sleep for twenty-four hours. See you in the morning."

"Whoa down there, big brother." She snatched a small stack of yellow slips from the wing of her L-shaped command center. "You need to return some calls."

He shook his head—Caitlin was the only person he intended to call—and he planned to do that from the comfort and privacy of his own bed. "Tomorrow."

"Not this one." She peeled off the top message and slapped it into his hand. "I promised you'd call the minute you walked in the door."

One glance at the cryptic message—"Vic-911"—and his vision of crisp sheets and soft pillows began to fade. *Damn*, no way he could ignore a 911 from Victoria Halle. "Why didn't she just call me on cellular?" *Stupid question*, he knew it the minute the words slipped past his tongue. When his best friend, who just happened to work for the National Security Agency, didn't want to talk on cellular it was either too sensitive or too private to broadcast over the airwaves.

Lara shook her head, not so much in answer as in dismay at the foolishness of his question. "What do you think, Dumbo?"

"Right." He turned toward his office, a place he saw very little of now that he spent so much time in Vegas. "Phone sex."

"Ha! You should be so lucky."

He dropped into his chair, punched 3 on his speed dial, and snatched up the receiver so Lara—who had followed him into the room—couldn't hear more than half the conversation. Vic's familiar voice interrupted the first ring. "You're back?"

He realized it wasn't a question, that she would be staring at a computer screen that not only gave his location and authenticated his voice, but would probably tell her the last time he'd been to bed—a fond but distant memory. "Like a bad pimple. What's up?"

"Hit your scrambler."

He reached over and punched the scrambler button on his console. "Done."

"What the hell are you up to?"

That was not a question he wanted to hear, and certainly not one he could answer. "What do you mean?"

"Your name has popped up twice in the last week."

"Popped up?"

"Stop playing question-question. You know damn well what I mean."

Of course he did—the computers at the NSA were constantly scanning e-mails and phone calls, searching for anything that might affect the security of the United States—but he needed time to think, to unlock his sleep-deprived brain and come up with some kind of reasonable answer without violating his pledge of non-disclosure. Equally important, he wanted to avoid lying to someone who had saved his skin more than once. "I'm not doing anything you need to worry about, Vic. You know me, just the same old back and forth, point A to B and home again."

"It's that point B that concerns me, Simon. Goods from *that* country, and I quote, 'may not be imported into the United States either directly or through third countries, without prior notification to and approval of the Office of Foreign Assets Control.' I checked, and no such approval has been issued."

"Come on, Vic, you know me better than that. I'm not importing *goods.*"

"I believe you, Simon, of course I do, but I don't understand why your name keeps popping up on my screen if this is just business as usual."

He wasn't completely surprised—any kind of talk between the US and North Koreans was bound to create chatter, no matter how much they tried to keep the lid on. It made sense that his name might be attached to their electronic communications. "Trust me, Vic, my client understands the law."

"You want to identify this client?" It was obvious from her tone she knew better.

"Let's just say it's a mutual friend." *Uncle Sam.* "A very righteous guy."

A good ten seconds ticked by while she thought about that. "A mutual friend?"

"That's all I can say." He was already stretching the boundaries of confidentiality. "What exactly are you seeing?"

She hesitated again, probably worried about her own disclosure limitations, before answering. "Not much, really, just a couple of open messages with an odd source code that our computers flagged. No one else would have paid any attention, but when I noticed your name I decided to track your phone. Then when I saw where you were, I became concerned."

Damn cell phone, he couldn't operate his business without one, but as long as it was turned on he had a target attached to his ass. "What do you mean by *open messages?*"

"Not encoded."

He didn't like the sound of that. Why would the State Department—if it was the State Department—be sending open messages with his name? Wasn't that the opposite of what they were trying to accomplish?

"Which in itself could be a code," she continued. "We watch everything."

That he believed, and it didn't make him feel any safer. "If you'd close your eyes once in a while, I'd sleep better."

"Understood."

He hoped so, he didn't need the NSA tracking his movements if he had to make two or three more trips to the land of *Juche*, a concept he had yet to grasp. How could the people be the *master of one's self* and live so obediently under the dictatorial thumb of Kim Jong-il?

"But I worry about you," she continued. "You have such a unique talent for trouble."

He could feel her smile over the phone. "And I appreciate your concern, Vic, but everything's copacetic."

"You going to be in town a few days?"

He hesitated, glanced toward his sister, who was listening intently, and realized what he needed to do. "At least three. I want to spend some time with Lara and the kids."

"How about dinner before you leave?"

"Absolutely. Let me get back to you with time and place."

"Ten-four, Bagman. Gotta run." There was a soft click and the line went silent.

The moment he racked the receiver, Lara was on him. "Three days! That's all you're staying?"

"I thought you'd be happy."

"Well yeah, but . . . I mean . . . well, it's been a little lonely around here since you ran off to the land of sin and sand."

Now that was unexpected, for his sister to actually admit she missed him. "I thought you liked working on your own."

"Well, I do, but—" She frowned, her high-octane personality replaced with an exhausted resignation. "Never mind." She turned and started toward her office. "Forget it."

Simon levered himself out of his chair and lurched after her, his legs so numb with fatigue they seemed to belong to someone else. "Spit it out, Sissie. What's the problem?"

"It's just that . . . that I never see any adults, that's all."

"And whose fault is that?" He didn't mean to sound so accusatory, but his brain felt like mush and the words escaped before he could engage the areas of *tact* and *sympathy*.

She sank into her new chair—a birthday gift from Billie and Jake Rynerson—an ergonomically correct, air-cushion design guaranteed to provide the ultimate in orthopedic comfort. "I said forget it."

"Don't you think it's time you—" He hesitated, not wanting to use the word *date*. "—got out a little?"

"Men my age aren't interested in women with kids."

"Trust me, Sissie, all men are pigs. When they see that finely tuned body, it's not kids they'll be thinking about."

She frowned, clearly not comfortable with the thought of romance. "I just want somebody to talk to."

"Talk is good. A good place to start."

"I'm not ready."

He wondered if she ever would be. Eth Jäger had been in prison for nearly two years, and she didn't seem any closer to putting the ordeal behind her. "Listen, I promised Vic we'd have dinner. You can join us. I know this really nice guy who—"

"No way! How pathetic would that look, getting set up and going on a double date with my brother?"

He couldn't blame her for thinking that, but he needed to do something to force her out of her shell. "Tell you what, I'll stick around a few extra days and—"

"No," she interrupted, "I know you want to get back to Caitlin. I'm just being a baby."

"And just who do you think baby sisters are supposed to turn to when they're having a problem? Why don't we—"

ZZZIT—ZZZIT.

He swiveled toward the security monitor as someone impatiently pulsed the building's outside buzzer. *ZZZIT—ZZZIT—ZZZIT.* The stocky Asian woman staring belligerently back at the camera was absolutely and without qualification the last person on earth he wanted to see at that moment. She was alone, a brown leather briefcase tucked securely beneath her left arm—a case identical to the one Lara had just placed in the safe. "Oh shit."

"Who's that?"

"That, I'm afraid, is the ghost of sleep deprivation, Ms. Jin Pak."

"Who works for the client I'm not supposed to know about?"

"Precisely."

"And from that constipated look on your face, you're thinking she's going to put you on the merry-go-round?"

Constipated was right, just the thought of getting

back on a plane was like sand in the gas tank of his stomach. "I don't think she's making a fashion statement with that scarred-up old briefcase." He reached over and pressed the outside door release.

Lara studied the woman as she snapped open the door and marched briskly toward the elevators. "I'm not sure about that, she looks tough as rawhide to me."

"You got that right."

"Why don't you slip down the back stairs? I'll tell her you're not back yet."

"I think she knows precisely where I am." In fact, he was almost positive two security officers—one man, one woman, both Asian—had shadowed him all the way to Pyongyang and back. That was not so unusual: clients would frequently add an extra layer of security when the consignment was irreplaceable, and though Simon was rarely told, he had learned to spot his surreptitious bodyguards. "Besides, she might just want to pick up the package."

"So why the duplicate briefcase?"

"Probably empty," he answered, trying to convince himself. "She doesn't want to be seen walking in empty-handed, then leaving with something." *Sounds reasonable*, he just didn't believe it.

Lara confirmed the thought with a roll of her hazel eyes. "You should be so lucky."

But five minutes later, in the privacy of his office, he realized luck was not on his side when Jin Pak began laying out a new set of travel documents. "You're kidding, right?"

"Jin Pak never kid."

"Of course you don't." The woman was about as funny as a brain aneurysm. "I could use a little sleep."

"Sleep on plane."

If only he could. "I never sleep when I have a package in hand."

"Package in hand?"

He reached over and placed his hand on the brief-case. "Package."

"Aaah." She nodded, a rare and dramatic show of animation. "No problem. You sleep on plane. Everything okay."

A statement, he thought, that seemed to acknowledge the presence of bodyguards. "This is really important?"

She acknowledged this with another drop of the chin, the only part of her body that seemed to get any mileage. "Big breakthrough in talks. Need documents Pyongyang. Very important."

Simon hoped they were talking about the same degree of importance. World peace, food for the masses, the reunification of North and South Korea, those were things worth losing sleep over, but if he read someday that all this hurry-up business was about apples—fruit or computers—he might seriously consider a move to Canada. "Okay, I'll be on the plane."

"Good." She stood up and extended her hand over the desk. "You sleep on plane."

"Right." But he knew that wasn't going to happen.

She turned toward the door. "Never turn off phone."

"Wait. What about the package I brought back?"

She kept moving toward the door. "You keep in safe. Too many eyes watch Jin Pak."

Was she assuming it was already in the safe, or was she telling him to put it there? "But—"

"Make arrangements later."

The minute she was out the door Lara was in his office. "What was that about?"

He shook his head, not sure himself, but he didn't like it. "I've only got about five hours."

"To do what?"

He folded his arms across the top of his desk and lowered his head. "Sleep."

CHAPTER SEVEN

Washington, DC

While the general ran down his checklist, Tucker kept his eyes on the van's surveillance monitors. It was one of those rare times they were actually alone, Captain Baggett off somewhere "on assignment." The general didn't elaborate, and Tucker couldn't ask without exposing his concern, but it didn't feel right. Buddy Baggett was like a circling shark, a threat Tucker preferred to keep in the crosshairs.

The general looked up from his notes, the wrinkles tightening around the corners of his eyes and across his forehead. "I'm still worried that Chairman Kim might decide to play it cozy."

Tucker ignored the comment. The general was just being a general, questioning and second-guessing. The driver turned left on Fourth Street, continuing to circle the National Mall and giving Tucker a perfect view of the traffic heading west on Madison and east on Jefferson.

"If he decided to keep his mouth shut," the general continued, "he'd have one hell of a bargaining chip. The President would give him damn near anything to bury those documents."

Tucker nodded, he'd heard it all before.

"Once this goes public, it's too late."

"You're right," Tucker agreed. "Given a choice, Kim might prefer to play it that way, but we're not giving him that choice. There are fourteen international film crews in the capital already, and there'll be more by tomorrow."

"Even so—" The general shook his head, unable to keep the anxiety out of his voice. "The man's erratic, he might change his mind and decide to boot everyone out of the country at the last minute."

It was possible, Tucker realized, but there was only so much he could control, and Kim Jong-il was not one of those things. "It's not going to happen, sir. He's the one who invited the foreign press to film the celebration. It's an opportunity to showcase his weapons."

"That's true," the general conceded, "but what he thinks is free advertising is going to end up being an international embarrassment. Once the—" He hesitated, searching for the right word. "Once the event takes place he might decide to confiscate the footage."

Event—mini-massacre would be more accurate— but Tucker could understand the general's effort to obscure the reality; it was simply a matter of evolution, from general to politician. "CNN will have a direct satellite feed, I've made sure of that. Once it happens, there won't be any way to stuff that rabbit back into its hole."

"No, but Kim could claim the event was nothing more than an attempt by the KUP to embarrass his government. We can't be sure he'll disclose the documents."

"Leonidovich is too high-profile. You can't kill a man like that in the middle of Kim Il Square and bury the story. The State Department will be asking questions and demanding answers. Kim will have no choice but to respond."

"The courier? High-profile?" The general glanced at his leather notebook. "What are you talking about?"

"You remember that Mira-loss scandal a few years back? The one that brought down Bain-Haverland."

"Of course I remember. I don't live in a vacuum, Corporal."

"No, sir, of course not. Leonidovich is the guy who discovered what the company was up to. He received a lot of positive coverage at the time. The press will pick up on that story and run with it."

"That's good." The general nodded slowly, absorbing the information. "Very good."

"More important, he's exactly the type of person the President would hire for such an important mission."

"But what if the Koreans grab him before your man has a chance to take him out? This guy sounds like someone people might believe when he says he's never talked to the President."

"That won't happen. I have two people assigned to do nothing but make sure Leonidovich never gets out of that square alive."

"It's going to be pretty chaotic. You sure these men

are up to the task? You trust them not to cut and run?"

Tucker kept his eyes fixed on the surveillance monitors, not wanting the general to read his anger. What did the man think, he was going to hire people he couldn't depend on? "Yessir, I trust them to do their job. Of course that doesn't mean they wouldn't talk if they were picked up. We have to protect ourselves against that possibility."

"Eliminate them, you mean?"

"Yessir, it's all arranged."

"Messier than we anticipated," the general mused, though nothing in his tone indicated displeasure over the plan. "But there's always collateral damage."

"Yessir, always." The trick, Tucker thought, was to avoid that fate himself. "If everything goes as expected, the President should be working on his memoirs within a month."

The general rolled his right hand from side to side. "Maybe so, maybe no. He might decide to fight the charges."

"Then he's not just an avaricious self-serving prick, he's an idiot. No President wants to go through an impeachment trial."

"Clinton survived."

"But that was political," Tucker pointed out. "Nothing to do with how he managed the country. It's one thing to have sex with an intern, but trying to overthrow a foreign government without authorization or provocation, that's a different matter. Both parties will want to fry his ass."

"If they believe the documents."

"Without the courier around to contradict the scenario, it's a slam dunk."

"I'd like to believe that."

"Trust me, General, once they find those documents in the courier's safe and the recording on his laptop, it's over. Once the dominos start to fall, the President will have no choice but to resign. All you have to do is sit back and watch it happen."

The general shook his head. "No, what I need to do is step forward and pledge my allegiance to the President. Then, if something *does* go wrong, I'd be the last person anyone would suspect of involvement. On the other hand, if the documents prove my devotion to be misplaced, well—" He shrugged and turned up his hands. "No one will blame me for being loyal to my commander in chief."

The transformation, Tucker thought, was now complete: from general to politician in one behind-the-scenes campaign. "You're right, sir, that's the way to play it."

The general closed his notebook, removed his glasses, and wearily rubbed his eyes. "This should be the last time we meet."

Tucker nodded, though something about the gesture and words bothered him—the finality—as if the general might be closing his book on Corporal Tucker Stark.

CHAPTER EIGHT

Kim Il Square, Pyongyang, North Korea

Sunday, 20 June 10:54:14 GMT +0900

Simon set the briefcase down—the damn thing was heaver than on the last trip—locked it between his feet and leaned back against the cool granite of the Korean Art Gallery, trying as best he could to blend in. Despite the immense size of the plaza—enough open space for seventeen football fields—and the gathering horde of humanity, his effort to disappear into the background seemed futile. In a country that venerated the old and drab, he was suddenly too old and too drab for such a festive occasion. Every year the city drew 100,000 colorfully dressed students and children to participate in the Mass Games and *Arirang*—a festival of ethnic dances, gymnastics, aerobics, and folk songs—and for some reason the State Department had chosen this time and this location to make the exchange, as if they had simply forgotten about his conspicuously white face. What the hell were they thinking?

Always a public place with lots of tourists, Powers had said. Among the thousands, Simon had spotted less than a hundred tourists—a few small tour groups here and there—but there were plenty of people: children and students and parents and spectators, all juxtaposed with huge displays of military weaponry and enough soldiers to start a medium-sized war.

Where you can make the transfer without being noticed . . . And just how was he supposed to turn his pasty skin to a nice shade of peach?

. . . *or photographed.* In fifteen minutes he had seen at least a dozen television crews.

Was the location an oversight? Had some idiot forgotten about the festival? *No,* the State Department might have, but not the Koreans; that would be like Americans forgetting the Fourth of July. So why, if they were so worried about *eyes everywhere,* would they stick him in the valley of eyes?

Even things that seemed right, now felt wrong and oddly inconsistent: the fact that there had been a breakthrough in talks, yet the State Department hadn't bothered to pick up the package in his safe; the fact that payment for the trip had already been deposited in his account. Since when had the government become so efficient at paying its bills? It didn't make sense, but he wondered if he might be trying to make something out of nothing. Had the eight-day marathon of international hop and skip turned his brain into a quivering mass of anxiety? He didn't think so—he actually felt surprisingly clear-headed, but even so, he didn't have the authority to cancel the exchange. *Should you have problem. Such as that.* He pulled the satellite phone from his shoulder bag and hit the preset number. Jin Pak answered almost instantly, her voice as clear as the cloudless sky above his head. "This Jin Pak."

That surprised him too, that she would use her name, even though the phone was preset to scramble their conversation. "There's a big festival going on here. Must be fifty thousand people." For emphasis, he borrowed a phrase from her own vernacular. "Too many eyes."

"Everything very well arranged," she answered without hesitation. "No problem."

Beyond the sound of her voice Simon could hear the low, echoing bong of a large clock as it hit the top of the hour and began to toll the numbers. "We've still got an hour, you could change the location."

"No. Location very good. Everything arranged. Everything go."

Damn, she didn't even think about it. "Are you sure? There are cameras all over the place."

"Everything go," she repeated. Uncompromising.

He wanted to debate the point, but couldn't conjure up a single argument to support his nebulous feelings of catastrophe. "Okay, it's your decision." He continued to count each echoing bong as the clock counted down the hours, then realized the line had gone silent and the sound was no longer coming through the phone. *Well, butter my butt and call me stupid*—no wonder she didn't hesitate, she knew exactly what was going on because she was there, somewhere among the throng. *Good,* that not only confirmed the importance of the documents, it meant she understood the situation and felt com-

fortable proceeding. It also meant that he now had
three people watching his back, assuming his surreptitious bodyguards had followed him from the
airport.

He slipped the phone back into his shoulder bag,
picked up the briefcase, and began to casually weave
his way through the crowd, toward the Grand People's Study House at the far end of the plaza. Like
the other buildings that bracketed the square, the
building was massive and gray and adorned with
huge colorful placards and flags to offset its austere
grandeur. Surrounded by thousands of Korean na-
tionals, mostly children, he had the unique experience of being taller than everyone around him. Not
that there was much to see—the formal activities
were not scheduled to begin for another two hours,
by which time he expected to be in a taxi on his way
back to the airport. *Ugh*, just the thought of eating
another meal wrapped in a cellophane condom made
his stomach clench.

He made his way through and around groups of
students as their adult leaders tried to assemble them
into some kind of order, each group identified by its
own unique color of traditional garb. Contrary to
other Asian cultures, the people were either unaf-
fected by the presence of a Caucasian or pretended
not to notice him. Despite this inattention, he felt
oddly exposed and scrutinized. He circled a small
group of flag-waving students near the Study House
and ran headlong into a CNN news team setting up
their equipment. He quickly reversed course, but not

before a female member of the crew spotted his out-of-place face and jumped forward to cut off his retreat. "Hi there!" She flashed a set of dazzling white teeth, her voice light and chirpy. "You're American, right?" She was dressed in khaki wash pants, an open-neck cotton blouse, and La Sportiva Makalu hiking boots.

He considered lying, saying he was Canadian, but had a feeling it didn't matter one way or the other, as long as he spoke English. "I am."

She gave him another flash of white teeth and stuck out her hand. "I'm Amy Carston, from Kansas City, Kansas." She was young, not yet thirty, cute as a baby tiger, aggressive as a rattlesnake, and clearly accustomed to having her way with men.

He knew exactly what she wanted. "Hello, Amy Carston from Kansas City."

"And you are?"

"Camera shy."

She was undeterred, locking his hand in a tight grip. "Just a few quotes for the people back home? How you're enjoying the festival, things like that."

"Sorry, I'm on a very important mission." He gave her a little wink, letting her know he was only teasing. "Very tight schedule."

"That sounds interesting," she responded with exaggerated enthusiasm. "What kind of mission brings you to North Korea, shy man?"

"I heard it was a good place to find a wife. The compliant, nonassertive type."

"Ha." She released his hand but stayed right in

front of him, up close and personal. "That doesn't sound like much fun."

He shrugged, looking for a graceful way to escape. "What's CNN doing in Pyongyang? Seems like a long way to come for a cultural event."

She rolled her eyes. "Tell me about it." She dropped her voice to a whisper. "My producer got a hot tip that the KUP was going to stage some kind of protest."

KUP? His brain made a quick search through its list of known acronyms and came up empty. "The KUP?"

"Korean Unification Party. It's a small underground group advocating the reunification of North and South."

Damn, that was all he needed, a political protest just when he was trying to exchange a briefcase full of political documents. "When's this supposed to happen?"

"Who knows?"

He gave her his best Simple Simon expression, positive she knew more. "Gee, you came all the way over here on the off chance there might be a little political protest? Things must be dull in the rest of the world."

She glanced around, as if afraid Fox News might be lurking among the brightly clad students. "We heard there might be violence. You know, a Tiananmen Square kind of thing."

"Oh." He bobbed his head to indicate he wasn't a complete doofus.

"Between you and me—" She glanced around again, this time toward the Study House and a large military formation. "I don't think it's going to happen. Not with all these soldiers around."

He nodded again. "You're probably right, looks like half the Red Army is here." He stuck out his hand. "I really need to go. Nice talking to you, Amy Carston from Kansas City."

She pulled a card from her pocket and slipped it into his hand as they shook. "You see anything newsworthy, that's my cell number." She gave him a sexy wink. "I'll make it worth your while."

He grinned, playing the game, but knew she was only keeping her news sources open with a little fantasy-frolic innuendo. "You're the first person I'll call."

She gave him a final flash of her camera-ready choppers. "Good luck with that wife thing, shy man."

He gave her a thumbs-up and moved off through the crowd. The children and students were now pretty much assembled into distinct and orderly groups, the parents and spectators having withdrawn to the perimeter of the square. He considered calling Jin Pak and warning her about the protest—*possible protest*—but decided against it. The chance of anything happening in the middle of so much military force seemed absurdly remote. He squeezed in behind a small tour group gathered on the steps of the Study House, slipped on a pair of dark glasses to hide his eyes, and began to methodically scan the massive crowd. In thirty minutes he saw no sign of Jin Pak or his bodyguards, and no sign that anyone had taken the slightest interest in his presence. He tried to tell himself everything was okay—*everything go*—but no matter how many times he repeated it, he couldn't shake the tingle across the back of his neck, the sense of being watched. Probably, he decided, the way a Korean would feel in Powderly, Kentucky, home to the Imperial Klans of America.

Eight minutes before their designated meeting time, Simon spotted his contact—or more accurately, his dirty white baseball cap—weaving between the colorful assemblage of young people. Dressed in baggy tan slacks and a washed-out cotton shirt, the now-familiar briefcase tucked under one arm, the old man stood out like a freshly excavated mummy at a convention of circus performers. If he had any concerns about drawing attention, he didn't show it, heading directly toward the rendezvous point, a nondescript location at the triangular epicenter of three large groups of performers. Simon took a deep breath, trying to calm the butterflies that were suddenly winging through his stomach, and stepped out from behind his shield of tourists. Not wanting to draw attention or arrive early, he cut across the square at an oblique angle, slowly winding his way through the crowd and then working his way back toward the target destination.

As he drew closer, Simon realized it was the same man from his previous trip: a rather distinguished-looking gentleman despite his peasant garb, his skin the color and texture of aged tobacco, his graying hair cropped close beneath the edge of his cap. He bowed slightly, his eyes sharp and watchful behind a pair of round Trotsky glasses. Simon smiled and mimicked the man's courtesy. For a brief moment it felt as if they were completely alone—East meets West—two men in a tiny bubble of space surrounded by an ocean of red and green and yellow tapestry. Then, before they could make the exchange, someone hissed what sounded like a warning, the voice close, somewhere within the sea of performers, but too mature to be that of a student. The old man's face went tight, pulling skin against bone and tendon. "This would not be a good time for sudden movement."

The fact that the man spoke English, with the unmistakable touch of a British accent, surprised Simon nearly as much as the threatening tone. He nodded, almost afraid to speak.

"Who do you work for?" the man demanded, his lips barely moving as he spoke.

"For myself," Simon answered without hesitation, trying not to sound evasive. "I'm an independent courier."

"Who hired you?"

It was a question the man should have known, and one Simon now realized he couldn't answer. "What's with all the questions? Is something wrong?"

Before the man could respond a shrill whistle broke through the din of murmuring voices, followed immediately by another warning hiss. "Do not move," the old man commanded, his hooded eyes darting from side to side.

Why should he move? He had no intention of moving. Where would he go? Whatever was going on, it was serious. He could feel it in the air, like ozone after a lightning strike. Had the KUP done something? Had the protest started? "What's happening?" he whispered, barely able to push the words past the tightness in his throat.

The man refocused his attention, his dark eyes intense and scrutinizing beneath his gray eyebrows. "Do you like the smell of coffee in the morning, courier?"

Simon nodded, the butterflies in his stomach reproducing at a massive rate. In the distance he heard someone shout, a commanding bark, and he couldn't stop himself from glancing around. Beyond a large mass of students, an army officer was pointing, soldiers were breaking formation, and what seemed like a million eyes were suddenly staring at paleface Simon Leonidovich. *Oh shit!* Never in his life had he felt so tall, so white, and so damn conspicuous.

"Would you like to see another sunrise, courier?"

He forced himself to turn back, to look the man straight in the eye because he had a very strong feeling his life now depended on what this old man saw and heard and believed. "Yes. I like to watch children laugh and sing and eat ice cream. I like Mozart's *Piano Concerto Number 21* and Van Morrison's *The Philosopher's Stone.* I'm in love with a woman by the name of Caitlin Wells and I haven't told her that nearly enough. Yes, I very much want to see another sunrise."

For a long moment the man said nothing, as if he had tripped over some distant memory, then he smiled faintly, the benevolent expression of a wise old judge with a soft heart. "Then do as I say."

Simon nodded. What choice did he have?

The old man shouted something in Korean and instantly a small wave broke free from the ocean of performers—middle-aged men and women hidden within the multitude—surrounding Simon and the old man in a cocoon of colorful tapestry. Someone slipped a brightly colored performer's cloak over Simon's shoulders and pulled the hood over his head. "Stay with me," the old man ordered as he clutched Simon's arm. "Do not let them get the documents."

Them? Who exactly was *them?*

"Better to die," he said as the group began to shift and move, trying to reintegrate itself into the ocean of student performers.

Whoa and slow! What kind of nonsense was that? Why should he risk his life for . . . ? For what? But it didn't matter, whatever the soldiers thought, they would only discover that the documents involved their own government. Their government and his. No big deal. He wanted to stop right there, hit the brakes, but the tiny group had him trapped, packed in like a sardine, and before he could mount a protest there was a muffled *POP-POP* and the forehead of the man on his right exploded, spraying bits of brain and blood over everyone within ten feet. For an instant Simon couldn't believe what he was seeing: the man standing upright and dead beside him, his eyes as cold and hollow as an empty fireplace. How did this happen? Why? Then he saw her—one of the two Asians he assumed the State Department had assigned to watch his back—not twenty feet away, standing like a lighthouse in a sea of students now cowering on the ground. Trapped in the crush of bodies, Simon could only watch as she calmly adjusted her aim, pointing a small black pistol directly at his head. With surprising strength, the old man jerked him to the ground just as the woman fired. There was another sickening *THUNK,* hard metal against soft flesh, followed by the high agonizing scream of a young girl.

Within seconds the entire square had dissolved into a frenzy of confusion: everyone screaming and diving for cover; whistles blowing and children wailing; soldiers shoving and shouting and trying to force their way through the crowd; students crying and crawling around like mice lost in a maze; parents fighting the tide of fleeing spectators in an attempt to reach their children; then more shots, followed by the high-pitched stutter of automatic rifles. Simon tried to stand, to somehow stop it, but two men held him down, covering him with their bodies.

The old man shook his head. "We can do nothing."

Another eruption of automatic fire seemed to confirm his words, followed by the staccato, high pitch of a whistle—some kind of warning or command—which was replicated immediately by echoing whistles from every direction. Even before the sound faded, the loudspeakers erupted with a barrage of words, the tone harsh and commanding.

"What's going on?" Simon whispered in the cold silence that followed.

"Everyone has been ordered to remain silent and still," the old man answered back, his lips barely moving. "Until the army has swept the area."

"What's this all about?" Despite the woman's attempt to kill him, Simon couldn't believe the overall madness had anything to do with him. "Why is this happening?"

"*Shh.*" The old man drew a thumb and forefinger across his lips, like closing a zipper. "They are coming."

Simon considered identifying himself—he was, after all, an American citizen, working as a conduit between his government and the government of Kim Jong-il—but rejected the idea almost instantly. Too many things didn't make sense. Why did the woman try to kill him? She obviously didn't work for the State Department. Who was this old man? He obviously didn't work for the Kim government. Where did Jin Pak fit into this mess? Too many questions, no answers. With an effort he pulled his right hand free from the tangle of bodies, ran it through a pool of blood and smeared it across his face and over his ears. The old man motioned his approval with a twitch of his gray eyebrows. Simon answered back in the same manner, then buried his head into the shoulder of the man with no forehead. He lay there, on top of a briefcase that suddenly felt like a bomb, listening to the soft groans and cries of the multitude and tried to make some sense of it all; but nothing seemed to fit, not the people, not the circumstances; and yet he could feel the pieces, like parts of a puzzle, but no matter how hard he tried, he couldn't squeeze everything together or even guess at the picture that might emerge when he did.

Then he heard the soldiers, methodically and silently working their way through the square. He held his breath as the sounds grew closer, his heart threatening to explode through the wall of his chest as the dead man suddenly moved, his body apparently prodded by one of the soldiers. Then someone shouted something and the soldier hurried away.

"They found the woman," the old man whispered softly. "The one who tried to kill you."

Simon cracked an eyelid and very slowly turned his head. There were at least half-a-dozen soldiers and one officer standing over the woman's body, the officer holding up a black pistol and speaking adamantly to his men. "What's he saying?"

"It is curious," the old man whispered back. "They do not know who killed her."

"It wasn't one of the soldiers?"

"Apparently not. She was stabbed."

Holy Joseph and Jesus, the puzzle was becoming more confusing by the minute.

Two hours later, after the soldiers had completed their search—for exactly what or who Simon was never sure—everyone was ordered to rise and exit the square through a checkpoint near the Study House. The shuffling exodus was eerily quiet, even the children afraid to speak for fear of drawing attention. Hiding the briefcase beneath his performer's cloak and slumping forward to disguise his height, Simon tried to dissolve within the old man's pocket of friends, but as they drew closer to the military officers checking identification cards—something even the children were required to carry—he realized the effort was futile. Knowing the State Department would quickly extricate him from any problem, he wasn't particularly worried, but he couldn't decide what to do with the documents. Should he complete the exchange? Despite the success of their previous meeting, the old man was clearly not with the government. *Jin Pak moment.* He pulled the special cellular from his pack and leaned close to the old man's ear. "I need to make a call before I'm taken into custody."

The man frowned and shook his head. "This would not be advisable," he whispered back. "Everything has been arranged."

Now that sounded familiar—*everything very well arranged*—and not very comforting. So far nothing had gone as *arranged,* but he hadn't broken any laws and couldn't think of any justification for doing so. "What do you mean, arranged?"

"We have a plan."

So did George Armstrong Custer. "Who's 'we'? What kind of plan?"

The old man nodded toward the line of officers

checking credentials, now less than twenty yards ahead. "You need to be ready."

"Ready for what?"

"You will see. Very soon now."

But *you will see* wasn't good enough. He had no intention of doing anything that might embarrass his government or land his butt in a North Korean prison. He reached down, ready to press Jin Pak's number when the oppressive calm was suddenly shattered by the loud rattling stutter of an automatic weapon, close by and behind them. The crowd, assuming they were under attack, surged forward, screaming and yelling and overrunning the line of military officers. The old man grabbed Simon's arm and yanked him forward. "Run!"

"Are you kidding?" Simon screamed. "This is your plan?"

The man grinned, his dark eyes disappearing into the wrinkles. "Very good plan."

Good plan or not, it was run or be trampled. As they surged through the opening and past the line of soldiers, Simon caught a glimpse of Amy Carston and her CNN news team, their camera pointing directly at his blood-smeared face.

CHAPTER NINE

The White House, Washington, DC

Sunday, 20 June 01:46:22 GMT −0500

The night steward rapped once, then opened the door and stepped aside. It was Tucker's first visit to the Presidential bedroom, and, he was sure, his last. The room was surprisingly moderate in size, with a single queen-sized bed, and except for an assortment of early-American watercolors, quite unremarkable. Though the quilt had been pulled up, it was obvious only one person had occupied the royal nest, confirming the rumor that the President and First Lady no longer shared a close connubial relationship. The steward motioned toward two overstuffed chairs in the far corner. "Coffee, Mr. Director?"

"Please," Tucker answered, positive he wouldn't be seeing his own bed anytime soon. "Strong as you've got."

The man nodded and stepped back. "The President is in his dressing room. He'll be with you shortly."

"Thank you." Tucker quickly pulled his laptop, laid it on the ottoman, adjusted the angle so the microphone was aimed directly at the other chair, activated the recorder, then sat back and tried to relax.

Even the best plans go sideways, he reminded himself. It was how a field commander adjusted to setbacks that ultimately determined the outcome of any campaign. *Contain the problem. Control the situation. Complete the mission.* The President could be handled—as long as he didn't get squirrelly and run to Estes—but the general was a different problem. Nobody *handled* the general. He would assess the situation, recalculate the odds, then make his decision: advance or retreat. He might push forward, as long as he believed the situation could be controlled, but if he believed otherwise, that his own position was compromised, he would withdraw before anyone realized he had taken the field—a tactical retreat that would necessitate the elimination of all evidence. Including, Tucker realized, his field commander. *Tucker Stark, KIA.*

The President emerged from a door near his bed. "Good morning, Tuck." Except for his dress—a burgundy-colored robe over silk paisley pajamas—he looked camera ready, his blackish gray hair neatly combed, his campaign smile already locked in place.

Tucker jumped to his feet. "Good morning, Mr. President. Sorry to disturb you at such an ungodly hour."

The President waved his hand, an imperious flip. "That's the job, Tuck, twenty-four/seven. God has a much better deal—He gets to rest every seventh day."

Tucker forced a smile. *Megalomania run amuck.* The greedy bastard was now comparing himself to the Deity. "Better union, I guess."

"Ha." The President lowered himself into the adjacent chair. "Trust me, Tuck, God is no unionist. The world would still be under construction."

"Yessir, and over budget."

Before the President could respond, the steward entered with a tray of miniature pastries and a carafe of coffee. He poured two cups and stepped back. "Will there be anything else, Mr. President?"

The President shook his head, then waited for the man to withdraw before turning back to Tucker. "So what's going on?"

"North Korea, I'm afraid. You should be getting a call from the Sit Room at any time."

"Oh." He leaned forward and dropped his voice, as if he expected his chief of staff to suddenly materialize out of the shadows. "Something to do with our . . . our, uh—"

"Technically, no," Tucker answered, wanting to downplay the situation so the President didn't go ballistic and call Estes. "The North Koreans have this big summer festival. *Arirang.* Yesterday—" He hesitated, searching for a way to keep it simple and as close to accurate as possible. "Today actually. They're fourteen hours ahead of us. Anyway, at one of the outdoor events in Kim Il Square, something happened. We're not sure what." *So much for accuracy.* "Some kind of protest against the government, we think. Things apparently got out of hand, shots were fired, and before it was over—" He glanced at his laptop, making sure he had the number right. "—one hundred and twenty-eight people were dead, mostly students and children. Trampled to death."

The President grimaced, the most sincere reaction Tucker had ever seen from the man. "That's terrible."

"Yessir, not a pretty scene."

"You said 'technically.'"

"Yessir, I'm afraid there's a minor complication." Not, Tucker reminded himself, the kind of words he could use with the general. "The independent we hired to deliver the plans and money to the KUP somehow got mixed up in the ruckus."

"He was there?" the President asked in disbelief. "At the festival? Why?"

Tucker shook his head in mock bewilderment, as if any reason defied comprehension. "We have no idea. He wasn't scheduled to make the exchange for another twenty-four hours. At a location nowhere near Kim Il Square. We assume he was sightseeing."

"Sightseeing!"

"Yessir, but I'm afraid that's not the worst of it."

"Please don't tell me he had the documents with him."

"Apparently so. I had one of our agents search his hotel room. They weren't there."

The President leaned forward, a white-knuckle grip on his coffee. "What the hell kind of operation are you running, Tuck? This is a goddamned catastrophe."

Tucker willingly accepted the reprimand, mild in comparison to what he expected from the general.

"It's not really that bad, Mr. President. He managed to get away without being picked up."

"You're sure?"

"The package contained a GPS transponder. We're tracking it now. We expect to have the courier and the documents back in our hands within the hour."

The President expelled a relieved sigh and slumped back in his chair. "Thank God for that."

"Yessir, but I'm afraid there's another complication." This time he avoided the word *minor.* "We think he may have been injured. CNN happened to catch him on tape as he ran from the square. His face was covered in blood."

"Serves him right," the President snapped. "The guy's obviously an idiot."

"Obviously, but now CNN is looking for him too."

"Let them look. Surely they won't identify him from a film clip."

"I'm afraid they have. They're getting quite adept at using facial-recognition software."

"You mean they had his picture on file?"

"Yessir, he happens to be the one responsible for exposing that Mira-loss thing a few years back."

The color in the President's face went from cinnamon to cranberry red. "Jesus, Director, why in the hell would you use someone that high-profile?"

"He's not really high-profile, sir. It's not like you would recognize him on the street."

"CNN did."

Tucker nodded, doing his best to look appropriately contrite. "Yessir, I'm afraid that's true. We didn't want any screwups, so we hired the best."

"Apparently the best wasn't good enough, Mr. Director. What kind of idiot goes to an outdoor festival with documents he's been hired to deliver?"

"Yessir, not very bright, that's for sure. In fact, before this happened he was spotted talking to a CNN staff person. Actually admitted he was on some kind of mission."

The President's mouth went slack, as if caught unexpectedly between expressions. "You must be joking."

"I'm afraid not. I haven't seen the tape, but I have it on good authority that that's exactly what he said, that he was—" He glanced at his laptop, reading the exact quote. "'On a very important mission.'"

"An important mission! Holy God in heaven, what kind of idiot is this guy?"

"First class, apparently. That's why we'd prefer the press didn't get their hands on him."

"So what if they do? He doesn't know what's in the documents and he doesn't know who he's working for. That's why you wanted to use an independent."

"Yessir, that's true enough, but the less he knows the more the press will dig. We don't need that."

"What are you suggesting?"

"I'm suggesting it might be best if we *don't* bring him in."

The President hesitated, the wheels turning behind his brown eyes. "I don't think I want to have this conversation, Mr. Director."

Tucker nodded in an understanding way, but he needed more, a smoking-gun quote that would convince the general to move forward. "Yessir, I agree. I just wanted to be sure you wouldn't be overly upset if something happened and we failed in our efforts to pull him out."

"Does he have a family?"

Tucker hesitated, surprised by the expression of concern—a reaction he hadn't anticipated—and clicked over to his Leonidovich file. "No, sir, divorced. No children."

"That's good. That makes it easier."

"Yessir." But not good enough for the general, Tucker was sure of that. "It's a hard decision, Mr. President, but when you put things in historical perspective—" He paused, just long enough to emphasize the point and get the President thinking about his legacy. "What could happen if the North Koreans start selling bombs to terrorists . . ."

The President bobbed his head. "Yes, you're right, of course. The loss of one person becomes insignificant when you consider the ramifications. Do what you have to do."

Bingo. "Yessir. Thank you, sir." It wasn't exactly a Presidential death sentence, but by the time the conversation had been edited and polished, it would sound like one.

CHAPTER TEN

Pyongyang, North Korea

Sunday, 20 June 18:15:51 GMT +0900

They walked south, staying with the crowd, moving at a steady but unhurried pace so as not to draw attention. Though Simon didn't feel like a prisoner, the small group of men and women kept him surrounded and hidden, so he didn't argue, not really sure of his options or what he should do. He wasn't even sure what caused the melee, couldn't imagine it had anything to do with him, yet couldn't dismiss the fact that someone had tried to kill him. But why? What could they possibly gain? And the biggest question of all: who were *they*?

As the throng began to disperse, the group turned east toward the Taedong, a large river running through the heart of the city, and joined another thick queue of people waiting to cross the Yanggak Bridge. Despite the large number of people and all the excitement of what had happened, no one spoke above a low whisper, the fear of government as palpable as the stifling humidity. As they moved slowly onto the bridge, the old man nodded toward a small ship moored along the north shore. *"USS Pueblo,"* he whispered. "Museum now."

Great, like he needed to be reminded that the North Koreans had captured and abused a shipload of American sailors for nearly a year before the State Department could negotiate a release. No, he didn't need that reminder, but he had a feeling that was exactly the message: do something stupid and you could disappear into a North Korean jail, your American passport as worthless as used toilet paper. "I really need to make a call."

The old man pretended to adjust his eyeglasses, hiding his mouth behind his hand. "Later. Too dangerous now. Better you not speak."

Simon nodded, knowing it was true, that if anyone overheard their conversation it would draw attention. Attention, he had a feeling, even more dangerous to the people around him.

It took nearly an hour to cross the bridge—the people packed so tight they could only shuffle forward a few inches at a time—and by the time they reached the other side, Simon could barely feel his legs from walking in a half crouch. They headed north on Songyo Kangan, the riverfront road, staying with the crowd until it began to thin, then they discarded their cloaks and turned west, toward the outskirts of the city. The boulevard was wide and clean and green, almost no cars, the air fresh and clear and smog free. Huge concrete apartment buildings lined each side of the street, each with its own park and playground. The capital, Simon knew, had been reconstructed after the war as a showplace of socialism—the city as the manifestation of the state, the state as the manifestation of the man—but was no more real than a Hollywood back-lot, with Chairman Kim playing the lead role, parading foreign dignitaries through his socialist fabrication while the rest of the country starved.

Eventually the high-rise buildings gave way to single-story brick and clay huts, and the small group began to dissolve away until there were only four younger men surrounding Simon and the old man. They moved from street to street—seemingly in no hurry, careful not to draw attention—and doubling back through the alleyways to make sure they weren't followed. Whoever they were, whatever their cause, they were experienced and cautious. Finally, as day faded into darkness, they turned down a long narrow alley, slipped through a wooden fence and into a tiny two-room house.

The place was dimly lit and depressing. Not dirty, but it had that ripe, lingering smell of too many bodies in too small a space. There was a battered wooden table and an assortment of mismatched chairs, but nothing else except for a few piles of old newspapers stacked neatly along one wall. The second room, from what Simon could see, looked even smaller and more spare, the floor covered with sleeping mats. The old man issued some kind of directive, his tone authoritative but gentle, and the young men disappeared out the door. Simon pulled the briefcase out from beneath his jacket, dropped it on the floor along with his shoulder pack, and collapsed onto a chair, his back so sore he could barely sit upright. "I need to call in."

The old man shook his head. "Talk first."

"But I—"

"Talk first."

Simon realized it was useless to argue, that he would first need to gain the old man's trust. "Okay, let's talk. My name is Simon Leonidovich and I'd like to thank you for saving my life."

The old man slowly circled the table, thinking about his response before finally selecting a chair and sitting down. "You may call me Lee."

"That's it, just Lee?"

"*Ye*, just Lee."

Safe choice, Simon thought, *Lee* being one of the five names that comprised more than fifty percent of the Korean populace. "Is that your given name or your family name?"

The man smiled, a slyly serene Buddha-like grin, unwilling to say more.

Okay, Simon thought, I can deal with that. "You speak very good English—" Though not sure the title was appropriate, he wanted to demonstrate his respect. "—Mr. *Just* Lee. Where did you learn?"

The man hesitated, clearly reluctant to share information, then for some reason decided to answer. "I spent the war in a British labor camp. Those who understood language were given better jobs and more food. I learned."

But what did he learn? Did he hate all things English, including their American cousins? One thing was obvious: he spoke too well for someone who rarely used the language. "So you came home and became an English teacher?" The old man tried to mask his surprise, but Simon could tell he had guessed right. "Okay, Mr. *Just* Lee, what happened out there today?"

"I would ask you the same, courier. Who was this woman who tried to kill you?"

"I have no idea."

Lee cocked his head, making no attempt to hide his skepticism. "But I was sure you recognized her."

Careful, Simon thought, the old guy might be a little long in the tooth, but he had the stamina of a pack mule and the eyes of a hawk. "I did. We were on the same plane."

"From Beijing?"

"From New York."

The man emitted a sound of surprise, a tiny hiss of air over his bottom lip. "Very interesting."

"Interesting how?"

"So this woman followed you all the way from New York, *ye?*"

"*Ye.*"

"Then tried to kill you in front of thousands of people in the middle of Kim Il Square?"

"*Ye.*"

"Why would someone do this?"

Good question, one Simon had been asking himself for hours. "Maybe I reminded her of an old boyfriend."

"You have an odd sense of humor, courier."

"My way of dealing with fear and anxiety."

"You have nothing to fear from us."

"That's really swell to hear, Mr. Just Lee, and I appreciate that, but someone tried to kill me and I don't have any idea why. I'm stuck in a country that hates Americans and has no American embassy. I'm in a house in the middle of I-don't-know-where, and someone by the name of Lee something, or something Lee, tells me I have nothing to fear. Sorry, but I'm a bit apprehensive about the situation."

The old man grinned. "Anything else?"

"Absolutely, I'm just getting started. I want to know who you are and—" He stopped himself. "No, I don't care who you are, that's your business. But I want to know who you represent."

The grin widened, revealing a full set of yellow teeth. "Represent?"

"You know exactly what I mean."

Lee nodded thoughtfully, tipped back in his chair and folded his arms across his chest. "Why should it matter?"

"Because I don't think you're with the people who are supposed to get this." He reached down and tapped the briefcase, a somewhat meaningless point since he had no way of stopping anyone from taking the damn thing.

"Knowledge can be dangerous, courier. Sometimes it is best not to know too much."

Especially in North Korea, Simon thought, but he felt like a blind lab rat caught in a maze, who would die running in circles if he couldn't figure out what was going on. "I'll take my chances."

"And I will consider your questions."

"And while you're doing that," Simon said, trying to sound more confident than he felt. "I'll make that call."

Lee hunched forward, the legs of his chair hitting the floor with an emphatic thud. "That would not be wise. All calls in North Korea are monitored by the government."

"This is a scrambler phone. The conversation is automatically—" Before Simon could finish one of the young men rushed into the room, his voice low and fast and urgent.

The old man listened without interruption, then turned to Simon. "We have a visitor."

CHAPTER ELEVEN

Washington, DC

Sunday, 20 June 05:42:37 GMT −0500

Not yet six o'clock and Tucker Stark felt like he had already put in a full day. A very hard day. He lowered the window a few inches, hoping the cool morning air might amp up his energy. In the last ten minutes the sky had gone from pewter to pink, his favorite time of day, and he wanted to enjoy it. *Just in case.* If that damn courier slipped through his fingers again, the odds of seeing another dawn weren't very promising. "Mose, do me a favor and take the Memorial." It was something he never tired of seeing—watching the sun come up over the Potomac—and something he was definitely going to miss.

Moses Williams—who had been an agent with The Company for so long no one remembered his actual name—glanced at the rearview mirror. "You sure, Director? Be awful slow this time of day."

"I'm sure." At that time of day there were only two speeds, creep and crawl, so he might as well enjoy the view. *Washington traffic,* something he wouldn't miss.

Twenty minutes later they were in Georgetown, less than a minute from Tucker's three-story brick

Victorian—something else he would miss. The neighborhood was old and settled, the lawns well land-
scaped and perfectly cut, with lots of trees to
dissipate the summer heat. He had always loved the
house, loved coming home to his wife and children,
but they were now gone—*sixteen months*—ashes in
three clay pots, and he realized it was time to move
on. Move on or swallow that hard silver pill.

Moses wheeled the big Cadillac—a bulletproof
hand-me-down from the Presidential fleet—up the
drive and stopped directly adjacent to the brick path-
way leading to the front porch. Tucker snapped the
lock and had the door open before the wheels
stopped turning. Though it was protocol for his
driver to handle the door and stand post outside the
car, it seemed demeaning, especially for someone like
Moses Williams, a man who had given so many good
years to the agency. Especially for a black man in this
tight-ass waspy neighborhood. "Relax, Mose, I won't
be long. Just need to shower and change before heading back to the office."

Moses twisted around, his lips curling into a self-
deprecating grin. "Maybe I could mow the lawn or
something." He hooked his thumb back toward the
street where a gray-haired woman with a dog was
eyeing the car suspiciously. "Put your neighbors at
ease."

Tucker laughed. "That's Mrs. Addington, our
Neighborhood Watch commander. A real busybody.
She comes nosin' around, you have my permission to
shoot the old biddy."

The grin widened, a slash of white against his dark skin. "Excellent. I could use a little target practice."

Tucker hurried up the walk, twisted the key in the lock and paused—the moment he could never get used to—coming home to an empty house. Too many memories. Too quiet. He took a breath, stepped inside and closed the door. Even the smells were different: no fresh flowers from the garden or enticing aromas from the kitchen, only the faint odor of furniture polish and the various cleaning products used by the housekeeping service. What had once been a home, a very happy home, was now just brick and mortar, dead and silent. He started toward the stairs when he suddenly realized the quiet house was too quiet—no familiar *beep-beep-beep* to greet his arrival. He stopped, frozen in place, trying to remember if he had set the alarm on his way out. Yes, he was sure of it, and damn sure he wasn't armed. He took a step back, reaching for the doorknob when a familiar voice echoed down the hall.

"For the Director of Central Intelligence, you sure got one piss-poor alarm system."

For an instant Tucker considered yelling for Moses, but immediately rejected the idea. If Captain Buddy Baggett had been there to kill, he wouldn't have deactivated the alarm, wouldn't have said anything, and wouldn't have hesitated. It would be over. *Terminato.* A part of him, Tucker realized, welcomed the thought. *One more pot of ashes.* He took a deep breath, willing his blood pressure out of the red zone, and tried to speak normally. "You're right, Captain, I should have upgraded the system when I had the minicams installed." In the answering silence, Tucker could visualize Baggett scanning the walls for some sign of the nonexistent cameras. "I'll have a team replace the system today."

Baggett stepped into the hall. Dressed in a navy watch cap, a dark blue jogging suit, and black Nikes, he looked more like a cat burglar than someone out for an early-morning run. "The general wants a status report."

"Sure." Tucker turned toward the den, letting the man see his back, that he wasn't afraid. The combination office/library/bar had always been *his room,* the place where he now spent most of his time—away from the echoing voices—and the place where he had hidden the tapes of his conversations with the general. *Life insurance,* as he liked to think of it. If things turned bad, he could pull them out, claim he had another set at his office in Langley, and hopefully buy himself some time. He dropped into his chair behind the desk and motioned for Baggett to have a seat.

The captain ignored the offer, moving around the room, looking at pictures, touching mementoes and acting as if he had never seen any of it. Tucker knew better, was sure the room had been thoroughly searched, but could see that his large freshwater aquarium behind the bar had not been touched, that the tapes were secure and well guarded by the school of Red-bellied piranhas circling back and forth over the watertight container hidden beneath the sand.

Baggett caught the look and followed it. "Those are the ugliest damn fish I ever saw."

Tucker smiled to himself—a little demonstration wouldn't do any harm—and pushed himself out of his chair. "They look a little hungry." He pulled a raw chicken leg out of the under-bar refrigerator, attached it to a three-foot piece of string, and lowered it into the water. The scout darted forward, snapped off a bite with its razor-sharp triangular teeth, then retreated. The others rushed in to claim their share, and within a minute the leg had been stripped clean, leaving behind only a five-inch sliver of white bone.

Baggett watched the spectacle with a mixture of fascination and disgust. "Holy Christ, why in the hell would you want those things?"

"Bar entertainment," Tucker answered, anticipating the question. "They're always hungry and willing to perform." He dropped the bone into the trash and returned to his chair behind the desk. "I need to get back to Langley, Captain. What is it the general wants to know?"

Baggett turned slowly, his eyes as cold and gray as dirty ice. "So what the fuck happened, Corporal?"

Tucker stood up, not too quick, not really wanting to provoke a fight, but knowing this was the moment he needed to establish his position. If he showed a lack of confidence, that would be the image Baggett would carry back to the general. "Do you really expect me to answer that, Captain?"

The gray eyes blinked in surprise. "What?"

"I was proud to serve under the general, and remain his loyal corporal, but that's a remembrance of past wars and simpler times—a title reserved for the general alone. You address me in that manner again and I'll feed your testicles to my fish."

Baggett grimaced, like someone had just shoved a hot poker up his ass. "Now just wait a—"

Tucker interrupted, not about to give Rambo-man time to recover. "I'm the Director of Central Intelligence for the United States of America and I expect to be addressed in a manner commensurate with that position." He paused, just enough to make his point. "Captain."

Not many people—not anyone who lived to talk about it—ever spoke to Captain Buddy Baggett in such a manner, but his military discipline overcame his obvious desire to maim and destroy. "Yessir, you're right. It won't happen again."

Tucker nodded, as if that settled the matter, and sat down. "Excellent."

"I hope you'll forget this ever happened," Baggett said as he lowered himself into a chair on the opposite side of the desk. "As I will."

Tucker forced a smile but knew better. Captain Buddy Baggett never forgave or forgot, and would attack the moment the general removed his leash. "Absolutely." *When you're shoveling coal and coughing smoke in the bowels of Hell.*

"So what should I tell the general?"

"You tell the general everything was well planned and well executed. The Korean Army took the bait, thought they had the leaders of the KUP trapped in the square, and moved in. Unfortunately, they moved too quick, the KUP realized what was happening and grabbed the courier. In the melee our shooter failed to take him out." No reason to sugarcoat the situation, Tucker thought, that would only make him look desperate and out of control. "In other words, a real cluster-fuck."

This produced a faint smile from the inscrutable Captain Baggett, who understood the vagaries of battle and knew that things seldom went as planned. "I've seen the video."

Tucker nodded, sickened by the thought that he had anything to do with the deaths of all those children. "Unfortunately, the courier managed to get away."

"With the documents?"

"Yes," Tucker answered. "We have him tagged with two GPS units. One with the phone we gave him, one with the documents. They're still together."

"So why haven't you taken him? It's been eight hours."

"We're not going to take him."

"What?" Baggett cocked his head, a dangerous edge coming into his voice. "You're not terminating the mission?"

"Why should we? The situation is better than we planned."

"Better? How can you say it's better?"

Tucker ignored the threatening tone. If he could convince Baggett, despite their antagonistic relationship, he could convince the general. "Because the situation has not only stabilized, it's improved. It now appears the courier has stopped for the night. We'll wait a couple hours, just to be sure, then tip off the KSP."

"KSP?"

"Korean Security Police. They'll go in thinking they're about to sweep up a bunch of KUP leaders and—" He paused for affect. *"Ta-da!* As a bonus they end up with an American courier and a stack of documents implicating the President in a scheme to overthrow their government. We couldn't ask for a better situation than that."

"But what about the courier?" Baggett asked. "We can't afford to have him flapping his gums to the press."

"I've got two agents tracking the units. Neither one knows about the other. They have orders to take him down as the security police move in."

Baggett shook his head, not buying the scenario. "Taking him out in the middle of a riot is one thing, but this would look suspicious. Too many questions."

Tucker smiled to himself. "I hope so."

"What?"

"The President has ordered his elimination."

The expression on Baggett's face was almost obscene with pleasure. "Are you shitting me?"

"Nope, from his mouth to my ear. Or maybe I should say from his mouth to my recorder. It'll look like he panicked when the courier showed up on CNN and he ordered the hit."

"Ha!" Baggett barked a laugh of utter astonishment. "That's perfect."

"Not perfect," Tucker said, not wanting to put himself in that tight a box. "We can't control the Korean Security Police, and we can't be sure our agents will be successful in taking out the courier, but whatever happens—" He paused to make the point, knowing his words would be repeated verbatim. "Nothing will ever lead back to the general."

Baggett smiled, the cold grin of a shark at feeding time, and Tucker knew without a doubt exactly what the man was thinking: *You lead to the general.*

CHAPTER TWELVE

Pyongyang, North Korea

"You know this man?" Lee asked.

Despite the blood on his face and the deep gash across his forehead, Simon recognized the man immediately. He had obviously put up a considerable fight but was now lying unconscious on the floor, two of the young Koreans standing by in case he regained consciousness. "He was on the plane from New York."

"With the woman who tried to kill you?"

"Maybe. They didn't sit together, but I assumed they were working together."

The old man cocked an eyebrow. "Eh? They were not sitting together, yet you noticed them and assumed they were working together?"

What could he say? He noticed things, a subliminal talent he could hardly explain, even to himself. How did he know the man lying on the floor was left-handed, that Lee had once been a teacher, that the woman who tried to kill him was right-eye dominant? How did he know they had passed thirty-eight grandiose picture-flags of Kim Jong-il on their long trek from the square to this little house? It wasn't magic, just things his eyes noticed and his brain processed. "I first noticed them on the flight last week. I assumed they had been assigned to protect the documents." His assumptions, he realized, were looking less reliable by the minute. "Maybe I was wrong."

Lee nodded emphatically. "The man is a hired assassin. He knew nothing of the woman."

Very wrong. "How do you know that?"

Lee answered with a look of silent admonishment.

Stupid question, they had obviously beaten the information out of him. "Did he say who hired him?"

"He did not know," Lee answered. "All arrangements were made by phone. Payment was made through a numbered account in Latvia."

A country, Simon was sure, with very liberal banking regulations and very stringent privacy laws. "You're saying he was hired to kill me?"

"Of course."

Of course, as if the name Simon Leonidovich had just gone to Number One on the international "hit" parade. "To kill me and take the briefcase?"

Lee shook his head. "He had no interest in what you carried."

"That doesn't make sense."

Lee hunched his thin shoulders. "Someone does not like you, courier."

"Apparently." Someone very rich and powerful, but he couldn't imagine who or why. It obviously had to do with whatever was in the case, but why kill him and leave it behind? He had a feeling something was getting lost in the translation. "How did he find us?"

Lee smiled, as if that was the question he had been waiting for. "I think we are about to find out." He opened his hand, exposing a beeper-sized black box with a single white button and a two-inch LCD screen. He pressed the button and the screen brightened momentarily, then dimmed away. "Aaah." He pressed the button a second time, this time holding it down, and the screen brightened again, exposing a directional arrow and a digital readout. The arrow was pointing toward the table, directly at the spot where Simon had dropped his shoulder pack and the briefcase. Lee stepped toward the table and the digital number began to scroll lower, apparently measuring the distance in meters.

Simon picked up the briefcase and moved to the other side of the room.

Lee nodded as the arrow followed the movement. "Empty it."

Though he felt as if he were somehow violating his fiduciary trust, Simon realized he could make no reasonable argument against exposing the contents. He snapped open the case, breaking the seal of security tape, and glanced inside. Though he didn't know exactly what to expect, it certainly wasn't money. Lots of money, a shrink-wrapped brick containing packets of hundred dollar bills. He had the queasy feeling he had somehow stepped into the middle of a major drug deal, the kind they always show on television, and about a thousand North Korean narco cops were about to come busting through the door.

Lee leaned forward, the wrinkles tightening across his forehead. "That is all?"

Interesting reaction, Simon thought, to a fortune in American currency. "And just what was it you were expecting, Mr. Just Lee?"

The old man shook his head, not so much in answer as disappointment. "Some things you do not wish to know, courier."

"Right," Simon said, knowing exactly what the old man was thinking. "Knowledge can be dangerous."

Lee glanced toward the man lying unconscious on the floor. "*Ye*, very dangerous." Then he smiled, his enigmatic Buddha-like grin. "Empty case, please."

Simon turned the briefcase over, then carefully skinned it back over the mini-mountain of greenbacks. Taped on the bottom—now top—was a 500-gigabyte digital card, which he recognized as one of the newer options in portable data storage. "Bingo."

"Bingo?" Lee repeated. "What is bingo?"

"A computer disc," Simon answered, keeping it simple.

Lee held out the tracking receiver. "For this."

Simon shook his head; unless the disc contained some hidden power source, it had no way to transmit a signal. "I don't think so." He picked up the briefcase and stepped to one side. The arrow followed his movements. "It must be hidden in the lining."

Lee turned to one of his compatriots and issued some kind of directive. The young man jumped forward and tried to take the case, but Simon held on. "What's he going to do?"

"Destroy it," Lee answered.

"I wouldn't do that. They—" He only wished he had some idea who *they* were. "—might have a fix on this location."

"What do you suggest?"

"You understand the expression *wild goose chase?*"

Lee flashed a grin of yellow teeth. "Excellent idea."

While Lee issued new and more detailed instructions, Simon tried again to make some sense of the situation. The State Department, he realized, had to have been the ones who tagged the case. No one else had access. That didn't bother him; it made sense they would want to track the shipment, but how would a paid assassin have gotten his hands on the GPS tracking code? And for what reason? Who would gain from the death of an itinerant bagman? Only one reason made a smidgen of sense: someone wanted to sabotage the talks. Someone on the inside. Assuming the United States government didn't hire people to play sacrificial lamb, it had to be someone on the North Korean side. Someone like Jin Pak, who despite the events of the day, hadn't tried to make contact. Perhaps she didn't need to call because she already knew where her pudgy little lamb had gone to ground.

Never turn off. No GPS locator.

Trust, he decided, went only so far. He dug the satellite phone out of his shoulder bag and powered it off. Just to be on the safe side, he did the same with his new smartphone, severing his umbilical cord to the digital world. *Ugh,* he felt instantly alone and trapped, as far removed from his world as ET must have felt in the land of oranges and palm trees.

"He will fly like the goose," Lee said as the young man disappeared out the door with the briefcase.

CHAPTER THIRTEEN

Washington, DC

Sitting at the van's control console, Tucker zoomed in for a close-up as the Ford Freestar pulled into the Capitol lot, but the windows were too dark to see inside. Using the joystick controller, he adjusted the microwave antenna until he had the vehicle directly beneath the crosshairs, then locked on, hoping to pick up some conversation or at least confirm the number of passengers. Dead silence. Either no one was talking or Captain Buddy Baggett had come alone. Either way, this time Tucker was ready.

If the general came through the door first, as he always did, Tucker knew he was safe, but if Baggett stepped through the door it meant the general had decided to sever their relationship. Tucker turned the matchbox remote over in his hand and released the safety on the pre-aimed directional charge. *No hesitation.* One false move and a thousand steel pellets would turn Buddy Baggett into Buddy Burgers.

Tucker toggled the communication switch marked DRIVER. "You hear anything out of the ordinary, just drive."

The woman glanced toward the pinhole camera,

her words clipped and without resonance, as if speaking were an exertion. "Out of the ordinary?"

"You'll know it when you hear it."

She nodded and Tucker turned his attention back to the Freestar. As it pulled into the spot alongside, he activated the internal recorder, killed the lights, and pulled open the door. Being careful not to expose himself, he reached out, tapped the dark glass, and stepped back, his thumb poised over the remote trigger. *No hesitation.* He could hear the soft skid of well-oiled metal as someone opened the side door of the Freestar, then the familiar silhouette of the general as he stepped into the van and slid the door closed behind him. "Captain Baggett won't be joining us tonight."

Tucker dropped the trigger into his pocket—barely able to contain a relieved rush of held breath—and snapped on the lights. "Good evening, sir."

The general nodded and lowered himself into his usual chair. "You think it's okay if we stay here? I don't have much time."

"Yessir, the next security patrol isn't due for forty minutes."

"Good. I like the view."

Tucker glanced up at the double row of surveillance monitors, at least half displaying some aspect of the Capitol. "Yessir, it's a beautiful building."

"It's not just a building, Corporal, it's the heart of America. The people's house. Not that pile of bricks where the President parks his greedy ass."

"Yessir, that's true. With you as an example, I

hoped we could remind people of that. The true meaning of public service, but—"

The general interrupted, a ditch forming down the center of his forehead. "What are you saying? You think we've failed?"

Tucker saw no reason to sprinkle sugar over shit—in the last twenty-four hours the smell had become overwhelming. "It doesn't look good, General."

"Tell me."

"Just when we thought we had everything pinned down, we lost contact with one of our agents and one of the GPS transmitters. We have no idea what happened. The other agent had no choice but to follow the remaining signal."

"The one in the phone?"

"No," Tucker answered, "the one in the briefcase. She found it seven hours later, buried in a garbage dump. Empty, of course."

"You're using a woman?"

Tucker nodded, angry at himself for letting it slip—the general still believed a woman's place was in the home—and angry that he should have to justify his decision. "Yessir. She's a Korean national, perfect for moving around the city without drawing attention. She's backtracking now, trying to pick up the trail, but . . ."

"I get the picture. It's been two days, they could be anywhere."

"Yessir, anywhere in Pyongyang. Even locals can't leave the city without a travel visa. If the courier's alive and he's still with the KUP, that would, of course, make it easier. Much easier."

The wrinkles tightened across the general's tan forehead, his tone doubtful. "You don't really believe he's alive?"

"Yes, I think there's more than a fair chance. The KUP is intellectually motivated, committed to the re-unification of their country. They're not street thugs."

"Still, this man . . . what's his name?"

"Leonidovich. Simon Leonidovich."

"Right. The man's a liability. He must stand out like a pink cow in the desert. The longer they keep him around, the greater their own risk of being ex-posed."

"Yessir, that's true, but I've been reviewing his jacket." For emphasis, Tucker reached over and tapped his Leonidovich file. "The man's described as resourceful and charming. He may have talked his way out of trouble."

"Not the idiot we thought?"

"Apparently not."

The general nodded slowly, thinking about it. "Where's the President sit on this? I haven't heard a peep."

"I've got him in a holding pattern. He won't do anything as long as he believes the situation is con-tained."

"Okay, good. He's probably too worried about his portfolio to give it much thought."

"I'm sure of it."

The general shook his head, as if to erase the thought. "Okay, let's assume you're right about Leonidovich, that he's still alive. What do you think he'll do?"

Tucker hated such speculation; no one ever remembered when you got it right, and they never forgot when you missed. "It's hard to say, General. He's scared, confused, and doesn't have a clue about what's going on. One thing for sure, he wants out of that country."

"Along with half the population."

"Right, it wouldn't be easy, but with the help of the KUP it's possible. They're smart, well organized, and have a pretty good pile of money to help grease the way."

"Counterfeit money."

"Yessir, but if I couldn't tell the difference, no one else will. That money won't set off alarms until it hits a bank, and no citizen of North Korea is stupid enough to walk into a bank with American currency."

"Okay, let's assume the worst: they bribe the right people and Leonidovich manages to make it out of the country. What's he do then?"

Tucker shook his head, trying to avoid specific predictions. "That's hard to say. He may come home, he may run. If he tries to come home, we've got him. If he runs . . . well, that's a problem. He's been to almost every country in the world, there's no telling where he might go. And he's got some powerful friends. Big Jake Rynerson, for one."

"Rynerson." The general snorted, as if the word gave him a bad taste. "He's nothing but a cowboy."

"Yessir, a very rich cowboy who could make every political dog in this city stand up and bark."

"Point taken. So what's your best guess? What's Leonidovich going to do?"

"I think it depends on whether he has the data card."

"Why would he?"

"What's the KUP going to do with it?" Tucker answered back. "Computers are tightly controlled over there. We really didn't expect them to have their hands on the thing for more than a minute before the army grabbed it. On the other hand, Leonidovich is a computer whiz and he's going to be curious."

"Damn." The general slumped lower in his chair, as if the calcium had just been leached from his spine. "If you're right . . . oh shit . . . once he sees those documents, you know what he'll do."

"Yessir, he'll go straight to the press."

"Exactly. And once he starts talking about the State Department and how he got his hands on . . . damn, that would be bad . . . then we've got ourselves a problem." He shook his head. "A serious problem. He's one of the few people who could really blow the roof off this thing."

Tucker nodded, aware he also fit within that narrow criterion. "Yessir, I'm afraid that's true."

"You need to get more people on this thing. We need to flush him out before that happens."

"That's a problem, General. I can't use Company assets, not for something like this, and it would take too long to pull together a team of independents."

"Then you've got to anticipate where he'll go and get there ahead of him." He pulled a pair of half-lens readers from his breast pocket. "Let me see the man's jacket."

Tucker handed over the file, watching quietly as the general flipped through the pages, his eyes burning through the text like a bar-code scanner. He suddenly looked up, peering over the top of his readers. "What about his sister, Lara Quinn? She runs his office, they must be close."

"I've got taps and auto-trace equipment on both her home and office. Also the woman in Vegas, Caitlin Wells."

The general nodded and resumed reading. Five minutes later he stopped again, thumping his finger on a line of text halfway down one of the pages. "Here you go. This guy could find him."

Tucker had read the file less than three hours before and had a pretty fair idea who the general might be referring to. "Are you talking about Eth Jäger?"

"Damn straight! Also goes by the name Retnuh, which is 'hunter' spelled backwards. That's what they call him: the hunter."

Tucker hesitated, trying to think of some way to avoid the minefield. "He's incarcerated at the ADX facility in Florence. Life sentence."

"Right. And Leonidovich put him there. You get him out and he'll do anything you want. Probably like nothing better than to put your courier in the crosshairs."

You get him out. *Your* courier. The implication was clear enough. "And just how do you propose I do that?"

"You're the director of the fucking CIA for Christ sake. Figure it out."

Oh yeah, he could figure it out—a little fancy paperwork, some made-up investigation—and he could get Jäger released into CIA custody, but then what? According to the file, the man was like a pit viper, silent and deadly, an expert in disguise, deception, and death. "Are you sure about this, General? The man is unpredictable and dangerous. Hard to control."

"Nothing for you to worry about, Corporal. We'll let Captain Baggett deal with Mr. Eth Jäger."

Great, two pit vipers loose in the same room. Someone, Tucker had a feeling, was about to get bitten in the ass.

CHAPTER FOURTEEN

Pyongyang, North Korea

Trudging along beside the old man—whose endurance never seemed to waver—Simon struggled to keep his mind from going the way of his legs, which felt like swollen bags of water. Though the temperature was mild, maybe sixty degrees, the air was leaden with humidity, making it difficult to breathe, like sucking the air through a wet blanket. As always, they were flanked by two of the younger men, the other two somewhere ahead in the darkness. No one spoke.

They had moved three times in thirty hours, usually at night when the city was eerily silent, staying in single-story clay huts and avoiding the high-rise apartment buildings where most of the population lived. The little homes were sparsely furnished—chairs and tables were generally reserved for schools and government buildings—so they sat cross-legged on the floor, on cushions, and slept on hard mats. The food was always the same: some kind of rice dish with beans, egg soup, and *kimch'i,* a spicy fermented cabbage. A dish, Simon realized, he had developed a taste for. If he made it home, finding a good Korean restaurant would be high on his list of culinary priorities. *If*—something he wasn't feeling especially confident about. Lee still refused to discuss his group, though they were obviously opposed to the Kim Jong-il government. Every attempt to get information was met with some variation of Lee's favorite aphorism— *"Knowledge can be dangerous"*—a precaution Simon understood and appreciated, but which answered none of the questions that kept buzzing through his brain:

Why someone would want to kill him?

Who would benefit?

Who was the package *really* intended for?

Who did Jin Pak *actually* work for? Did she betray her government, sabotage the exchange, or . . . ? Lost in his constant tangle of questions, he didn't notice that the younger men had disappeared until the old man took his arm and began to steer him through a maze of tight alleyways. Just as the first faint rays of sunlight began to dampen the eastern sky, they slipped behind a fence and into another small home. Though still dark, Simon immediately sensed a change from the other places where they had stopped. He could smell it, a mixture of human and household scents: water and soap, noodles and nut oil, *ppang* bread and eggs boiled in vinegar, garden vegetables and fresh flowers, old books and new papers.

Mr. Lee ignited a toy-sized kerosene lamp, its pale yellow light barely enough to turn back the shadows. The room was small—a traditional Korean combination of living room, dining room and kitchen—with only a few select pieces of furniture. Despite its spareness, the room was spotlessly clean and warm in texture, with hardwood floors and an abundance of colorful, hand-embroidered cushions. Lee glanced around, the proprietary and pleased look of a traveler relieved to be home from his journeys. He motioned toward a cluster of cushions at one end of the room, then disappeared through a door on the opposite wall. It was the first time Simon had been left alone in two days, and he realized a level of trust had finally been established.

He barely had time to remove his shoes—Koreans, he had learned, never wore shoes in the home—before Lee returned with a white-haired companion. She was a tiny woman, somewhat frail and slow of step, her body encased from neck to ankles in a turquoise silk robe. "Courier, this is my wife, Hee-Won. She wishes for me to express her apology for not speaking your language."

Knowing Korean women never shook hands with men, Simon lowered his head, trying his best to imitate the customary greeting. *"Annyonghasimnikga."* Though he had learned to recognize a number of words and phrases, *good morning* was one of the few he felt comfortable expressing. "Please extend my gratitude for allowing me to visit your home, and my apology for understanding so little of your language."

Lee translated, the woman smiled and bowed, then retreated into the kitchen, her slippered feet shuffling silently over the polished wood. Lee lowered himself slowly onto one of the deep cushions, showing his age for the first time. "Time now," he said, "we decide about you, courier."

Thirty hours earlier those words would have sounded ominous, but now that Lee had dismissed his young brigade, Simon felt more confident in his safety. "I have friends. If you would permit me to make just one call—"

Lee shook his head vigorously. "Phone identify location. Many people now searching for American with bloody face."

Though he wasn't entirely convinced, Simon could tell that any further argument would be useless. He also realized that if the North Koreans got their hands on him, it could endanger Lee and his organization. "What do you have in mind?"

"Only two options," Lee answered. "First option, walk."

Knowing that all roads led north or south, and that south led to the DMZ and more land mines than Gates had dollars, it didn't take a genius to figure out what the old man was thinking. "Are you talking China?"

Lee nodded. "Over mountains."

After two days of trudging through the back streets of Pyongyang, *over the mountains to China* sounded somewhat daunting. "What's the second option?"

"Boat."

Simon had a strong feeling they weren't talking

about a leisurely cruise aboard the *Queen Mary 2*. "Tell me more."

Hee-Won interrupted, shuffling forward with a tray containing two bowls of bean-curd soup spiced with pork intestine, and a pot of tea. She slid the tray onto a low table next to her husband, poured the tea, then silently withdrew to her room. They ate in silence, no one saying a word until the soup was gone, then Lee picked up the conversation exactly where they had left off. "Many small boats now trade between North and South. Arrangements can be made."

Arrangements, Simon was sure, meant money. Real money, not the plastic never-leave-home-without-it kind. "I'm a little short on cash."

Lee waved his hand dismissively. "Money not important. I arrange everything."

Though Simon knew it wasn't a good question— that looking the old gift horse in the mouth thing— he couldn't stop himself. "Why are you doing this?"

The old man gave him a puzzled look. "This?"

"Why are you helping me? I know you're taking a risk."

Lee shrugged, as if the matter were of little consequence. "Confucius say, 'To know what is right and not do it is the worst cowardice.'"

Before Simon could think of an appropriate response, a young woman entered the room by the same door through which Hee-Won had disappeared. She was a lovely girl with raven-black hair that hung well below her shoulders and dark eyes that sparkled like onyx beneath her hooded lids. Barefoot and dressed in a white pull-over blouse and loose-fitting drawstring trousers, she looked about sixteen, with an angelic face and a girlish figure that would turn any teenage boy into a stuttering erectile fool. The old man smiled with unrestrained affection. "Courier, this is my granddaughter, Soo-Yun." He turned to the young woman. "Soo-Yun, this is my friend, Simon Leonidovich, from the United States of America."

Recognizing that he had passed some kind of test—*friend*, the first time the old man had dropped the "courier" moniker—Simon jumped to his feet. "Ms. Yun, my pleasure."

The girl smiled modestly and bowed her head. "Soo-Yun first name, sir." Her dark eyes strayed momentarily toward her grandfather. "Family name Lee." Her voice was beautiful, the texture of silk, and though her English came off somewhat abbreviated, it was precise and clear and filled with youthful confidence. "You would please call me Soo-Yun."

Simon returned the bow. "Thank you for correcting me, Soo-Yun. Please call me Simon."

"Thank you, sir. I have many questions of your country."

"I would be very pleased to answer them."

The old man reached out and squeezed his granddaughter's hand. "Later, child, if there is time."

She bowed politely, struggling to mask her disappointment. "Yes, Grandfather." She turned back to Simon. "It has been my honor to make your acquaintance, sir." She bowed again, then disappeared back through the same door from which she had entered.

"She lives with you?" Simon asked.

The old man nodded slowly, his eyes reflective. "My daughter's husband come from South. They escape there when Soo-Yun was but a year."

Simon wasn't sure what to say—most Korean families had relatives on both sides of the DMZ—but to leave a baby daughter, even for freedom, was a decision beyond comprehension. "That must have been extremely difficult."

Lee nodded again. "No one could think—" His voice faltered as he pulled the memory out of its lockbox, prying open the lid. "—think it could be so long."

"You should be proud," Simon said, trying to lift the man's spirits. "Soo-Yun is obviously a remarkable young woman."

"Most remarkable. She deserves more than—" He stopped himself, his dark eyes suddenly misty. "She is my treasure."

Not even Shakespeare, Simon thought, could have expressed so much love in so few words.

Lee took a deep breath and exhaled forcefully, as if to close the lid on that box of memories. "So, we agree. Boat. Best option."

Simon nodded, though he realized there was at least one other choice. It would be easier, probably safer, to turn himself in, explain that he had been caught in the disturbance at the square and in his rush to escape had gotten lost in the city. The story was weak—no one would believe an international courier had been lost for two days—but he had to believe the State Department could arrange his release. *Or not*. It had taken them a year to get the *Pueblo* crew home. A year of imprisonment and torture. Still, he might have seriously considered it if he knew it wouldn't endanger Lee and his family, but that was something he couldn't be sure of. "*Ye*, the boat."

"Good. I make arrangements. Everything settled."

Not quite, Simon thought. The money had disappeared, but he still felt an obligation to protect whatever secrets the data cartridge might contain. "What do you intend to do with the computer disc?"

Lee hunched his thin shoulders. "Computers are beyond our reach."

"I would like to have it."

"Knowledge can be dangerous," he replied. "Better we destroy."

Something Simon had considered, it was probably the smart choice, but he couldn't bring himself to destroy something that might contain so many answers. Answers that might save his life. "In North Korea knowledge can be dangerous. In America, knowledge is power."

Lee hesitated, the wheels turning behind his dark eyes, then he reached over and extracted the data cartridge from his canvas backpack. He held it up, inspecting it, as if trying to ascertain its value. "You may have the disc—"

Simon extended his hand, pulling the word for

thank you from his mental phrase book. "*Gomapsum-nida.*"

Lee drew the disc out of reach. "But it comes with a price."

Always, though Simon was certain the old man wasn't talking about money. Mr. Just Lee recognized things of value, not the stuff people bought and bartered and left behind. "Name it."

"I would like for you to deliver a—" He hesitated, searching for the right word. "How do you say in your business?"

"A package?"

"*Ye,* a package. A most valuable package."

"That's my specialty, Mr. Lee. Valuable packages. You get me out of this country and I'll deliver your package anywhere you want. Any country, county, or hamlet. You have my word."

"*Most* valuable," Lee repeated.

This time the words sent a warning tingle through the pit of Simon's stomach. "How big is this package?"

Lee spread his hands and shrugged. "Forty-five, forty-six kilos."

"Forty-six kilos . . . that's—" It took Simon a moment to access the conversion number from his cerebral database and make the calculation. "That's a little over a hundred pounds."

Lee nodded, a look of determined resignation that melted into an old man's sadness. "A treasure."

CHAPTER FIFTEEN

Super Max (ADX) Control Unit, Florence, Colorado

Wednesday, 23 June 15:22:15 GMT –0700

Captain Buddy Baggett wheeled the rental van—an inconspicuous Dodge Caravan—out of the small airport and onto state Highway 61, heading south. The road shimmered in the midday heat, turning the black asphalt into caloric waves of silver. "Doesn't look like any part of Colorado I'm familiar with."

Though he didn't say it, Tucker couldn't have agreed more. Hot, dry, and windblown, the washed-out landscape looked as if it belonged farther south, in the Chihuahuan Desert. There was even a bit of symmetry: like New Mexico, the government's favorite dumping ground for Native Americans, the area around Florence, with its nine state and four federal prisons, had become the country's favorite out-of-sight, out-of-mind penal landfill.

Baggett took his right hand off the wheel, turning it from side to side. "Jesus-fuck, I look like the god-damn Pillsbury Doughboy."

Tucker smiled to himself. It was true: the hybrid, fast-acting steroid had temporarily turned Baggett's hard-ass body into a fleshy marshmallow that not even his mother would have recognized. "Don't think about it. You'll be back to normal in forty-eight hours."

Baggett muttered something unintelligible and Tucker let it go, in no mood to cross swords with the ex–Army Ranger. When that moment came, and Tucker knew that it would, he intended to pick the time and place. "Better step on it, the warden's expecting us by four."

"What do you know about this guy?"

"Typical bureaucrat, afraid of Washington but can't wait to get there. Shouldn't be a problem." He tried to sound confident, but just the thought of getting trapped in some obscure lie was enough to liquefy his bowels. Christ, he could see the headlines: *Tucker Stark, Director of the CIA, caught* . . . What in the hell was he thinking?

Ten minutes later they were trapped in a small sally port, surrounded by razor wire–topped fences while guards methodically checked the van's underside with long-handled mirrors. Baggett leaned forward, staring up at the antihelicopter shield over the exercise yard. "Holy shit, just look at all those fucking cameras. I don't like this."

Tucker nodded. He didn't like anything about the whole damn operation, even though he felt confident no one would be able to identify them from video footage. The changes to his own appearance—a pair of thick-framed tortoise-shell glasses over colored contact lenses and a bald skull cap—had been dramatic. A pair of irregular lifts, which added an inch to his height and gave him a slight but memorable limp, completed the makeover. "What's to like? You're looking at home-sweet-home to the worst of the worst." And it was—from the individual zealots like Unabomber Theodore Kaczynski, to members of the most violent and vicious gangs in America: the Aryan Brotherhood, the Black Guerrilla Family, the Mexican Mafia, and the Dirty White Boys—the ADX Control Unit had them all. "It's the most secure prison in the world."

"That's what bothers me," Baggett said, with that special dropping inflection that made it an understatement. "Something goes wrong and we're not getting out of this joint."

"Nothing will go wrong," Tucker answered, trying again to sound more confident than he felt. "Just keep your mouth shut and let me do the talking."

Baggett scowled but said nothing, the depths of his anxiety revealed by his abnormal lack of response.

Once the guards had satisfied themselves that there was no contraband inside, outside or under the van's hood, the second row of gates opened and they were allowed to pull forward into a small parking area. From there, two guards escorted them to the warden's office, a room as sterile and bland and government-issue as the man sitting behind the desk. "Gentlemen." William Hulburt jumped to his feet. "Come in, come in. Welcome to Super Max."

Tucker stepped forward, being careful not to overexaggerate his limp. "Good afternoon, Warden. I'm Paul DeMott and this is my associate, Agent Joseph Kravec."

Everyone smiled, shook hands, and exchanged greetings. Before Hulburt could invite them to sit, Tucker motioned toward a small conference table, wanting to get the man away from his seat of power and to let him know, in the most subtle way, who was in charge. "Why don't we sit here? I'll need some room to organize my papers."

Hulburt nodded agreeably. "Excellent idea. Would either of you gentlemen like something to drink? Coffee, soda . . . ?"

Baggett shook his head. "I'm good."

"No thanks," Tucker answered. "As I'm sure you've been told—" Aside from the fact that two high-ranking FBI agents would be arriving from Washington, the man had been told absolutely nothing, but being out of the loop was not something most bureaucrats liked to admit. "—we're on a pretty tight schedule."

"I understand," Hulburt said, in complete contrast to his expression. "Let's get right to it."

While Baggett and Hulburt settled in, Tucker opened his briefcase and pulled two thick files, mostly bureaucratic scrap paper, but indexed, tabbed, and banded with a conspicuous *Top Secret* ribbon. "Okay." He looked up, straight into Hulburt's eyes. "Ready?"

Hulburt shifted uneasily in his chair. "Do I need a lawyer?" He smiled, as if he were making a joke, but it congealed in the middle of his face, revealing his discomfort.

Tucker laughed, as if that was a real hoot, but was

relieved to have the man on his heels. "I like your sense of humor, Bill." He hesitated, as if catching himself. "Is that okay? May I call you Bill?"

"Absolutely, please do," Hulburt answered, his voice rising in relief. "Now how can I help you gentlemen?"

Tucker flipped open the smaller file. "You have a prisoner." Though he had the number memorized, he glanced down at the cover sheet, just to demonstrate his access to official records. "Inmate number 89170–054."

Hulburt nodded cautiously. "Eth Jäger."

Tucker barked a laugh of honest astonishment. "Wow, you know the numbers of all your inmates, Bill?"

"No," Hulburt answered, without any pretense of retentive powers, "only the special ones."

"When you say 'special' . . .?"

"Eth Jäger is an alias. He has others. Retnuh. The hunter. To the best of my knowledge he's the only inmate currently in the system that we've never been able to identify."

Tucker thumped the file with his finger. "That we know. What we'd like to know is what isn't in the file. Tell us about him."

"Not much to tell," Hulburt answered. "The guy's in lockdown twenty-three hours a day. The only time he's out of his cell is when he's in the exercise yard, which is nothing more than a twelve-by-twelve wire cage. And when the weather's bad, he doesn't get that."

Tucker made a face, trying to look appropriately impressed. "Christ Almighty, that's gruesome. How's he pass the time?"

"You want to see?" Without waiting for an answer Hulburt jumped to his feet, stepped to his desk, swiveled his computer monitor around so they could see, then punched in a series of numbers on his keyboard. The ADX screensaver dissolved instantly, replaced by a full-screen visual of an eight-by-ten cell. Everything was steel and concrete, white and gray and black, including Eth Jäger, who was stretched out on the bed in white boxer shorts, a gray T-shirt, and a black patch over his left eye. Despite his age—late thirties or early forties—and twenty-three-hour-a-day confinement, he could have passed for an athlete, his lean body toned and hard.

"What's with the eyepatch?" Baggett asked. "I've forgotten."

"The cat," Tucker answered quickly, trying to cover up the fact that Baggett hadn't bothered to read the file. "You remember: Madrid, the flight attendant . . ."

"Oh yeah, right. The flight attendant."

"Doesn't seem to bother him," Hulburt said, as he settled back into his chair. "The man reads at least twelve hours a day."

This was exactly the opening Tucker had been hoping for, but he forced himself to go slow. "That much?"

Hulburt nodded. "He's very disciplined in that regard. He jogs in place and does isometrics at least two hours every morning. Then he takes a sponge bath and reads until the midday meal. That's the only time he eats. After lunch he'll take a short nap, exercise for another two hours, take another sponge bath, then reads until lights-out."

"That is disciplined," Tucker agreed. "What kind of stuff does he read?"

"The classics. Eastern philosophy. Western poetry. A lot of high-tech computer stuff."

Tucker flashed a smile, a pay-dirt grin, and glanced at Baggett. "That's our boy."

Baggett bobbed his head enthusiastically. "No doubt about it."

Hulburt glanced back and forth between them, a look of amazement. "You know who he is?"

"Sure do," Tucker lied, knowing no more than what was in the file. "We know everything about the man."

Hulburt looked relieved, the way a confused person does when they finally figure out what's going on. "That's great. Really great. Who—"

"Sorry, Bill. I'd like to, but—" Tucker ran his index finger over the *Top Secret* ribbon. "It's a matter of national security."

"National security." Hulburt repeated the words softly, as if he were reading from the Dead Sea scrolls. "Really?"

Tucker nodded and leaned forward, as though to share a secret. "We're here to take that bad boy off your hands, Bill."

Hulburt's pupils popped like a pair of umbrellas. "You are? I mean—"

"I know." Tucker bobbed his head as if he understood exactly what the warden was thinking. "Most unusual."

"Most unusual," Baggett repeated in a way that made it sound like a colossal understatement. "*Very* sensitive."

"And the reason," Tucker explained, "we didn't want to use federal marshals to make the transfer. We simply can't afford a leak."

Hulburt frowned, the pained expression of a man who treasures rules and regulations. "What exactly are you asking? I can't just—"

Tucker cut in, not wanting to give the man a chance to start throwing up bureaucratic roadblocks. "Bill, we're not asking you to throw open the vault. Of course not. We have the necessary paperwork." Tucker pulled the "transfer of custody" order out of his file and pushed it across the table. "All we're asking for is a little discretion."

"Depending on it," Baggett added.

Hulburt quickly read through the document. "Excellent. Looks good."

No, Tucker thought, it looked *perfect;* the signature of Justice Harold Reese so dead-on, not even the judge could have identified the document as a forgery.

"But what—" Hulburt hesitated, a look of embarrassment. "I'm sorry if I'm being dense here, but what exactly are you gentlemen asking? What do you mean by 'a little discretion'?"

"It's very important that word doesn't slip out that we've taken him," Tucker answered. "This guy's a hard nut. It'll take some effort to uh . . . you know . . . extract the information we need."

"And we'll need time," Baggett added, "to take down the network."

Tucker scowled, as if Baggett had revealed too much. "That's really all we can say, Bill. Believe me, your cooperation will be recognized and duly rewarded when this thing goes public."

Hulburt made a dismissive motion with his hand, as if such things didn't matter to him, though they clearly did. "Glad to help." He pursed his lips and made a little motion with his thumb and forefinger, the lock and key. "Strictest confidence."

"Great, I had a feeling we could count on you, Bill."

"So how do you want to handle this thing?"

"We'll need to interview him first," Baggett answered. "Just to confirm there's no mistake."

"Privately," Tucker added. "No video or audio. This is all classified."

Hulburt smiled knowingly and shook his head. "Trust me, that guy's not going to tell you anything. We've been at him for nearly two years and he hasn't even given up his age."

Tucker leaned forward, his tone confidential. "We have information you don't, Bill. We know which buttons to push."

"I hope you're right."

Tucker nodded, though he knew hope had nothing to do with it.

While Baggett checked the air vent, Tucker booted his laptop and activated his audio jammer, just to be on the safe side. The room was small and sterile and gray, a concrete box without windows, used by attorneys for private meetings with their inmate clients. The only furniture—a stainless-steel table with a bench along one side, and a single stainless-steel chair beyond the reach of anyone sitting at the table—were bolted to the floor. Hulburt cracked the door and poked his head inside. "Ready?"

Tucker nodded. Despite his training and all the old-boy spy crap he put up with at the agency, he couldn't suppress a feeling of anticipation at meeting the enigmatic Eth Jäger: the man with no name. How many professionals would be so good at protecting their secrets? Not many, he was sure of that.

Jäger came in flanked by two uniformed guards, his leg restraints limiting his movement to a shuffle, his hands cuffed to a steel cable encircling the waist of his orange jumpsuit. With his steel-gray hair, light brown skin, and black eyepatch, he looked like a Bedouin pirate—the kind of man women found attractive, in a formidable, dangerous way.

No one said a word as the guards seated and locked him to the chair, leaving him virtually immobilized. Throughout the process Jäger showed absolutely no emotion, his face as impassive as a stone god. Hulburt pointed to a button adjacent to the door. "Whenever you're through just hit the buzzer." He followed the guards out of the room and closed the thick, soundproof door.

Though Jäger had been through the exercise half a dozen times, he sensed immediately that this was different. The warden had dropped his pompous I'm-in-command persona the moment they entered the room, as if outranked by the two strangers sitting at the table.

The older of the two, a bald-headed man with heavy tortoise-shell glasses, spoke first. "Mr. Jäger, I'm Paul DeMott. Federal Bureau of Investigation."

Jäger stared straight ahead, not about to give anything before he knew what was going on. Something about the situation felt staged, the two men nothing like the starched-shirt, mousy investigators who had questioned him previously. Two men, judging from their body language, who didn't like each other.

DeMott cocked his head toward the man on his left. "And this is my associate, Agent Joseph Kravec."

Joseph, even the name sounded wrong. In contrast to his soft puffy skin, there was something dangerous in his eyes and the way he sat, all stiff and silent in coiled readiness, a cobra measuring its prey.

DeMott hesitated a moment, waiting for a reply, then smiled as if he found the silence amusing. "What would you do to get out of here?"

That had to be the stupidest question Jäger ever heard, but it was also unexpected and startling in its implications, and it took all his willpower not to react. "That would depend—"

DeMott interrupted, his voice rising impatiently. "Don't start feeding me that jailhouse bullshit! You want to talk or you want to live in this fucking cage the rest of your life?"

Jäger struggled to contain his anger. Did this fool really believe he lived here, in this concrete coffin? The hunter lived in his mind, far removed from the smell of kept men and arrogant keepers. But still, there were times he could not ignore the wire, could not block out the cage and key, and he could not stop himself from asking, "What is the cost of this freedom?"

"Simple," DeMott answered, his expression going from anger to satisfaction. "You have a reputation for finding people. We would like to retain your services."

Too simple. Before they came to him, other people would have tried and failed. "One person?"

"Yes."

Much too simple. It would have to be someone beyond the reach of government. High-profile. Protected. A drug lord or politician. Someone they wanted dead, not found. "And if I were to locate this person?"

DeMott let out an exasperated sigh and pulled off his glasses. "If you need to ask that, I'm talking to the wrong man."

Jäger nodded, the only part of his body he could move more than an inch. "I understand." What he didn't understand was why the man was hiding his identity—the indentation on his nose was much too light for such heavy glasses. "And if I agree to do this?"

DeMott smiled and slipped the glasses back on. "Goodbye. *Adiós. Arrivederci. Au revoir. Auf Wiedersehen. Hasta la vista.* Pick your language. Get lost. Have a nice life."

It sounded too good to believe, and Jäger didn't. "A pardon?"

"No," DeMott answered without hesitation. "But we can make you disappear from the system. You understand computers—" He splayed his fingers into the air. *"Poof.* There one minute, gone the next."

Jäger doubted that any FBI agent would have such power. More likely they planned to make *him* go *poof* once the job was done. That would explain the other man, the silent one with dangerous eyes.

"Of course," DeMott continued, "you're thinking that once you're out of here you could just disappear without fulfilling your part of the bargain."

Jäger frowned, as if the thought had never entered his mind, but that was exactly what he was thinking.

DeMott leaned forward, his voice low and penetrating. "That would be a very stupid mistake. I would just hunt you down and throw your ass back in this fucking hole for the rest of your fucking life."

Jäger wanted to scream, *I am the hunter, I am the one who sets traps, I am the one who . . .* but something in the man's voice, something not yet said, made him listen.

"You can run, but you can't hide." DeMott's lips tightened, the smile of a man about to drop the bomb.

"Because I will know where you are every minute of every day."

Now Jäger understood: some kind of electronic tag. The police did it all the time, with ankle bracelets, but he had a feeling this man had something more sophisticated in mind. He wanted to resist, to pretend he had something to negotiate against their electronic leash, but he had nothing and they knew it. "How soon would I be released?"

"Within the hour."

He could barely contain the rhythm of his heart. "I accept your offer."

DeMott sat back, no expression, clearly expecting the answer. "You don't want to know who you're looking for?"

Jäger didn't really care—he would hunt, someone would die—but he tried to appear interested. "Of course."

"Simon Leonidovich."

The name vibrated through his skull like the closing notes of La Bohème. He had dreamed of revenge for two years—*an eye for an eye*—and now he would have it.

CHAPTER SIXTEEN

Pyongyang, North Korea

They had been walking since midnight, northwest, toward the river and the industrial part of the city; Mr. Lee out front, setting his normal double-time pace, Soo-Yun close at her grandfather's heel, Simon a few steps back. The air was cool and damp, the sky clear, the moon casting a glow of dim yellow light over the gray landscape and the endless rows of nondescript cement houses. In the soft light Soo-Yun looked like a mature young woman—blue jeans, white T-shirt, backpack, her long hair woven into a fishtail braid—but occasionally, in a silent catch between footsteps, Simon could hear a quick shuddering breath and realized she was only sixteen, a frightened teenager struggling to hold back the tears. The scene at the house had been heart-wrenching, Soo-Yun holding her grandmother as the old woman tried and failed to conceal what they all knew to be the truth: that they would never see each other again. It had to be a terrifying experience for the girl, to leave her country and home and the only parents she had ever known, but also exhilarating: the adventure, the escape, the thought of living in freedom and meeting her mother and father for the first time.

As they moved from residential to industrial, ghostlike wisps of fog began to drift out from between the buildings, the air heavy with the sulfurous odor of factories and the smell of the river, a combination of damp rot and putrefied fish. It was nearly three o'clock before Lee finally slackened his quick pace and stopped behind an unbroken line of old buildings. He motioned for them to wait, then disappeared into the building they were standing behind.

Simon pulled a water bottle from his shoulder pack and offered it to the girl, who was still struggling to catch her breath. "You okay?" he whispered.

"Ye." She took a sip and passed it back. "Grandfather"—quick breath—"very strong, no?"

"Very strong, yes. The man's a jock."

"Jock?" She shook her head, the dark braid swinging like a pendulum. "I am not familiar with this word."

Before he could answer, the rising voices of Lee and another man reverberated through the porous and rotting wood. Though Simon couldn't understand the words, he could tell by the tone that something was wrong. "You understand what they're saying?"

"Grandfather very angry," she whispered back. "The other man—" She hesitated, searching for the right words. "—is wanting money."

"More money?" The agreed-to price—five thousand for each of them—had already been paid from the shrink-wrapped bundle of American currency.

She bobbed her head. *"Ye.* More money."

That was not what Simon wanted to hear. He could accept the fact that they were dealing with people who smuggled desperate souls in and out of North Korea—which seemed almost honorable considering the political and economic conditions—but he didn't like the thought of entrusting his life, and especially the life of Soo-Yun, to profiteers who only cared about money. Once they reached the sea, what would prevent them from simply dumping their human cargo into the blue abyss? He tried to mask his concern. "Don't worry, your grandfather is a very smart man. He'll work something out."

She nodded, her expression a mixture of relief and disappointment; afraid that he would, afraid that he wouldn't.

Lee was back two minutes later, his voice low and angry, his faced contorted with the effort of not screaming what he clearly wanted to say. "Captain now claim price too low. All foreigners pay double."

"Does he know you have more money available?"

Lee frowned, offended by the question. "You think I am stupid, courier?"

"Sorry, dumb question. What we need is a carrot." He could see the wheels turning in the old man's head, trying to decipher this need for a vegetable. "A reward," Simon explained, "once we're safe in Seoul."

"Ah, this is carrot. You have idea?"

Simon nodded, quickly working it through his mind before answering. "I keep an emergency fund with American Express. I'll pay him another twenty thousand when we reach Seoul."

"He ask only five more."

"I understand, but for twenty thousand he won't be thinking about anything but getting us to Seoul."

"Ah, big carrot." Lee glanced at his granddaughter and smiled, as if to reassure her. "This very good plan." Then he pulled a paper bag from his shoulder pack and handed it to Simon. "Here phones. Best not to use until out of Democratic People's Republic." He immediately turned his head and spat, as if to excise the offensive words from his tongue.

Soo-Yun said something in Korean, her tone admonishing but her dark eyes teasing and full of love. The old man hung his head, accepting the reprimand with a good-natured smirk. "Sorry, child, very bad habit." He turned to Simon and winked. "Time to feed the rabbit."

They followed him inside, stopping just inside the door to let their eyes adjust to the darkness. The building was long and narrow, the air stagnant and foul, thick with the smell of mold and rat droppings. After a moment Lee motioned them forward, leading them through a maze of crates and discarded equipment and out the back, onto a loading dock that cantilevered out over the river, a dark-brown clog that looked thick as molasses in the moonlight. Two young men, not more than twenty-five, with brawny bodies and simple-minded expressions, were busy loading crates onto the deck of what looked like a converted tugboat, old and weather-beaten, no more than thirty-five feet in length and ten abeam. Though adequate for the river, it hardly looked substantial enough for sea duty, especially in rough water. "Kind of small," Simon whispered, trying not to sound overly apprehensive.

"Boat stay close to coast," Lee said, as if reading his thoughts. "Weather good."

A third man, sea-grizzled and hard-looking, obviously the captain, emerged from the pilothouse. He flashed a big car-salesman grin and stepped onto the dock. His eyes took a quick sightseeing trip over the nubile landscape of Soo-Yun before settling on Simon. He smiled again and stuck out his hand. "My name Choi. You English man? I talk good English."

Though nearly asphyxiated by the man's foul breath, Simon forced a confident smile and took the man's hand, a calloused lump as hard and knotted as a piece of oak burl. "My name Smith. Canadian man." He was pretty sure Choi had exhausted his reservoir of English. "You talk Canuck?"

Choi stared back in trancelike bewilderment. "Smit?"

Simon nodded, as happy with Smit as Smith. "Ye. Smit."

Choi turned to Lee and immediately began jabbering away in Korean. They argued back and forth for a couple of minutes, Lee holding firm to his offer. By the time Choi realized he wasn't going to get any more up-front cash, the two deckhands had finished lashing down the cargo and were sitting and smoking and leering openly at Soo-Yun.

The negotiations now over, Choi smiled agreeably and led them onto the stern of the boat, where he pointed to a metal cargo container, indicating that this was where Soo-Yun and Simon should hide. Though Simon had never had a problem with claustrophobia, there was something about being locked in a metal box no larger than a trash Dumpster that did the trick. In his mind he could hear Choi ordering his men to push the thing overboard the minute they came in contact with a North Korean patrol. "You must be joking."

Lee obviously agreed, and there was another spirited exchange with the captain, but this time it was Choi who refused to compromise. Lee nodded, not happily, and turned to Simon. "Captain Choi promise to release you after passing Namp'o harbor." Lee pointed to the ten on his watch. *"Yol si."*

Simon still didn't like it, didn't like anything about it, but he had the feeling staying in North Korea would be even more dangerous. *Seven hours.* He could take about anything for seven hours. "Okay, but I think you should let Soo-Yun decide for herself." He flicked a glance toward Choi. "In my language."

Lee nodded his understanding, turned to his granddaughter and smiled hopefully. She tried to return the smile but it came off flat, like a young child facing a dentist for the first time. "Whatever you think, Grandfather."

Lee shook his head slowly, as if the effort were painful. "No, child. Mr.—" He caught himself. "Mr. Smit is right. You are young woman now. Must decide for yourself."

She hesitated, struggling to choose between the safety and protection of the grandparents she loved for an uncertain future with the parents she had never known. It was a pitiful choice, one no child should have to make, with no right answer. She took a deep breath, the kind one takes before plunging into an unknown darkness. "I should like to stay with you, Grandfather." She released the breath, an outrush of air that sounded like a sigh. "But I understand why you think I should go. It is the right decision."

Lee pulled the girl into his arms, his Trotsky glasses magnifying the tears that burst into his eyes. "I hold you in my heart, child."

She held on, desperately, the tears burning behind her eyes. "And I you, Grandfather." Then without another word she pulled away, as if knowing she must do it now or never, and ducked into the container.

Struggling to keep his own emotions in check, Simon took Lee's hand and bowed his head in respect. "Your treasure is safe with me, Just Lee. You have my word."

Blinking back tears, the old man returned the bow. "I promised you a sunrise, courier. I wish you many."

"And you, my friend." He bowed again, threw his shoulder bag in beside Soo-Yun, who was scrunched against the back wall, and crawled inside. Choi pushed the door closed, and the light faded into blackness.

CHAPTER SEVENTEEN

Los Angeles

Thursday, 24 June 13:15:04 GMT −0800

Jäger came awake slowly, drifting back and forth between dreams and reality. He felt weak, his mouth dry as chalk, but he forced himself not to swallow or move before he could make some sense of it. All the sounds were muffled and far away. No human sounds. Even his bed felt different, as if . . . then it all came rushing back, a mini slide show playing across the back of his eyelids: the prison, the interrogation room, the two FBI agents. *Leonidovich.* They wanted him to kill Leonidovich. The last slide flickered across the screen, the silent one with dangerous eyes rising from his chair, the spring-loaded syrette, the sting of the needle . . .

He cracked the lid of his good eye. The curtains were closed, but there was a small gap where they came together, allowing just enough sunlight to make out his surroundings, one of those mini-suites for the executive traveler: small kitchen and dinette, full bar with four stools, a six-chair conference table, and a comfortable conversational area. *Prima classe.* But where? How long had he been unconscious? His throat felt hot and raw, like he'd been asleep for a week with his mouth open. The glowing red numbers on the bedside clock read 1:17. He rolled onto his side, found the television remote and began scrolling through the channels until he found the information channel.

Welcome to the *Royal Ambassador at LAX*
Thursday, June 24

Local time (PST): 1:18 PM
Current Temperature: 76 F

Guest Services: channel 215
Transportation: channel 216
Events: channel 217

LAX? It took a moment to process the information. *Los Angeles International Airport.* He threw back the blanket, saw he was naked, and stood up. A lightning bolt ripped through his midsection, from his rectum to the pit of his stomach, and it was all he could do not to cry out. *Merda!* It felt like they had given him to the *iarrusi*, the faggots on D Block, for a night of rip and rape. Then the reality registered: no ankle bracelet, no electronic tags. The *bastardi americani* had gone inside, through his *Bsino*, attaching some kind of micro-transmitter to his intestinal wall—a violation he would make them regret.

Moving carefully, he crossed to the windows and edged back the curtain. Despite the proximity and the fact that he was up ten floors, the distinctive gateway arch at LAX could barely be seen through the brownish gray smog. He stared down at the freeway—twelve lanes of motionless cars and trucks—and wondered how anyone could choose to live in such a vile city, where they devoted sixty-five percent of the land to machines that belched out carbon monoxide. *Americani!*—they would trade their own children for a new automobile.

He dropped the curtain back in place and snapped on one of the bedside lamps. The closet doors were open, revealing a leather travel bag, two pairs of Italian shoes, and an assortment of shirts and slacks. All new, all expensive. Somehow he knew everything would fit perfectly, and that it was a message: *Do not underestimate our power.* That he believed; any organization that could pull him out of Super Max had to be powerful. But not the FBI, he was sure of that. The ramifications of exposure were too great. Too great, he suspected, for any bureaucratic agency. More likely it was one person, someone well connected. Rich, powerful, and well connected. The question was, who? Even more important, why? Why Leonidovich? Why did the man disappear? What did he have? What did he know? Normally Jäger didn't concern himself with the whatfors and the whys—that was not the job of the hunter—but this was different. This time he needed answers. They would provide insurance. His bargaining chip. His permanent pass to freedom.

He started toward the bathroom when he noticed the array of items strung out across the surface of the large rosewood desk:

A notebook computer, lightweight and state-of-the-art, with built-in Wi-Fi.

A Globalstar satellite phone.

Six packets of used currency, with a total value of one hundred thousand dollars, divided equally between British pounds, Euros, and American greenbacks.

Two passports: one American, one British.

A carton of Fatima cigarettes, his personal choice in Turkish tobacco—something few people knew—and a luxury he had been denied for two years. *Another message.*

And a black calf's-leather billfold, containing a complete set of identity cards: California driver's license, Safeway Club card, Blue Shield insurance card, Macy's credit card, Citibank Visa card, and an American Express card, the kind with no limit. Everything looked distressed and used, all issued in the name of Adam Huntsman. *First hunter.* Were they just being clever, or was this another message? Either way, it was clear enough. They had power and wealth and resources, and they wanted him to know it, to think twice before he ran. *Bastardi americani!*

He closed his eyes and pictured his villa in Taormina, his panoramic view of the Mediterranean and the coast of Italy. *Favoloso,* the best vista in all of Sicily. He could almost taste the salty air, feel its rejuvenating effects against his skin. And now he was free, next to one of the largest airports in the world, only a flight away from . . .

No, better to play the obedient bloodhound until he could find a way to sever his electronic leash. Until he could find Leonidovich. Just the thought made Jäger's heart quiver with anticipation, like a hunting dog on point to the scent of its prey.

CHAPTER EIGHTEEN

Korea Bay

Thursday, 24 June 13:30:17 GMT +0900

Despite the intensity of the sun—within hours the metal skin had gone from cool to sizzling hot—not a sliver of light managed to penetrate the walls of their iron box. Simon tried to control his breathing, but it was useless; he was panting like a dog trapped in a car with the windows up. To make matters worse, the stench of past human cargo seemed embedded in the metal—urine and sweat and excrement—and he couldn't get the smell out of his nostrils. "Shouldn't be long now." The moment the words cleared his lips he realized his exaggerated confidence sounded foolishly stupid. A couple more hours and they'd be dead, literally baked alive.

Soo-Yun, who was scrunched along the opposite wall, attempted to respond but it came out strangled and he realized she was crying, trying desperately to hold back the flood. He wanted to reach out and pull the girl into his arms, to assure her everything would be okay, but she was at that vulnerable age—half woman, half child—too mature to be cuddled, too immature to properly interpret the intentions of older men. As a compromise, he reached over, found her knee and gave her a couple of reassuring pats. "He'll release us once we're at sea." The words sounded false, even to himself.

"Jigum myosimnikga?"

In her fear she had slipped into Korean but he recognized the common phrase: *What time is it now?* He pressed the stem on his watch, momentarily illuminating the dial. "One-thirty."

"Gomapsumnida."

"You're welcome." *Eleven hours,* they should have been on the open sea by now. He tried to tell himself there had been some unexpected delay, but he knew better. Despite the boat's battered appearance, the engine sounded surprisingly strong, the steady vibration not having wavered since they reached the main channel of the river. That was good, every minute brought them closer to Seoul and to freedom—but so what? A successful escape involved not just getting away, but arriving somewhere. *Alive.* Though he knew other boats might be in the area, this was clearly no time for caution. He pulled off a shoe and began pounding the container wall. A moment later Soo-Yun joined in, but the hot iron absorbed their blows like a sponge, the dull echoing sound lost beneath the steady growl of the diesel. Within a minute they were both exhausted, puffing and wheezing like a couple of overweight boxers, and they abandoned the effort.

The next thirty minutes disappeared into a black hole, neither of them making any attempt to communicate, the struggle to breathe consuming all their energy. Then, just when it seemed they couldn't survive another second, someone slid the bolt aside and pulled open the door, drowning them in a bath of fishy, salty, and moist air. Blinded by the intense light, Simon found the edge of the door and managed to pull himself upright and onto the deck. Shielding his eyes against the sun, it took a few seconds to make out the features of Captain Choi and his two deckhands, who were staring with unrestrained lust at Soo-Yun as she emerged out of the darkness, her face dripping with sweat, her white T-shirt soaked through, her perfect pear-shaped breasts clearly visible through the thin cotton. Realizing he needed to divert their attention before things turned ugly, Simon stepped back, blocking their view. "Where are we?" he demanded, speaking with an authority he had no way to support.

Choi gave him a puzzled, slightly wary look. *"Modaradurossoyu."*

Soo-Yun, who suddenly recognized her exposed condition, pasted herself against Simon's back. "He says he doesn't understand."

Simon nodded—he could see the coastline fading in the distance—and kept his gaze fixed on Choi, giving the man an angry glare. "Tell him I'm very upset. That I'm a very rich *migugin* and if he wants his money he better start treating us like honored guests." Simon wasn't worried about the exaggeration; all Koreans considered Americans to be rich. "And Soo-Yun . . ."

"Sir . . . ?"

"You must say it with great conviction, as if . . . as if your virtue depended on it. You understand?"

She hesitated, but only a moment, then her words came hard and fast, with surprising strength. Choi's eyes narrowed ominously, looking Simon up and down for some sign of weakness.

"And tell him," Simon continued before Choi could muster a rebuttal, "that I demand the very best stateroom available on this fine boat of his." Though Simon realized the weatherbeaten old tug had nothing remotely close to a stateroom, he suspected Choi lived on his vessel and had some kind of personal accommodations.

"Are you sure? I don't believe—"

"I understand," Simon interrupted, "but I want you to say it, Soo-Yun. To say it as if you believed this crazy *migugin* was about to explode and sink this garbage scow."

She did as instructed, her tone reasonable but insistent, with a touch of feminine guile. Choi shook his head so hard his leathery jowls lagged behind his chin. *"Aniyo! Aniyo! Aniyo!"*

"Ye, ye, ye," Simon fired back.

Soo-Yun, who had now figured out the game, took up the argument, her stubborn tone reminiscent of her grandfather. The captain continued to shake his head and didn't stop until she finished. "It's no use," she said. "He says we must remain in the box. He promises to leave the door open—" She extended her arm over Simon's shoulder, showing him a four-inch gap between her thumb and middle finger. "—for air."

Simon expelled a breath of resignation, as if beaten, but he had no intention of spending another twenty-four hours in that iron coffin. Not another minute. Knowing he had an excellent chance of ending up dead or locked away in a North Korean jail, it seemed like a propitious time to splurge on better accommodations. "Tell him I'll pay another five thousand dollars for the use of his room."

Soo-Yun relayed the offer, and though Choi tried to mask his feelings, his dark eyes gleamed with greedy enthusiasm. He glanced over his shoulder, dismissing his deckhands with a gruff order, then redirected his attention back to Simon. *"Aniyo!* Ten thousand!" When it came to the subject of money, neither his intentions or his English could have been clearer.

Simon nodded without hesitation, anticipating the demand. *"Ye."*

Choi held up his index finger—*"Hana!"*—then pointed to Simon and barked out some new demand.

"He says ten thousand is for one person only. That it would not be proper for us to be in the same room."

Simon smiled and nodded, as if he found this sudden moral concern to be perfectly reasonable. "Ask him if another five thousand would make it proper." He realized it would cost him ten.

Once again, Choi needed no interpretation when it came to numbers. *"Aniyo!* Ten thousand!"

Simon flopped his arms, a gesture of concession, letting Choi know he had won the battle. *"Ye."*

Choi waited while they retrieved their packs, then escorted them to his quarters below deck. Located near the stern, adjacent to the engine compartment, the room was loud and small, without a porthole to the outside—a combination bedroom, kitchen, and bathroom—if a hand sink and a two-burner hotplate could be considered a kitchen; if a vacuum toilet could be considered a bathroom, and a wooden cot, a bedroom. Everything was filthy, either smeared or covered in a fine layer of oil. Choi gestured grandly around the minuscule cabin, said something to Soo-Yun, then cackled uproariously and bolted the door.

"What did he say?" Simon asked, his words barely audible above the vibrating rumble of the engine.

Holding her backpack over her chest, she averted her eyes. "He says—" Embarrassment tangled her tongue. "He says we should enjoy our honeymoon suite."

"Captain Choi is a pig, pay no attention to him." He gave her shoulder a reassuring squeeze. "Soo-Yun, you have nothing to worry about. Not from me and not from those idiots on deck. That's the reason I offered Choi so much money. He won't do anything to jeopardize his newfound wealth."

"But it's so much, sir. Do you really—" She hesitated, not knowing how to say it.

"Yes, I have the money. And if Choi gets us to Seoul he's welcome to it, the whole forty thousand." Though he realized getting the money and keeping Soo-Yun safe might be mutually exclusive. "But we still have a problem. The good captain is never going to let me go alone to get the money. I could just disappear."

She nodded slowly, the picture coming into focus. "He'll want to go with you?"

"No question about it. Which leaves you alone with the slobbering twins."

She grimaced.

"Right, but not to worry. I've got a plan."

"What sort of plan?"

"As soon as we're out of North Korean waters and it's safe to use my phone, I can arrange for someone to meet us in Seoul. If Choi keeps his end of the bargain, he'll be paid. But if he tries anything funny, this person will notify the harbor patrol."

"Aaah," she sighed with relief, like someone slaking a thirst. "This sounds like a very good plan."

"Right, except the hull of this boat is metal. My phone may not work."

Her relief dissolved into apprehension.

"In which case we'll go to plan B."

"Plan B?" She cocked an eyebrow. "What is plan B?"

"I'm still working on that one," he admitted, "but as a last resort we can always jump"—an inadvertent but somewhat revealing choice of words—"to plan C."

Her eyebrow found a new direction to cock itself. "You have a plan C?"

"Plan C is always the same—run like hell." He gave her a confident smile, as if this was just an adventure, something he did all the time. "In this case—swim."

She studied his face, trying to judge his seriousness, then she smiled and shrugged, as if to say, *why not?* "Soo-Yun very good swimmer. What about you, sir?"

"Like a fish." More like a sea slug, but why quibble over details? Teenagers could be so finicky about life-and-death decisions.

CHAPTER NINETEEN

Los Angeles

Thursday, 24 June 07:21:41 GMT –0800

Stretched out on the bed, the laptop beside him, Jäger had been dozing when a sharp *ping* jolted him awake. He rolled onto his side as a world globe bloomed onto the monitor and began to rotate toward its target, identified by a scrolling line of text along the bottom of the screen.

................cellular contact: s. leonidovich...................
.........cellular contact: s. leonidovich..........................

Jäger watched as the globe locked in place over Southeast Asia and began to zoom in on the Korean peninsula. *Find him! Find him!* The picture seemed to expand as the details grew sharper, zeroing in on an area near the DMZ, when a small red dot and informational dialog suddenly ballooned onto the screen.

Target Acquired

Latitude	**37°**	**43' North**
Longitude	**126°**	**41' East**

Jäger smiled to himself, savoring the moment. *I am the hunter.* He started to magnify the area when the dot suddenly disappeared.

Target Lost

But he had what he needed. He pushed himself into a sitting position and quickly typed in the coordinates. The program instantly zeroed in on the location, a spot approximately twenty miles northwest of Seoul, directly over the River Han. *Buongiorno,* courier. What are you doing in South Korea? Why are you running? What do you know? What do you have that these rich and powerful *Americani* want so badly? Information, Jäger knew, Leonidovich would not easily surrender. But that was just part of the hunt—the trap, the capture, the extraction of information—his reward for two years behind the wire. *Dolce vendetta.* Long before the angel of death swooped in to save him, Leonidovich would scream his secrets.

Soon, courier. Very soon.

CHAPTER TWENTY

River Han

Friday, 25 June 14:21:14 GMT +0900

Sitting cross-legged on the narrow cot, Soo-Yun watched in hopeful silence as Simon circled the tiny cabin, moving his cellular from one spot to another, searching for a signal. He had been trying off and on for five hours, without success, and the battery was rapidly heading toward the dead zone. He hit the power button and lowered himself to the toilet—the only place to sit—and forced a confident smile. "I need to save some power for emergencies." He couldn't imagine things getting much worse.

"Nothing?"

"I caught a signal for a few seconds, but it disappeared before I could make a connection."

"What about that one?" she asked, pointing her chin toward the satellite phone.

"Same thing," he answered, "I checked it while you were sleeping." He didn't like lying, but the phone remained his only link to Jin Pak and the answers to why someone wanted him dead. When he used it, he needed to be ready, to turn a trap into a lair.

Soo-Yun nodded stoically. "Plan B?" Though her

face remained frozen, in that inscrutable expression of Asian detachment, her cheeks reddened noticeably, embarrassed just thinking about it.

"Unless you can think of something better." There wasn't anything *better*, they had gone over every possible scenario, but he wanted her to make the choice, to at least feel they had come to the decision together.

"You are sure we are on the river?"

"Absolutely." He couldn't be sure of anything, not really, but the surface seemed smoother and they could now talk without shouting, so he knew Choi had reduced speed. "If we're lucky we'll be out of the water before they turn this thing around."

"Assuming . . ." She smiled, just a little, pleased to use the word he had taught her only hours before.

"Yes," he admitted, "assuming." Assuming they actually made it out of the room and over the side. Assuming one of the slobbering twins didn't jump in after them. Assuming Choi didn't have a gun and decide to turn his golden goose into shark pâté. "It's your decision."

"Then we will do it," she said, her voice flat and without resonance.

"You're sure?"

She lifted her chin in a self-mocking way. "It is time for Soo-Yun to be a woman."

He wasn't sure about the rite of passage, but he wasn't about to argue the point. "We need to get ready." Using an old razor blade he had found earlier beneath the sink, he quickly cut a square of oilskin from the back of Choi's rain slicker and laid it on the cot. "Okay, give me your papers and identification."

Soo-Yun pulled her papers and a small bundle of photographs from her backpack; then, looking a bit sheepish, she peeled open a seam and extracted two packets of American currency. "For my new family."

Simon immediately recognized the money as part of the shrink-wrapped bundle, and knew that each packet contained ten thousand dollars. "I understand."

"Grandfather said—"

"You don't have to explain, Soo-Yun. I would have been surprised if your grandfather had not given you some of the money."

"You may offer it to Captain Choi if you think—"

"No," Simon interrupted, "that might put us in even more danger. But—" He picked up one of the packets, broke the paper seal, and stuck the bills in his pocket. "—just in case."

Within a minute he had everything—including his wallet, passport, phones, and the 500-gigabyte digital data card—tightly wrapped in the oilskin and sealed with zip ties from his emergency kit. "You ready?"

She nodded.

He pulled off his shoes and stuffed them into her backpack along with her canvas tennies, then began to pry loose a rusty three-foot section of pipe that ran from the ceiling into the back of the toilet. Behind him he could hear Soo-Yun peeling off her clothes. The pipe broke free with surprising ease and instantly began flooding the cabin with greenish, sour-smelling water. "Okay if I turn around?"

"Ye."

Completely naked, she was doing her best to cover herself with one of Choi's oily towels but the material wasn't quite large enough for the job. Simon tried not to look but that was impossible as she squeezed past him to position herself by the toilet, and he saw enough to know that any man who wasn't momentarily mesmerized by such a beautiful face and perfect body would have to be gay or stone-cold dead. At least that's what he hoped. As he stretched out on the cot, the water began pouring beneath the door and into the passage beyond. "You remember the signal?"

"Ye." Her voice quivered, like a child lost in the dark.

Tucking the pipe in close to his body, he turned to the wall as if he were sleeping, then took a deep breath and closed his eyes, trying to control a rising sense of panic. Now that they were actually doing it, the plan seemed ridiculously flawed, everything depending on one person noticing the water and opening the door. In theory it seemed reasonable—if they were on the river, Choi would be at the wheel, and only one person ever checked the engine—but what if that person called for help? What if . . . Then he heard it, the muffled sound of someone splashing through the water. *Oh shit—oh shit—oh shit!* His heart shifted into overdrive, the sound like a kettle drum—*KA-BOOM, KA-BOOM*—so loud he could barely hear the bolt as someone snapped it open.

One person, he was almost sure. He grabbed a quick breath and held it, forcing himself to focus. *Not too hard,* he sure as hell didn't want to kill anyone. *Not too soft,* he couldn't give the man a chance to call for help.

The next two seconds seemed to last forever, every impression magnified: the sound of the door as it jerked open . . . the flush of water as it spilled into the passageway . . . then a dead beat of silence, intense and electric . . . followed by a yelp of surprise— just as they planned, not too loud—and Simon made his move . . . rising and turning . . . the pipe a blur as it came out from behind his body . . . Soo-Yun standing there, naked, making no attempt to cover herself . . . the big deckhand frozen in midstep halfway through the door, eyes bulging in voyeuristic astonishment . . . and then the dull *thunk* as the pipe ricocheted off the side of his head. Unfazed, the man turned, stared at Simon in silent disbelief, then reached for the boning knife at his belt. Simon jerked the pipe back, ready to swing again when the man suddenly closed his eyes and pitched forward, face down into the shallow stream of green water.

Soo-Yun, still making no attempt to cover herself, looked at Simon with an odd expression of little-girl embarrassment and womanly pride, then she blushed and turned away. Thankful he hadn't killed the slobbering fool, Simon struggled to heft the inert body out of the water and onto the cot as Soo-Yun scrambled back into her T-shirt and jeans. They had decided, after some debate, to wear their clothes, making it harder to swim but easier to disappear once they were out of the water. Nearly exhausted by his efforts to get the huge man out of the water, Simon took a moment to gather himself. "You ready?"

Soo-Yun nodded, her face flushed, fear mixed with excitement.

He leaned close, keeping his voice low. "Once you're in the water, don't wait for me, no matter what happens."

She gave him a suspicious look. "You not good swimmer?"

"I'm an excellent swimmer," he lied, "but my body's built for endurance, not speed. You just go like hell. Plan C. I'll catch up."

"But—"

"No buts," he interrupted, trying to sound parental. "You take this." He pushed the oilskin bundle into her hands and hooked the backpack over his shoulder. "We need to get out of here before slobbering beauty wakes up." Before she could delve deeper into his aquatic skills, he glanced into the passageway, saw that it was clear, and started toward the ladder located directly behind the pilothouse.

The air was hot and muggy, stagnant with the odor of motor oil and machinery and . . . ? Then he caught it, the faint after-scent of a thundershower as it wafted down through the open hatch. Motioning for Soo-Yun to wait, he crept up the ladder, just far enough to grab a quick peek over the edge. They were definitely on the river, a reddish brown muck that stretched out wide behind the boat, the nearest bank not more than forty feet off the starboard side. Nei-

ther Choi or the second slobbering twin were anywhere in sight, both apparently inside the pilothouse.
Thank you, God.

Simon motioned for Soo-Yun to follow, then pulled
himself up onto the deck—still damp with rain—and
crouched behind a container of freight. Within seconds Soo-Yun popped through the hatch, nimble as a
cat, and together they began crabbing their way toward the stern, in and out between the crates, trying
as best they could to keep something between themselves and the rear windows of the pilothouse.

Almost there, Simon thought, suddenly realizing
how fast the boat was churning through the muddy
water. He glanced toward the riverbank, which now
seemed ominously deserted and remote. Only forty
feet, he told himself. *No sweat.* So why didn't he believe it? He crouched behind the last stack of crates
to catch his breath, trying not to think about the
jump, the shit-brown water, and the churning backwash of the propeller—but could think of nothing
else.

Soo-Yun hunkered down alongside, a look of concern clouding her face. "You okay, sir?"

"Sure. No problem." Nothing like a *sir* from the
mouth of a delectable young nymph to make a middle-
aged man feel old and feeble. "How about you?"

Before she could answer, the angry, high-pitched
howl of slobbering beauty rose up over the sound of
the engine. The man clearly did not have the sense to
be knocked senseless. It was all the motivation Simon
needed to get past his fear of drowning. Jumping to

his feet, he swooped Soo-Yun into his arms and stepped to the rail. "Plan C!" Then he spun around, a complete 360, mimicking his old shot-putting style, and tossed her as far as he could away from the boat. She seemed to hover in mid-air, clutching the oilskin package like a parachute before disappearing into the dark water.

He twisted around for the backpack, but Captain Choi and the slobbering twins were coming on fast and he realized he would never make it over the rail before they had him. *Plan D!* Thank God he had the wind at his back! He yanked the ten thousand in currency from his pocket and tossed it into the air, fanning the bills as he let them go. They dipped and swirled in the breeze—a mini tornado of greenbacks—spreading out over the deck, directly into the path of Choi and his two lackeys, who immediately set about trying to save them from a watery grave. Simon snatched up the backpack, scrambled over the rail, took a deep breath, and jumped.

He hit the water and went under, but popped up almost immediately as the warm current swept him downstream. Once free of the boat's backwash, the current slacked considerably and he realized he would make it unless Choi suddenly decided to give chase, but all three of the men were still scrambling around on deck, pushing and shoving and fighting over the wealth like a bunch of crazed monkeys, seemingly unconcerned at the loss of their human cargo. Relieved, Simon twisted around, searching the dark surface for Soo-Yun.

A good sixty yards downstream, already halfway to shore, she raised an arm and shouted—"Simon! Simon!"—the first time she had used his name.

He gave her a thumbs-up; then, clutching the backpack like a football, began a one-arm dog paddle toward the shoreline.

CHAPTER TWENTY-ONE

CIA Headquarters, Langley, Virginia

Saturday, 26 June 13:18:57 GMT –0500

"He's here?" It was all Tucker could do to hide his surprise. "In the building?"

The voice of Sara, his weekend secretary, reverberated back through the intercom. "Yessir, along with his military attaché, a Captain Baggett. They're already on the elevator."

Shit. "Thank you, Sara. Please show them in the moment they arrive."

"Yessir."

Before he could even think through the ramifications—there were so damn many—she pushed open the door. Tucker jumped to his feet, trying his best to look pleased. "General, what an unexpected pleasure."

The general smiled slightly, as if it amused him to catch Tucker by surprise. "Good afternoon, Director. I hope I'm not interrupting anything important."

"Absolutely not," Tucker answered. "I reserve weekends for paperwork." He motioned toward the round, six-chair conference table in the corner. "You're always welcome, you know that."

"I had some business in the building," the general explained, putting on a show for the secretary, "and just wanted to say hello to one of the best damn soldiers to ever serve under my command."

"Thank you, sir, but I think you're being overly kind." He waited for Sara—who was obviously impressed to be in the presence of such a luminary figure—to close the door before continuing. "This is really not a good place to meet, General."

The big man held up a hand, waiting for Captain Baggett, who began circling the room with an electronic wand, obviously searching for active recording equipment. Tucker could have assured them otherwise, but realized they were actually checking on him, making sure he hadn't activated any hidden recorders before they came in. Baggett completed his three-sixty sweep and gave the general a thumbs-up. "All clear."

The general nodded and dropped into one of the tan leather chairs that surrounded the conference table. "I received your four-one-one flash and thought something critical might have happened."

Tucker knew better—a 411 information flash was not the same as a 911 emergency flash—but he couldn't very well imply the general was being disingenuous. "Yessir, something critical has happened." He lowered himself into a chair on the opposite side of the table. "But nothing that couldn't have waited until our meeting tonight."

"Well, like I said, we were in the building." He glanced at Baggett—who was now standing at modified attention near the door—as if to confirm the fact. "It would have been rude of me not to stop by. Noticeably rude." He leaned forward over the thick glass. "I can't imagine there's a more secure place in all of Washington."

Tucker understood the implied question and nodded. "Yessir, the walls are soundproof, but—"

"Good," the general interrupted. "I'm getting awfully damn sick of that van."

"Yes but—" Tucker stopped himself. It was too late now, the damage was done. "But we need a good cover story. Someone is sure to ask why you were here and what we talked about."

"No reason to make things complicated," the general answered. "We served together in Nam. I stopped to say hello and we chatted about old times. Simple as that."

Right, simple as that, but nothing was ever *simple* when it came to the general. "Yessir, that should work."

The great man leaned back in his chair, his eyes taking on their familiar intensity. "So, what's happened?"

"Some of the counterfeit money popped up. In Seoul. We traced it to a small boat crew who work the waters between North and South Korea. They were hired to smuggle Leonidovich out of North Korea." He could have mentioned the girl but saw no reason to further complicate what was already a debacle.

A frown creased the general's forehead. "I thought that sort of thing was impossible."

"No, sir, it's quite possible if you have the money to pay for transportation and bribes."

"So he used our money to get away?"

"Yessir, that's exactly what he did."

"Clever bastard. So he's in Seoul?"

"Probably. He left the boat about fifteen miles northwest of the city, but we know he's heading in that direction."

"Who's 'we'? How do you know?"

"I have an agent right behind him," Tucker answered. "The same one who traced the money and found the boat crew."

The general narrowed his eyes, which suddenly looked cold as blue ice. "You're talking about that female agent?"

"Yessir, Jin Pak. She's very good." Tucker regretted the words instantly, that he should once again feel the need to justify his decision to use a woman. "She'll find him."

The general nodded slowly, accepting the news with surprising calm. "It's a setback all right, but it's not a catastrophe. There's no possible way Leonidovich could know what's going on."

Tucker could hardly believe his ears. Not a catastrophe? Had the general suddenly gone daft? "No, but he may have the data disc, and it wouldn't take a genius to break the encryption. We set it up that way. And if he—"

The general interrupted. "Don't panic, Corporal. No one is blaming you."

Panic? Blame? Who the fuck was talking about blame?

"You'll just have to find the man and recover the disc before he has a chance to do that."

"And we will," Tucker answered, forcing himself to speak with a confidence he didn't really feel. "One of them should have him by tomorrow."

"Them?"

"Jin Pak or Eth Jäger. That's the guy—"

"Yes, yes." The general waved his hand impatiently. "I know who he is."

"As you know, we've got him tagged with two internal GPS units. He arrived in Seoul just a few hours ago."

"Good. Excellent. So these two are working together?"

"No," Tucker answered. "Neither one knows about the other."

"That's even better. Let's keep it that way."

"Of course, but—"

"It sounds to me like you're right on top of things, Corporal." He glanced at Baggett and nodded meaningfully, as if to say, *we're impressed.* "You eliminate Leonidovich. You destroy the disc. Everything's go."

Everything's go! Tucker felt like he was talking to an ostrich with its head buried in concrete. "The plan is no longer operational, General. We needed Kim Jong-il to hold up the documents in front of the world and accuse the President of conspiring with the KUP. That's not going to happen. There's no way we can get Leonidovich back in North Korea."

"Who cares about Leonidovich? All we need is a new courier."

"Sir, it's not that simple."

"Sure it is. We've lost some time, nothing more. So

it takes a little longer than we planned. You crank up the machine and start over."

Start over! "It's too late, sir. That window has closed."

"Nonsense. The country has lasted this long, it'll survive a few more weeks."

A few more weeks! It had taken him a year to set up the network—most of which had already been dissolved—and the man wanted to start over. "It would take months."

"No, you're just feeling negative right now. That's understandable." The general smiled and shook his head, as if speaking to a stubborn child. "We have a perfectly good plan. Everything is still in place. I have full confidence in your ability to pull this off."

But it wasn't that simple. They had the phony recordings of the President talking to Leonidovich and a briefcase full of incriminating documents locked in the man's safe. The *Arirang* festival was over, and after the last fiasco Chairman Kim was not likely to invite the international press into his country anytime soon. What the hell was the general thinking? "It's too late, sir. There's too much risk. We'll all end up in the ADX facility in Florence. No one will understand what we were trying to do. We'll be branded traitors and criminals." Tucker could see that he wasn't getting through and tried to appeal to the general's more vainglorious view of himself. "All your years of service and all you've done for this country will be forgotten."

The general straightened his shoulders and raised

his chin. "We can't think of ourselves at a time like this, Corporal. The country is too important. We *have* to move forward. It's our duty. Our sacred duty."

But Tucker realized it wasn't duty or country the general was thinking about. The man was already hearing *Hail to the Chief* in his dreams. "Yessir, you're the boss. I'll start putting the pieces back together." But he wouldn't. Couldn't. The general was no better than the President, both of them corrupted by power. Somehow he had to stop the madness, stop it before they were all in cells, waiting for the needle.

CHAPTER TWENTY-TWO

Westin Chosun Hotel, Seoul, South Korea

Sunday, 27 June 20:04:25 GMT +0900

"Hi, it's your favorite brother." The connection was bad, and Simon could hear the faint echo of his own voice reverberate back through the receiver. "Is everything okay? How are the kids?"

There was a dead beat of silence, the momentary delay of transcontinental communication, before Lara's sleep-fractured voice came snapping back over the line. "Is everything okay! How are the kids! Damn you, Boris, we see you on television with your face all bloody and then you disappear off the face of the earth for eight whole days! Just how do you think we are?"

"Sorry, I didn't mean to worry you. Everything's fine, but—"

"Everything's fine! So why didn't you call? Where have you been? Where are you? What's going on? When . . . ?"

He waited until the questions ran out—realized she was only venting her anxiety—then gave her the summarized and sanitized version of what happened; but, if anything, his attempt to allay her concerns only seemed to irritate her more.

"That's your story! You and a teenage girl escaped from North Korea aboard a cruise ship!"

"You've got the gist of it."

"And you stayed in the same room?"

"Captain's quarters, actually. First class all the way."

"And you're now staying in a hotel room that's registered in her name?"

"Hey, someone's trying to kill me. Until I figure out what's going on I didn't want to announce my whereabouts."

"And she's with you! A sixteen-year-old girl! Are you crazy, Simon!"

"Christ, Sissie, you don't have to say it like that, like I'm some kind of child molester. It's a two-bed-room suite and she's got her own room."

"That's not the point, Simon. It's the perception. False name, underage girl—if someone—"

"I understand," he interrupted. *Perception is reality.* And the perception, he had to admit, sounded pretty bad. "But it's a moot point. She called her parents the minute we arrived. They live in a small town about six hours south of the city. They'll be here this evening."

"With the police, no doubt."

"Now stop that. This is a nice family and she's a wonderful girl. There's nothing to worry about."

"Right. First you tell me someone's trying to kill you. You don't know why, you don't know who. Then you tell me you're in a hotel room with a teenage girl. Just when do you suppose it might be appropriate to worry?"

"I love you too."

She humphed, trying to sound disgusted, but the effort lacked conviction. "Speaking of love, you better call Caitlin. She's been worried sick."

"I already did."

A slight pause, then a soft "Oh," cool as cream.

Only one word, but he recognized the sound: *wounded female.* "Come on, Sissie." He tried to keep his tone light and chiding, but felt like he was sticking his head out of a foxhole. "I would have called you first, but I didn't want to wake the kids."

"I understand."

Meaning she didn't. *Women!* They had such a knack for making a man feel about two feet tall. "I'll let you know what's going on as soon as I talk to someone at State."

"You better call Victoria first. She's been hearing some things."

"What kind of things?"

"You know Vic, she's so cryptic. Just said you should call her *before* making any kind of travel arrangements."

He didn't like the sound of that. "Okay, I'll give her a call."

"And she doesn't have kids. You don't have to worry about waking *her* up."

Before he could respond the line went silent. *Damn*—what was it with women? Always the last word, one more twist of the knife. "Soo-Yun!"

She poked her head out of the bedroom. "Sir?"

"Don't grow up."

She shook her head, the silky mass of black hair. "I do not understand."

"Me neither."

She gave him an indulgent half-smile, apparently getting used to his odd sense of humor, and disappeared back into the bedroom.

He pulled his cellular, tapped ADDRESS BOOK, scrolled down to Vic's home number, then punched the numbers into the hotel phone, knowing she would never say anything over the airwaves.

She answered on the second ring, her voice thick and furry. "This better be important."

"Are you paying too much for long distance? Would you like to save—"

"Bagman!" There was a faint *click*—lamp switch—and the sound of covers being thrown aside. "You okay?"

He allowed himself, if only for an instant, the delicious vision of the luscious Victoria Halle sitting on the edge of her bed—nude. "Some women actually think I'm better than okay."

"The weird, kinky ones, no doubt. Where are you?"

"The Westin in downtown Seoul," he answered. "A place where they understand a little English."

"Thank God, I was starting to think we'd lost you."

"Trust me, if I was lost God wouldn't be the one to come looking."

"So how did you manage to get out of Pyongyang?"

"I took the scenic route, by land and by sea."

"I can't wait to hear the story." Her tone mutated from chatty to businesslike. "You've talked to Lara?"

"Not five minutes ago. She said you wanted me to call before—"

She interrupted. "Are you on cellular?"

"No, I'm using one of those old-fashioned hotel hookers."

There was an extra beat of silence beyond the normal intercontinental hiccup. "Hotel hookers?"

"Yup, the ones that charge you ten bucks a minute whether you make a connection or not. Very expensive, very frustrating, very unsatisfying."

She laughed, a throaty chuckle. "You really are a sexual pervert."

"Maybe, but I'm fun and safe. Just like this phone."

"Nothing's safe."

"You're just paranoid because—" He stopped himself, knowing he shouldn't mention the NSA, land line or not. "Because of who you work for."

"Damn straight." Her voice modulated in pitch as she stood up and began to move. "You figure it out."

Damn, sometimes it was just impossible to subdue the male-pig chromosome and he had a vision of her striding across the room, her long naked limbs, her firm . . . *No,* he felt like he was cheating on Caitlin and forced himself to turn off the picture. "I get the message. So what's this about travel arrangements?"

"There's been an International O and R attached to your passport."

He ran the acronym through his mental database and came up empty. "O and R?"

"Observe and report."

"I don't understand."

"It means that any time you pass through customs, anywhere in the world, it's going to get reported."

The distinctive *Welcome to Windows* melody resonated in the background, and he realized she was now at her computer. "Reported to who? For what reason?"

"That's what's odd," she answered. "There's no explanation attached to the directive, and though the document appears to be US in style, it doesn't identify the agency of origin."

"So who does the information get reported to?"

"Good question. It's an unlisted international 800 number. Frankly, I didn't know such a thing existed until I tried to track its source. The number leads to an unidentified voice-mail box, the only option being to leave a message. When I tried to trace the number, it disappeared behind a firewall and a shield of ghost numbers while their computer tried to countertrace my call. Very cutting edge and just a bit too familiar."

"Familiar?"

"To the software they use at Langley."

"CIA?"

"You got it." Her voice dropped a notch, to a secretive whisper. "What are you up to, Bagman? Why would the CIA be interested in you?"

He could understand why the State Department would be interested—but the CIA? Unless they were working together. He didn't want to lie, certainly not to Victoria Halle, but he couldn't say much without violating his pledge of nondisclosure. "I don't know, Vic." At least he couldn't be sure. "Really don't."

"But you have an idea."

It wasn't a question. "Well—" He hesitated, trying to filter his response through the restrictions of the nondisclosure agreement. "—of course I understand why someone might be looking for me. Lara said the thing at the square was all over the news. But I don't know why the CIA would be involved. What do you think?"

"I think you use that passport and someone's going to be waiting for you at the other end of the rainbow. They might be friendly, they might not. They might be CIA, they might not. But until you know, you better be damn careful about making travel arrangements. You get my meaning?"

Loud and clear, and he didn't like it. He wanted to go home, he wanted to believe it was the North Koreans who wanted him dead—though he couldn't imagine why—and now that he was out of the country he was safe, the matter behind him, but he had a feeling it was all wishful thinking, that he was a pawn in a game he didn't understand. "Yeah, that's clear enough, Vic, even for a dummy like me."

"I mean it, Simon. You're always getting involved in some kind of weird shit. You need to be careful."

"I will," he promised. "Don't worry."

"But I do. Is there anything I can do to help?"

He hated to ask, didn't want to get her involved,

but without his laptop and the security of his passport, he suddenly felt marooned, helpless to fight back against . . . against the *weird shit*. "Well, since you're sitting there anyway, maybe you could run a quick search on—"

"Hey," she interrupted, "how'd you know I was at my computer?"

"I'm clairvoyant."

"And I'm serious."

Screw serious. Serious was for accountants and judges. "You remember that little dinner party you threw last month?"

"Yeah, sure."

"While you were busy in the kitchen I attached a Secret-cam to your monitor."

Four or five seconds ticked by in utter silence. "A Secret-cam?"

"Yup."

"I'm in the spy business, you idiot. There's no such thing."

"Whatever you say."

She hesitated again, as if considering the possibility. "Okay, smart guy, what am I wearing?"

From idiot to smart guy in ten seconds, a new record. "Not a damn thing. You're naked as a snow lily."

"In your dreams."

True, but those were pre-Caitlin dreams, and a man shouldn't be held responsible for old fantasies about young women. "Believe what you want. I'm looking straight at you."

"Okay, lucky guess," she admitted. "Excuse me while I get a robe."

"Good idea. You stand up I get to see your ass."

"Okay, that's enough, Leonidovich, you're freaking me out."

"Sorry about that."

"You get rid of that broad in Vegas and I'll play this game."

"Careful now, I happen to like that broad very much."

"I like her too, that's why I'm not doing this."

"Doing what?"

"Having phone sex with you."

Phone sex! Is that what she thought? Is that what it was? "I was just teasing you."

"Bullshit. I know good foreplay when I . . . Forget it."

"So you're experienced?"

She ignored the question, her voice back to business. "A quick search of what?"

"Two names," he answered, turning off the image of her naked body. "See what you can find on a Stanley Powers and a John Clayton."

"Get real, those names are way too common." She began tapping at the keys, apparently logging into the NSA mainframe. "Give me more."

She was right. *Way too common.* Was that just a coincidence? *Probably.* "Add US government to your search criteria."

"Still too wide."

"Okay. Why don't you start with the State Department?" He tried to make it sound like a guess, the first of many possibilities. "Maybe we'll get lucky."

Her fingers hammered away at the keys, followed by a few seconds of silence, followed by a double *ping* as the search engine successfully completed its mission. "Well, well, well, aren't you the lucky one." It was obvious from her sarcastic tone she didn't think luck had anything to do with it.

"Oh?" He tried to keep his voice casual. "What did you get?"

"Just a minute."

He waited, knowing she was scanning the document for clearance restrictions before disclosing any information. From the corner of his eye he saw Soo-Yun glance into the room, apparently checking to see if he was still on the phone, before disappearing back into her bedroom.

"Okay," Vic said, "what do you want to know?"

All he wanted was confirmation that the men actually worked for the US government, which she apparently had, but he had to ask something. "Anything stand out?"

"Well, let me see. Clayton, John. He was a—"

"Wait a sec. Hold on. What do you mean 'was'?"

"He retired in 2004," she answered.

"John Clayton? C-L-A-Y-T-O-N?"

"Yup."

"That doesn't sound like the guy I'm looking for."

"He's the only John Clayton listed in the State Department database."

Simon told himself not to overreact—the man

might be working as a special consultant, or part-time—one of a dozen perfectly good explanations. "What about Powers?"

"Okay. Powers, Stanley. Looks like a typical mid-level bureaucrat. Works in the Office of Protocol. That the guy?"

Midlevel? Office of Protocol? It didn't sound like the man Simon had met in the offices of the North Korean Trade Legation. "Maybe. Works in DC?"

"No," she answered. "The last two years he's been assigned to the embassy in Mexico City."

Oh shit, that did not sound good. He thought back, running each page of the nondisclosure agreement through his mind scanner, making sure the NKTL hadn't been mentioned before throwing out the name. "What do you have on the North Korean Trade Legation?"

More finger tapping. More waiting, then a single *ping* as the search engine completed its mission. "Not a thing," Vic announced. "You sure you have the name right? North Korean Trade Legation. L-E-G-A-T-I-O-N."

"That's it," he answered, trying his best not to telegraph his rising sense of panic.

"Sorry. Nothing. The organization doesn't exist."

But it did. He had been there, seen the place. He thought back, replaying the images in his mind. The austere waiting area, the circular reception counter, the pretty receptionist dressed in her traditional Korean hanbok. The smell of incense and beneath that . . . what? Then it came to him: fresh paint. He focused closer, seeing the magazines fanned out across the top of the Tansu-style table and realized they were new, all of them, never opened, their spines perfect, no subscription labels on the covers. He could imagine the woman carefully peeling them off—the people of the Far East possessed a patience beyond the concept of most Westerners—but for some reason he knew that wasn't the case. He remembered Stanley Powers—tall, urbane, his well-tailored suit, his casual "and I'm Stan"—and thinking how inappropriate the nickname sounded.

"Simon?"

He remembered following Powers down the narrow hallway, the high nap of the carpet, the lack of impressions, the faint smell of newness. He remembered the conference room, the long glass table, and the surveillance cameras—all, he now realized—facing the chair where he sat. Jin Pak and Ang Lee Han and Stanley Powers all sitting together at the opposite end, *below* the cameras, never turning, never showing their faces. *Everything staged. Everything new.*

"Earth to Simon, you still there?"

"Sorry, got lost in Neverland for a minute. I was just thinking about . . . wondering if maybe you could send me those files?"

"Sorry, Bagman, no can do."

He knew better than to argue. "How about a picture?"

"Of what?"

"Stanley Powers."

She hesitated, thinking about it, apparently considering how far she could stretch the boundaries of confidentiality. "Yeah, sure, I could do that. Hold on."

He listened to the keys and waited, wondering exactly what kind of *weird shit* he had stepped into this time. *Seriously weird,* he was sure of that. If Powers and Clayton didn't work for the State Department . . . ? If the North Korean Trade Legation didn't exist . . . ? Why the elaborate ruse? Why North Korea? Why . . .

"Okay," Vic said, "you should have it."

He tapped the e-mail icon on his smartphone, scrolled down through his messages, found it, and gave the attachment a double-tap. The face that pixilated onto the screen—a black man in his thirties—was clearly not the person Simon knew as Stanley Powers.

"Get it?" Vic asked. "That the guy?"

"Yes and no."

"You're sure?"

"Yes," he answered, "I'm sure."

"Maybe it's a bad picture."

"The picture is fine, Victoria. I remember the guy very well."

"Right, of course you do," she said, her tone a bit caustic. "I momentarily forgot about that camera in your brain."

"Now don't start with that. I *do not* have a photographic memory. There's no such thing."

"Okay, eidetic recall if you want to be picky. And I'm awfully damn jealous."

"Anyone can do it." In the background he could

hear the irritating buzz of an alarm clock. "You can train yourself to notice the little things."

"Bullcrap," she said, the sound of the alarm growing louder. "I've tried."

"Nice ass," he said, knowing she was moving across the room. "Turn around, will you?"

"Naughty, naughty." The alarm went silent. "I'll tell Caitlin."

"Some friend you are. I give you a nice-ass compliment and you threaten me with conjugal obstruction."

"You keep it up," she snapped back, "and I'll give you a conjugal obstruction you won't soon forget."

"Promises, promises."

"I need to get dressed, pervert. Call me at the office when you figure out—" There was a faint click and the line went silent.

"Vic?" Nothing. He toggled the cradle button. Nothing. *Now what?*

CHAPTER TWENTY-THREE

Westin Chosun Hotel, Seoul, South Korea

Sunday, 27 June 20:38:16 GMT +0900

The moment Simon racked the receiver, Soo-Yun stepped into the room. "Sir, you are sure this is proper thing?" She made a flat-footed pirouette, a schoolgirl showing off her new clothes: a sea-foam colored sundress with spaghetti straps that hit her legs about mid-thigh, and low-heeled espadrilles. She had pulled her long, silky hair into a ponytail and wore no makeup—the perfect combination of tomboy and adolescent heartthrob.

He tried to concentrate, knew she was nervous about meeting her parents, but couldn't ignore the queasy feeling that something was wrong. "Trust me, it's a lot different here. Besides jeans, that's exactly what girls your age wear. And you look great." He seriously doubted she would look any less adorable in sackcloth. "Your parents will be so excited they won't even notice what you're wearing."

"But, perhaps—"

He held up a hand. "Hold on." He punched the hotel's main number into his cellular. "This will only take a second."

A woman answered, her voice polite and refined,

with only a trace of accent. "Westin Chosun. *Anny-onghasimnikga.*"

"And good evening to you. Do you speak English?"

"Yes, sir. How may I direct your call?"

"I'm in Room 1704. The phone isn't working. Are you having problems?"

"Hold, please." There was a click, followed immediately by the sound of music. He gave Soo-Yun a wink, trying to hide his anxiety. "You ready to go?"

She nodded. "Thank you again for new clothes and packback."

"It's a backpack. And you're welcome. I still owe you ten grand."

"This is not necessary."

"Of course it is." Ten thousand to escape North Korea felt like a bargain, much less than what he expected to pay Captain Choi. "Your parents can give me the name of their bank and I'll wire the funds first thing tomorrow."

The music stopped as the operator came back on the line. "Sir?"

"Yes?"

"We are unaware of any problems. I will try your room now."

He waited. Silence. "It's not ringing on this end."

"I apologize for this inconvenience," she said. "I will notify maintenance immediately."

"Thank you."

"It will be at least two hours."

"That's fine." He disconnected and turned to Soo-

Yun. "I think we should wait for your parents in the lobby."

"Is there a problem, sir?"

He realized he was being paranoid, but decided this was no time to start second-guessing his instincts. "Just some mechanical glitch," he answered, trying to keep his tone casual. "But your parents said they would call when they reached the hotel. We don't want to miss them."

"Ah." She bobbed her head, her black ponytail bouncing. "Very good idea." She started toward her room. "I will get my bag."

"And stop calling me 'sir.' It makes me feel like an antique."

She glanced back over her shoulder and grinned, a dimple in each cheek. "I will try."

He reached down beside the chair for his new shoulder bag just as someone rapped on the door. Soo-Yun came flying into the room, her new backpack over one arm, her face glowing with excitement. "They are here, sir! They are here!"

"Wait!" He smiled, not wanting to ruin her big moment. "Make sure it's them before you open the door."

She leaned forward, eye to the peephole, then stood back, her shoulders sagging with disappointment. "Ye?"

A man's voice barely penetrated the thick door. "Telephone repair."

Though Simon didn't recognize the muffled voice, he realized instantly that something was wrong. The woman had said two hours—*at least*—and the response had come in English. "No!" But it was too late, Soo-Yun had already turned the knob.

The door burst open, knocking Soo-Yun to the floor as a man quickly stepped inside and closed the door behind him. Dressed in dark-blue maintenance coveralls and aviation-style reflector glasses, he waved a small-caliber automatic pistol back and forth between them. "Speak—" There was a distinct *click* as a stiletto blade materialized in his left hand. "—and I will cut out your tongue."

Though he spoke in a soft monotone, there was something chilling and familiar about the voice. And something else, Simon thought, something about his posture, the way he balanced his weight, like a cat waiting to pounce. *Eth Jäger!* But that was impossible; Jäger was locked up in some escape-proof prison, a life sentence, no parole. *Couldn't be.*

The man grinned triumphantly and pulled off his glasses, revealing his black eyepatch. *"Buongiorno,* courier."

Jesus, Mary! How? The thought trailed away as he considered the impossible combination: men masquerading as State Department employees . . . the Korean Unification Party . . . the government of Kim Jong-il . . . Jäger free. Nothing fit. He opened his mouth, then thought better of it, though he doubted Jäger had come halfway around the world just to slice him into pieces. No, he wanted something. Then he would kill; of that, Simon had no doubt. Soo-Yun would also die, but at least she didn't know it, and didn't have to think about it. *Better that way.* And her parents too, if they arrived before Jäger finished his work. The man liked blood.

"What is your problem, courier? You are not happy to see the hunter?" He laughed, a kind of mirthless bark. "Sit!"

Simon slid back into the deep armchair he had just vacated, his mind struggling to make some sense of the situation. Why would the government release a man like Eth Jäger? For what possible reason? Or did they? Escape seemed unlikely; Vic would have known and mentioned it in the first two seconds of their conversation.

Jäger glanced down at Soo-Yun, lying frozen as a field mouse beneath his feet, then back to Simon. "How is your sister, courier? The *delicious* Mrs. Quinn." He licked his lips and laughed again, the sound as obscene as the gesture.

Simon forced himself not to overreact. "She speaks of you often." *I hope they keep that pervert locked in a cage until his testicles rot off.* "With enthusiasm."

Jäger smirked, as if reading Simon's thoughts, then pointed the tip of his stiletto at Soo-Yun. "And who is this little morsel?"

Simon feigned a look of surprise, careful not to overdo it. "You don't know?" It was his best stalling tactic, to answer a question with a question while he tried to conjure up some story that would fit the facts of their journey and make Soo-Yun too valuable to harm.

Jäger hesitated, clearly not wanting to expose what

he did or did not know. "My interest is in what you know, courier. You will answer my question."

The problem with a story, Simon realized, was getting caught in a lie, but he couldn't imagine things getting worse. "She's uh—" *What? What? What?* His brain felt stuck, his neural conductors frozen in cytoplasmic glue. "—the package."

"Package?"

"My consignment," Simon answered. "That's what I do, deliver packages."

"And this—" Jäger again pointed his stiletto at Soo-Yun. "—is what you are paid to deliver?"

Simon nodded, realizing from the response that Jäger knew nothing of the girl.

"And who paid for this delivery?"

That was a perilous question, but it offered Simon the opening he had wanted, something to establish Soo-Yun's value. "I don't get paid until I make delivery," he answered, avoiding the real question. "Five million in gold Krugerrands."

A spark of surprise flashed through Jäger's dark eye, there and gone. Soo-Yun had a similar reaction, though Jäger failed to notice. "Krugerrands? Why Krugerrands?"

Simon shrugged, feeling more confident in the story he was slowly weaving together in his mind. "I don't ask those kind of questions."

Jäger waved his knife back and forth like a windshield wiper, as if to say *unh-unh-unh, don't play games with me*. "But you know."

Simon tried to look appropriately fearful, which

took no effort with his heart pounding at mach speed. "Not really. But gold is hard to trace. Maybe that's the reason."

"Of course that is the reason," Jäger shot back, as if nothing could be more obvious. He looked down at Soo-Yun. "And you, my little cherry, what makes you worth five million in gold, eh?"

Soo-Yun opened her mouth but Simon cut her off. "She doesn't speak English." One slip, one contradiction to the outrageous story he was about to tell and they would both be dead.

Jäger kept his dark eye fixed on the frightened girl. "Is this true? If you lie—" He waved the knife back and forth in front of her face.

Soo-Yun glanced at Simon, her eyes wide with fear, then back to Jäger. *"Modaradurossoyu?"*

"What did she say?"

It was one of the first Korean phrases Simon had learned—*I don't understand*—but decided to play dumb. "I don't have a clue." An answer, he realized, that wasn't far off the mark.

"What makes this little bitch worth so much?" Jäger demanded.

"I assumed they told you," Simon answered, watching for any reaction to his use of the word *they*, which there wasn't, and which seemed to confirm that Jäger had been intentionally released. "This is the daughter of Kim Jong-il." Though he kept his attention fixed on Jäger, Simon could see Soo-Yun's eyes expand in astonishment. *Simon says:* if you're going to tell a lie, tell a whopper. "She's defecting to the South."

Though he tried to hide it, Jäger looked equally surprised. "Defecting?"

Simon nodded. "It's a major propaganda coup for South Korea. Her father is the—"

"You think the hunter is a fool?" Jäger snapped. "You think he does not recognize the name, Kim Jong-il?"

If not a fool, Simon thought, certainly a legend in his own mind, always referring to himself in the third person. "No, of course not. I was just surprised they didn't tell you."

Jäger hesitated, apparently noticing the *they* and thinking about it. "Who hired you for this job, courier?"

Simon mentally braced himself for an eruption in case he was wrong. "I assume it's the same people who hired you. The US government."

Jäger nodded, as if that was exactly what he thought. "So they fear you will talk, eh? That you will expose their part in this—" He struggled to find the appropriate word, then gave up the search and simply motioned with his knife toward Soo-Yun.

"Apparently," Simon answered. "You take care of me, and then—" He paused for effect, surprised at how reasonable it all sounded. "—well, you know how it works."

Yes, Jäger thought, he knew very well how it worked. They had set him up to do their dirty work and tagged him with an electronic locator so they could find and eliminate him once the job was done. *Bastardi americani!* They would find out soon enough who was the hunter and who was the prey. "What are the arrangements?"

Stalling for time as he worked through the ramifications of adding Jin Pak to the mix, Simon gave the man his best Simple Simon look. "Arrangements?"

"*Sì*, arrangements." Jäger reached down and lifted the hem of Soo-Yun's dress with his knife—a rabid dog inspecting his next meal. Soo-Yun closed her eyes, her body rigid with fear, her face waxy. "For delivery, courier. What are the arrangements?"

Nothing he did, Simon realized, could make matters worse. "I'm to call them with a location—" From the corner of his eye he could barely make out the numbers—8:53—on the small desk chronometer. "At precisely nine o'clock. We're to meet in the lobby thirty minutes later."

Jäger straightened, a look of suspicion. "In the lobby?"

"I'm not stupid," Simon fired back, knowing this would be his only opportunity to get Soo-Yun out of the room. "We're talking five million in gold here. Naturally I insisted we meet in a public place." Soo-Yun dropped her chin slightly, letting him know she understood what he was trying to do.

Jäger glanced at his watch. "At nine o'clock?"

"Precisely," Simon answered. "They even gave me a special phone so no one could monitor the transmission."

Jäger cocked his head to one side, as if he found that particularly interesting. "Special phone?"

Simon pointed to his Gore-Tex shoulder bag. "Right there."

"You—" Jäger nudged Soo-Yun with his foot and pointed his pistol toward a chair next to Simon. "Sit."

She feigned a look of confusion. Simon reached over and patted the chair. "Come. Sit." It sounded, he realized, like he was talking to a dog.

Still on her backside, her pack over one shoulder, Soo-Yun scrambled backwards to the chair, never taking her eyes off Jäger, who never took his lecherous dark eye off her long, bare legs. Once she was sitting, he slipped his knife into a side pocket of his coveralls, picked up the shoulder bag, and retreated to a small table near the door. He glanced inside, cautiously, as if expecting a bomb, then reached in and pulled the satellite phone. "This phone?"

Simon nodded, already anticipating the next question.

"Why is it not turned on?"

"Because I was told not to use it unless I needed to." *Should you have problem. Such as that.* "Those things broadcast a location and—" He motioned toward Soo-Yun. "There's a lot of people looking for her."

Jäger nodded, apparently satisfied, and glanced again at his watch. "Two minutes." He tossed the phone to Simon. "Make your call." Then he smiled, a ghoulish grin, and ran a finger across his throat. "Location only. Nothing more."

At least, Simon thought, he now had something to throw if it came to that. He turned the phone over and pressed the power button. *Hello, God. If you're up there, now's the time to answer. I'm not asking for myself, but there's a sweet girl here who could use a bit of help right now. Nothing big, no fires, floods, or famine, just a little signal to let us know you're on the job.* The phone answered with a sharp *beep* as it found a signal. *Thank you, God, that's a start.* Tilting the phone, as if to better see the keypad, he punched in Jin Pak's preset number and pressed the phone to his ear. She answered on the second ring. *"Ye?"* Though tentative and obviously surprised, the connection was clear and he recognized her voice immediately.

"The Westin Chosun Hotel," he said, carefully enunciating the name. He wanted to identify the city, but decided the time—which he hoped would act as a deadline—was more important. "Nine-thirty." Unless she was in Seoul, it wouldn't matter anyway. He pressed the END button but purposely left the power on. "Okay, everything's set." But he knew better— couldn't imagine Jäger walking into the lobby with either of them, not even for five million.

Chapter Twenty-four

Washington, DC

Sunday, 27 June 05:02:48 GMT –0500

It took a moment for Tucker to separate the soft buzz from the familiar and steady hum of the aquarium's filtration unit. Without opening his eyes, he listened hard for any unfamiliar sounds, but the rest of the house was silent, as dead as his wife and children. He cracked one eyelid, watching with a sense of detachment as the blurred shapes on his desk solidified into mountains of paper. *Holy Christ,* his head felt like a pumpkin. Never much of a drinker, he should have known better than to mix alcohol with his all-night effort to scan and digitize two years of documentation, all the evidence he had managed to accumulate relating to the President's profiteering. A job, Tucker now realized, he should have done earlier, instead of letting the general talk him into "a better way." *Fuck that.* It might be circumstantial, and it might not land the President in Leavenworth; but it was enough for the press, and once they started to dig, the corrupt bastard would have no choice but to resign. Making sure the general didn't end up at 1600 Pennsylvania would be trickier, but Tucker was confident he could accomplish that as well; his last act of patriotism before joining his wife and children in the great abyss.

What the hell was that buzzing? Or was it nothing, a figment of his imagination, a false echo, just part of the discordant orchestra wailing away inside his skull? He slowly raised his head, brushed away a Post-it note that had stuck to his left cheek, and glanced around. Except for the desk lamp and the glow of the aquarium, the room was dark, the heavy curtains blocking out all but a faint glow of early-morning light. Then he saw it, the pulsating light on the phone console—his secure line. The luminescent numbers on the display read 5:03. He cleared his throat and snatched up the receiver. "Yes."

"This Jin Pak."

The orchestra fell silent, his senses going into high alert. "Did you find him?"

"*Aniyo,*" she answered. "He find me."

He listened as she described the phone call. "That's it? That's all he said?"

"*Ye.*"

"You're sure it was him? You recognized his voice?"

"*Ye.*"

"And this just happened?"

"*Ye.* Something . . . how you say? . . . smell like Denmark."

Rotten in Denmark. Tucker was sure of it. He also realized—a revelation, he silently admitted, that had come a bit slow—that Leonidovich was not the type to make foolish mistakes. "I think he's in trouble and he's looking for help any place he can find it."

"*Ye,* big trouble."

"And something is going to happen by nine-thirty your time."

"*Ye.* Twenty-six minutes."

"Are you close?"

"Moving now," she answered. "Two minutes."

"It could be a trap."

"*Ye.*"

The woman was like a machine; she didn't waste time wanting to *talk about it,* like most women. "You'll just have to be careful. We need to clean this up."

"*Ye.* The girl?"

Shit, the girl from the boat, he had completely forgotten about her. Who was she? What was she doing with Leonidovich? "Yes, if she's still with him." He hoped to hell she wasn't; he didn't need the death of a young girl on his conscience. "We can't afford any loose ends."

"Loose ends cost extra."

Christ, all she cared about was the money, but maybe that's the way someone in her business made it through the night. "Understood. And the disc. He might have it, he might not. You need to check everything."

"*Ye.* I go now."

"Just—" He hesitated, tempted to tell her about Jäger, but realized there wasn't nearly enough time to explain that complication. "Just be careful. Clean it up. No loose ends." If he was lucky, Jäger would be one of the loose ends that got cleaned up.

"Jin Pak always careful."

"Call me when—" But she was already gone.

He swiveled around, nudged the mouse to wake his computer, then logged on to a Company network with a secure server. Within seconds he had a satellite visual of South Korea, including a white dot that pulsated directly over the city of Seoul. Using his joystick controller, he centered the crosshairs over the blinking target and zoomed downward to an elevation of twelve miles. Instantly, the white dot separated into three: one red and one blue, representing the two internal GPS transmitters attached to Jäger's upper and lower intestine, and one green, representing the satellite phone. All were blinking—indicating a strong signal—and tightly clustered over the central part of the city.

Tucker leaned forward, reading the latitude/longitude markers, confirming what he already suspected, that all three tags were located within ten meters of each other. Despite his personal feelings of repugnance, he had to admit, if only to himself, that Eth Jäger was very good at what he did. Jin Pak would have to be equally good to take him down. Between the two of them, Leonidovich didn't stand a chance.

CHAPTER TWENTY-FIVE

Westin Chosun Hotel, Seoul, South Korea

Sunday, 27 June 21:26:00 GMT +0900

Jäger circled the room, closing drapes and turning off lights, leaving on only one floor lamp, which he moved directly behind Soo-Yun, casting her in a shadowy circle of yellow light. "Four minutes, courier."

And then what? But Simon wasn't at all sure he wanted to know the answer to that question. For twenty minutes he had been weighing options, but there were only a couple and they both seemed suicidal: to try to coldcock the guy with the satellite phone, or charge him and hope his first shot missed a vital organ. The first seemed ridiculously optimistic. The second, he decided, would at least give Soo-Yun a chance to escape, but even that seemed foolishly optimistic. What he needed was a distraction, to somehow exploit the fact that Jäger had no peripheral vision on his left side, but aside from Jin Pak riding in on a white horse . . . *no*, he dismissed the thought. It wasn't going to happen. Even if she was in Seoul, even if she could get there in time, she wasn't there to save his ass, no use kidding himself about that.

"Then," Jäger continued, "you will make a second call, insisting to meet here, in your room."

Simon now understood—the hunter had chosen his ground and was setting his trap—using Soo-Yun as bait. "They'll never go for it. We agreed to meet in a public place."

"No, courier, *you* insisted. That is what you said, eh?"

"Well, yes," Simon admitted, sensing he had already lost the argument and his best chance of getting Soo-Yun out of the room, "but—"

"No," Jäger interrupted. "No buts. You will insist to meet here."

"They won't go for it," he repeated, struggling to come up with a more compelling argument. "It's too late. Everything was agreed to."

"For the daughter of Kim Jong-il—" Jäger smirked, his voice confident, as if nothing could be more obvious. "They will agree."

Except *they* didn't exist, Simon thought, and he couldn't imagine how Jin Pak might react to another nonsensical call. He glanced at Soo-Yun, who looked frozen and pale with fear, and tried to convey with his eyes what he couldn't say—*everything will be okay*—and was having trouble believing himself.

Jäger stepped behind the bar, giving himself a clear view of the room, the door, and his captives. "Make the call, courier."

Telling himself the situation couldn't get worse, Simon punched the preset number. It rang, the sound echoing in both ears, and for an instant he found himself in one of those confusing, out-of-sync moments—like he had walked into the wrong theater in the middle of a performance—and then realized what was happening, that the sound wasn't an echo at all, but a phone ringing just beyond the door. Even then, it took a moment for him to realize what it meant. He started to reach for Soo-Yun when the door blew open, the explosion surprisingly muted, a low *whuump* that instantly filled the room with a diaphanous cloud of smoke and dust. Pulling Soo-Yun into his arms, Simon threw himself backwards, overturning the chair and knocking over the lamp. In the sudden darkness Jäger opened fire, four flashes of light and sound in rapid staccato—*pop-pop-pop-pop*—then silence. Simon leaned forward, cupping a hand to Soo-Yun's ear. "You okay?"

"*Ye,*" she whispered back. "Plan C?"

Though he had to admire her spunk, there was only one door and no place to run. He peeked out from behind the chair: the door hung at an awkward angle, on one hinge, the opening framed in light from the hall, no one in sight . . . Then he saw it, Jin Pak's hand as it appeared and disappeared behind the doorframe, the flash-bang canister as it spiraled through the air and bounced off the carpet toward the bar. He rolled over, shielding Soo-Yun with his body and covering his ears. The explosion was like a burst of white noise, so loud he could feel it resonate through his bones and see the flash of light behind his eyelids, but the heavy chair absorbed much of the impact and he knew this was his only chance, that

Jin Pak would be moving toward the bar and the threat. Seeing that Soo-Yun was too disoriented to stand, he managed to get his legs under him, pulled her body onto his shoulders in a fireman's carry, and ran.

It couldn't have been more than fifteen feet to the door, but it felt like a mile on the thick carpet, as if he were running through a sandy battlefield at night—smoke and dust and darkness, and the smell of burnt cordite—but fortunately the war was off to his left, muzzle flashes and the distinctive sound of two automatic weapons, one higher pitched than the other, and the crash of glassware. *Almost there!* He reached out, snatched his shoulder bag off the side table, and darted into the hall. Nearly blinded by the light, he ran as hard as he could toward the elevators, shouting "Fire!" and ignoring the puzzled expressions of hotel guests—some in sleepwear, some in street clothes—emerging from their rooms.

He didn't look back until he reached the elevators, but could see no sign of Jäger or Jin Pak in the growing number of people now streaming into the hallway. He punched the CALL button, debating whether to take the stairs or wait, then noticed one of the doors was slightly ajar, a small screwdriver jammed into the track. All set, he assumed, for Jin Pak to make her escape. He yanked the tool free and the door popped open. *Thank you, God.*

He stepped inside, lowered Soo-Yun to the floor and pressed the LOBBY button. As the door slid closed, he caught a glimpse of Eth Jäger in the crowd of people now moving toward the elevators. He didn't appear to be in any special hurry, as if not wanting to draw attention to himself, but for a brief moment Simon felt the intensity of that one dark eye and all that it promised.

CHAPTER TWENTY-SIX

Incheon International Airport

Monday, 28 June 17:14:19 GMT +0900

"You think he is here?" Soo-Yun whispered.

Though Simon hadn't used his name, his passport, his phone, or a credit card in twenty hours—anything that would leave an electronic footprint—he checked the enormous room for a third time. The airport was new and shiny and clean, the building a modernistic solarium of marble and glass and steel. Done in multiple shades of gray—from the marble floor to the high domed ceiling—the lack of color would have given him an instant case of sensory deprivation if it hadn't been for the frenzied din and movement of modern-day travel: people of every color and size and age, dressed in every conceivable and inconceivable style, the rapid shuffle of their footsteps, the constant drone of luggage carts and rolling suitcases, the murmur of conversation and whispered goodbyes. "No, he doesn't have any idea where we are." A situation, Simon realized, that would change the instant he used his passport. "And it's nothing for you to worry about. He knows by now that everything I told him was a lie. The minute I clear customs, he'll be on the next plane out."

She turned toward the huge glass wall overlooking

the tarmac, pretending to watch a 747 as it pulled into the gate. "You will not forget Soo-Yun when you are back in the United States of America?"

"Of course not," he answered, trying to sound upbeat. "I get to this part of the world at least once a year." That wasn't always true, but he was determined to make it happen. "I'll schedule an extra day and we can spend some time together whenever I'm close."

"Once a year," she repeated. "This you promise?" Her eyes flicked a peek at his, then ricocheted away, embarrassed.

"Absolutely." He crossed his heart with a finger. "Scout's honor." He understood her anxiety—he had become her bridge between the past and future—and he was now leaving her to face it alone: new school, new country, three new siblings and a mother and father she didn't know. He glanced over at the parents—standing about twenty feet away—giving their daughter and this stranger from America a semiprivate moment to say goodbye. "You're going to like it here. Your parents are very nice."

"Ye, very nice," she agreed, though the expression did not match the apprehension in her beautiful dark eyes. "It is all very strange here in the South. I did not think it would be so different."

He nodded, knowing she missed her grandparents and the familiarity of her old life. "Freedom can be intimidating when you're used to someone always telling you what to do and how to think. Give it a chance."

She smiled awkwardly, dread mixed with excitement mixed with hope.

From the corner of his eye he caught a flash of champagne color as Big Jake's flying penthouse—a BBJ 2, the rich-and-famous version of a 737—settled gently onto the nearest runway. "That's my ride."

Soo-Yun stared wide-eyed at the plane, the muted Sand Castle logo on its tail the only clue to its lineage. "One person needs such a very big plane?"

"It's called a whale taxi."

"Whales?" She looked so confused she didn't know what questions to ask. "I do not understand."

Exactly his reaction when he first heard the term. "My—" he hesitated, never quite sure how to characterize his relationship to Caitlin. "My friend uses it to ferry big-time gamblers back and forth to Las Vegas. They call them whales. I was just lucky the plane happened to be in Shanghai when I called."

"Your friend must be very rich."

"She isn't, but the man she works for is. B. J. Rynerson . . . ?"

She shook her head, her dark braid swinging back and forth.

He should have known; though Big Jake was one of the richest and most well-known figures in the world, he was a poster boy for capitalism—poor boy makes good—and not someone the socialist press of North Korea would write about. "Well, now that you have access to a computer, you can look him up."

She nodded blindly, her almond-shaped eyes glittering with moisture.

Jesus-damn, how he hated moments like this; there were no right words, no good way to say goodbye. "Now don't be sad, young lady. We had quite an adventure."

She nodded again, as if she couldn't quite believe it herself. "I do not still understand what everything was about."

He didn't either, but had a feeling if he didn't figure it out pretty damn quick he was going to end up as a trophy on the hunter's wall. "I'll call you as soon as I figure that out." He pulled a small box out of his shoulder bag and handed it to her. "And just so I know where to find you."

She turned the box over in her delicate hands, a look of surprise and bewilderment.

"It's just like mine," he said, tapping the phone on his belt. "All the latest bells and whistles."

"But—"

"And don't worry about the bill, everything will be charged to my account." It was a privilege he knew she would never abuse. "So if I don't get a call at least once a week, I'm going to be very angry with you." He felt like a parent, sending his first-born off to college. "I want to know how you're doing, how you like your new home, your new school, what kind of grades you're getting. Everything."

"This would interest you?" she asked, a tone of disbelief.

"Of course I'm interested. We're friends aren't we?"

"Oh, yes, sir. You are my very best friend in all the world."

He smiled to himself, knowing he would soon be replaced by many new friends vying for that honor. He reached out and pulled her into his arms. "If I ever have a daughter, I want her to be exactly like you, kid." He wanted to say more, something meaningful and poignant, but that was all he could squeeze past the lump in his throat.

She held on, clutching him like a life preserver, then slowly backed away and bowed, tears streaming down her cheeks and dripping onto the gray marble floor.

CHAPTER TWENTY-SEVEN

Washington, DC

Monday, 28 June 03:52:54 GMT –0500

Exhausted but pleased to be finally done, Tucker dropped the last stack of documents into his shredder, waited for them to feed through, then dumped the basketball-sized clump into the fireplace. The confetti-like pieces burst into flames with a dull *fumph,* sending shadow ghosts flying up the walls before melting back into the corners of the room.

Satisfied that God Himself couldn't have deciphered the ashes, Tucker slipped the final two CDs into separate ziplock freezer bags and carefully sealed the tops. Maybe now he could sleep, but he hadn't gotten more than an hour at a stretch in over a week and he didn't have much hope. Not until he heard from Jin Pak, and he had a feeling that wasn't going to happen. He glanced at the clock. Something had obviously gone wrong.

He levered himself up from his chair, waited a moment for his head to clear, then stepped behind the bar. Instantly the school of Red-bellied piranhas adjusted their swim pattern, aware of his presence and the prospect of food. Tucker pulled a fresh chicken leg out of the refrigerator, attached it to a precut piece of string, and dropped it into the water. As the fish swarmed in to claim their share, he buried the discs beneath the sand on the opposite end of the tank, using a long-handled skimming net. By the time he smoothed the sand in place, the leg had been picked clean. *Good boys.* They might be ugly little bastards, but they were damned efficient and they didn't sleep on the job.

Just as he dropped the bone into the garbage, his computer began pinging like an airport metal detector, letting him know that one of the search engines had found a match. He hurried back to his desk, reading the seven lines of text now emblazoned on his monitor.

> **LEONIDOVICH/SIMON/NYC/NY/USA**

> **CUSTOMS/PASSPORT CONTROL/REPUB-LIC OF KOREA**

> **DEPARTURE GATE/INCHEON INTER-NATIONAL AIRPORT**

> **MONDAY, 28 JUNE 17:34:19 GMT +0900**

> **DESTINATION/LAS VEGAS/NV/USA**

> **NON-STOP PRIVATE CARRIER/RYNER-SON ENTERPRISES, INC**

> **ETA MONDAY, 28 JUNE 14:00:00 GMT -800**

Damn, the bastard had gotten away. How was that possible? Either the man had more luck and lives than an Irish cat or was smarter than anyone thought. And now that rich-ass cowboy from Vegas was involved, what more could go wrong? *Shit*, the answer to that was obvious enough.

He lowered himself into his chair, hit ALT/PRT-SCRN to save the image, pasted it onto his scanner desktop, hit CTRL/P-ENTER to print, then logged on to his satellite overview of South Korea to verify Jäger's location. Everything was still the same, his GPS coordinates unchanged in over twenty hours. Was the man dead, dying, or . . . ? One thing for sure, Leonidovich was in the open and on the run, and no one was doing anything about it.

Jäger rolled carefully onto his right side, trying not to irritate the wound to his left shoulder, and snapped on the light. Though somewhat austere—the black walnut furniture was old and scratched, the Oriental rugs faded and threadbare—the hotel was small and private and no one asked questions. Stretching out, he caught the satellite phone just as it vibrated off the bedside table. Instantly, the wound to his shoulder began to throb. *Ahi madre!* He took a deep breath—determined not to expose the fact that the woman had gotten lucky—and pressed the CON-NECT button. *"Allô."*

Tucker hesitated, the French accent catching him by surprise, then remembered that Eth Jäger was a man of many faces and many tongues. "You know who this is?"

Of course Jäger knew; the one who called himself DeMott, a name as fake as his FBI credentials. *"Oui."*

"So what's going on?" Tucker asked, trying to sound casual, then realized how false it sounded and quickly adding an edge to his voice. "We *expected* you to report in."

Expected! Report in! Did this *stupido americano* think they could send someone to kill the hunter, then pretend it never happened? He took a deep breath, forcing both his temper and his pain down beneath the surface of his voice. "This I believe is a question for you to answer."

Tucker hesitated, sensing an ambush, but was too tired and could think of no way to avoid it. "What do you mean?"

"The woman," Jäger snapped, unable to contain his temper a moment longer. "That *gouine* bitch you sent to kill me!"

"I have no idea what you're talking about."

Did they think the hunter was some kind of idiot? Some helpless pet they could jerk around on their electronic leash? "Then you tell someone who does. The hunter is waiting. *Au revoir.*"

"Hold on!" Tucker realized he was trapped. Jin Pak was dead—*had to be*—and there was no way to know how much information Jäger might have extracted before he killed her. "Okay, okay, I know about the woman. But I have no idea why she would try to kill you. She didn't even know about you. She was looking for Leonidovich, same as you."

"I had Leonidovich," Jäger snapped angrily. "The bitch let him get away."

"We should have told you about her," Tucker admitted, trying to calm the man down. "That was a mistake."

"Your mistake. Her life."

"That's unfortunate," Tucker said, being careful not to sound accusatory. "We accept responsibility."

Though Jäger knew there was more, that things were never so simple, he realized the situation was not as he first suspected. "How generous of you."

Tucker ignored the sarcasm. "Nothing has changed. We still need Leonidovich."

"And the girl?"

"The Korean girl?"

"Oui."

"No, of course not," Tucker answered, clearly surprised by the question. "She's of no importance."

No importance! Jäger suddenly felt as if Leonidovich were standing over him on the bed, pissing down on his face. *Fucking bastardo!* So it was all a story, a fabrication to make the hunter look foolish. "It would be my pleasure to kill this man."

Tucker released a long, silent breath, bubbles of relief bursting in his chest. "That's excellent. We know he cleared customs at Incheon International less than an hour ago."

Jäger pushed himself into a sitting position, being careful not to stretch the sutures in his shoulder. "You have the airline and flight number?"

"He's on a private plane, heading to Las Vegas."

"What are the interim stops?"

"There are none," Tucker answered. "It's a non-stop flight."

"This I doubt."

"I'm sure of it. They're scheduled to land at two o'clock this afternoon."

Jäger knew better; Leonidovich was too clever to place himself in such a box. "So why do you need the hunter?"

"It's complicated," Tucker answered. "We can't really arrest the man."

Of course not. They didn't want the courier found, they wanted him to disappear—permanently. *"Oui,* I understand."

"I'll have a team at the airport. They'll follow. You call me when you get here, I'll give you his location."

Jäger smiled to himself. *Stupido americano,* did he really think the hunter needed a pack of point dogs? "Of course."

"And you keep me informed."

Jäger didn't bother to respond; the hunter did not *report in.* He disconnected and immediately placed a call to the hotel's travel desk. "Airline reservations, *s'il vous plaît.*"

The woman responded in perfect English. "Your destination, please?"

Jäger hesitated, but only an instant. Leonidovich was clever, that was his strength—but foolishly attached to his sister. That was his weakness. "New York City."

CHAPTER TWENTY-EIGHT

Over the Pacific Ocean

Monday, 28 June 22:13:51 GMT +1100

Simon hit the phone's MUTE button, took a deep breath and counted to five, trying to control his growing impatience. He was sitting in one of the plane's semiprivate work areas—complete with computer, fax, scanner, printer, and scrambler phone—trying to avoid the six whales who had boarded the jet in Shanghai and clearly did not appreciate the unscheduled stop in Seoul. He knew Caitlin would soothe their inflated egos and make sure they were well compensated for their loss of gambling time, but for now he preferred to stay off their radar screens.

He took another deep breath, released it in a long, slow exhale, and tapped the MUTE button. "Please, Sissie, don't give me a hard time about this. Just close the office, take the kids, and go to Vegas. I want you to bring my laptop and the briefcase that's in the safe."

There was a double beat of silence, the time it took for his voice to make the hop and skip over the satellite network, and for hers to bounce back. "But why? I can overnight the briefcase and laptop.

There's no reason for me to haul the kids all the way to Vegas for that."

"It's not just that." He tried to hide his exasperation but could hear it bleeding into his voice. "I need your help with some stuff."

"Stuff!" She barked the word back. "What stuff? There's nothing I can do in Vegas I can't do in New York."

That was the problem with relatives—sisters in particular—they felt entitled to explanations. "I'm the boss, dammit. Just do it."

"Don't you give me that kind of adolescent horse-shit, Boris. I'm your sister. Now what is it you're not telling me?"

Women! Why did they make everything so difficult? He couldn't lie, couldn't fire her, and didn't have a clue how she might react to the news. "You're not going to like this."

"Spit it out."

"Eth Jäger is out of prison."

This time the silence lasted a good ten seconds. "How do you know?"

"I saw him."

"What do you mean, *saw him?*" She clearly did not want to believe it. "Like on the street? Maybe you just thought it was him. There's no way they let that maniac out of prison. No way, no way, no way." She was trying desperately hard to convince herself. "Not possible."

"No, Sissie, this was up close and personal. He's out and he's looking for me."

"It's not possible," she repeated, though it was obvious from the sinking tone of her voice that she knew better.

"I don't know how he did it, but he's on the street and he's looking for revenge. You take the kids to Vegas, stay at the Sand Castle. You'll be safe there with all the security." He paused, waiting for a response, then realized he wasn't getting one. "Sissie?"

"I'm thinking."

"There's nothing to think about. The guy's a psychopath. When he can't find me he'll come after you."

"You're just trying to scare me," she snapped back defensively. "You don't know that."

"No," he admitted, "I don't. But he did it the last time and he's likely to try it again."

"The guy's insane, Simon. He's not going to do the same thing twice."

"Dammit, Sissie, that's exactly what insanity is, repeating the same action and expecting a different result."

"You're overreacting. He's probably forgotten me by now."

"Not hardly. You've been squirreling around in that crazy brain of his for two years. He mentioned you."

"Mentioned me?" Her voice suddenly sounded small and far away, like it was filtered through cotton. "What did he say?"

But Simon couldn't repeat it—*the delicious Mrs. Quinn*—didn't dare conjure up any more memories.

"I don't remember his exact words, but he hasn't forgotten you. That was clear enough."

She expelled a hissing, between-the-teeth sigh. "Okay, okay, I believe you."

About time!

"But I'm not leaving New York," she continued. "The kids are in summer camp and I refuse to disrupt their lives because of that psycho." She took a deep breath, the sound of a person marshaling their resources. "Now that I know he's out, I'll be extra cautious."

"Extra cautious doesn't make it, Sissie. This guy's as smart as he is crazy. You need to—"

"No!" she broke in, "I'm not letting that bastard dominate my life. It's gone on for two years and I'm sick of it. I'm sick of thinking about him. I'm sick of being afraid. It's having an effect on the kids." Another deep breath. "Let him come, I'll be ready this time."

Great, as if he didn't have enough to worry about, he now had to contend with Ms. I'll-be-ready Rambo. He argued the point for another five minutes, then gave up and called a personal protection service, a little peace-of-mind investment that would diminish his savings account at the rate of ten grand a week, but worth it to know she would be safe. "Damn woman!"

Vicki, the whale's longtime Scandinavian hostess—who spoke Japanese, English, Swedish, and two dialects of Chinese—poked her head around the partition and smiled. "You called?"

"Sorry, Vicki. I'm just . . . just—" He threw up his hands, too frustrated to articulate the thought.

"Must be Caitlin."

"No, Caitlin I can handle." Vickie cocked an eyebrow and he made a little backpedal. "Okay, maybe *handle* isn't the right word."

"Not if it's the Caitlin I know." Her lips widened into an amused slash of perfect white teeth. "Little chest, big balls."

"That's the one. And my sister's just like her. They seem to take special pleasure in breaking *my* balls."

The grin dissolved into a grimace. "Sounds painful."

"You can't imagine. I'm thinking of writing a book." He spread his hands, painting the title. "Simon Leonidovich: My Life as a Eunuch."

She laughed and groaned at the same time. "Can I get you anything to ease the pain? Champagne? Aspirin? Aspirin floating in champagne?"

"No thanks, I'm good." He rocked back in the chair, suddenly conscious of the ebullient gleam in her green eyes. "So what's going on with you? I haven't seen you in months."

She grinned, clearly anxious to share something, and wiggled the fingers of her left hand, showing off a substantial diamond. "I'm getting married."

"Congratulations!" He jumped up and gave her hug. "That's wonderful." He immediately thought of Caitlin and where they might be heading. Would marriage make things better, or would it screw up a perfectly good relationship? And what about children? Was it too late? He thought of old Just Lee and his treasure, and realized how much better life could be with a wife and children. "So, what's the plan? Are you going to give up life in the stratosphere for a cottage in the burbs?"

"Not right away," she answered. "We—" She hooked a thumb toward the front of the plane. "Dex and I think—"

"Dexter, the copilot?"

She smiled again, and her entire face glowed with happiness. "That's the lucky guy."

"Ah-ha." He could only imagine the beautiful bronze-skinned babies those two would make. Dexter Hightower was as handsome as Vicki was beautiful, as black as she was fair. "So there's been a little hanky-panky going on in crew cabin, eh?"

She blushed like a schoolgirl. "I admit to nothing."

"You just did."

Her cheeks darkened to a deeper shade of pink. "Speaking of the crew cabin, there's a bed available if you want to use it."

"No, thanks." He needed to think, to try to make some sense of things and come up with a plan. "I need to do some work."

She cocked her head toward the main cabin. "They're really nice guys. I'm sure they won't mind if you want to sit in the lounge or use the exercise room."

"No, thanks, I'm fine here. I need to check my

e-mail." After two weeks of being incommunicado, he expected to find his in-box overflowing. "And make a few more calls."

"Okay." She pointed to the SERVICE button on the communications console. "Just hit the buzzer if you need anything."

"There is one thing."

"Name it."

"I need to get off this thing before we reach Vegas."

Her smile faltered. "You're kidding?"

He shook his head. "It's important, Vicki. Real important." He hit the *real* hard enough to let her know he wasn't joking.

She slid into a chair, smoothing her short skirt over her long thighs. "You're serious?"

"As a heart attack."

She nodded slowly, thinking about it. "That's pretty much what it would take."

"Precisely. What I need is a little help."

She leaned forward, dropping her voice to a conspiratorial whisper. "What do you have in mind?"

Good girl. "It's important nothing gets called in until the last possible moment. I was thinking of a little cardiovascular problem about a hundred miles west of San Francisco. You tell the pilots, they get emergency clearance and we're on the ground fifteen minutes later."

She bobbed her head, the mass of blond hair. "That would work."

"Right. I get off the plane and you get right back in the air."

"And it turns out to be a temporary case of indigestion."

"Exactly. No harm, no foul."

She grinned wickedly. "Sounds like fun. I've always wanted to use the defibrillator."

He waved a finger just beyond her freckled nose. "You get near me with that thing and I'll tell Caitlin you and Dex have been making whoopee in the crew cabin."

She stood up and stuck out her hand. "You keep my secret and I'll keep yours."

He spent the next hour wading through e-mail, dumping the junk and the jokes, then spent another twenty minutes organizing his thoughts before calling Vic.

As usual, she picked up on the first ring. "Bagman?"

"How'd you know? I'm on a scrambler phone over the—"

"A calculated guess," she cut in. "I can see where the call is coming from, and I knew where you were."

"Oh?" But he realized immediately how she knew. "Lara called you?"

"About an hour ago. She's pretty freaked out."

"Good. She should be. When I talked to her she was acting all bravado, ready to go toe-to-toe with the one-eyed devil of darkness."

"Reality has set in. I told her you were right, she should go to Vegas, work out of that office."

"And?"

"No way," Vic answered. "Wouldn't even consider it. She might be scared, but she's stubborn as a mule and harder to turn than a stampede."

He wasn't surprised. "I hired a personal protection firm. You think you could at least convince her not to fight me over that?"

"That I can do. So what's going on? How did that maniac get out of prison?"

"I was hoping you could tell me."

There was an extra beat of silence before she answered. "Actually, I've already checked the federal prisoner database. He's still listed on the inmate roster at the ADX facility in Florence, Colorado. But—" Her voice took on a sarcastic edge. "—knowing you're never wrong, I cross-checked the roster against the daily prisoner count. That's a figure that can't be fudged. The count is one short of the manifest. Has been since the twenty-third."

"So he was released—" He paused, working it through his mind. "—but they're trying to hide the fact."

"I don't know what other explanation there could be."

"Who has that kind of power, Vic?"

"I've been thinking about that . . ." Her voice trailed away.

"And?"

"You can forget the judiciary and the legislative—they wouldn't or couldn't, in that order. So it has to be someone on the executive side. Someone with a lot of juice."

His thinking exactly. "Makes sense."

"And I have to assume this has something to do with that international O and R on your passport."

"Which you said looked like the work of the CIA."

"Sounds like a clue," she answered, obviously not wanting to speculate further. "But I'll keep digging."

"Thanks. There's something else."

"Why am I not surprised?"

He hesitated, wondering if he still had a nondisclosure obligation, and decided he didn't. Nothing had been as it was presented, including, he had to believe, the possibility that he might be committing treason or other high crimes and misdemeanors. "I've got this 500-gigabyte data card that might give us a few answers. I tried to access the contents, but it's encrypted." He paused, waiting for a reaction, but she obviously wasn't going to make it easy for him. "Any suggestions?"

"Okay, okay," she said, obviously wanting to know what was on it, "send it to me. I'll see if I can break the encryption."

"Thank you, Victoria."

"But I won't promise to share the information. Not if it's classified."

"Understood. You'll have it in the morning."

"Okay. Call me late tomorrow. Stay safe, Bagman."

As he dropped the receiver back in its cradle, he noticed the clock had reset—00:31—and realized they had crossed the international date line. Without conscious thought—the action so familiar to his lifestyle—he pressed the zone button on his watch and adjusted the time and date backwards from Seoul time—Tuesday, June 29, 2:31 A.M.—to Vegas time: Monday, June 28, 9:31 A.M. *Ugh,* most days were hard enough without having to live them twice.

Make it better. He swiveled around toward the computer. *Figure it out.*

CHAPTER TWENTY-NINE

Rye, New York

Thursday, 1 July 05:24:37 GMT –0500

After a long, uneventful night, the dark sky had finally given way to the blue gray of dawn, and the soft contours of the neighborhood had solidified into distinctive shapes. Jäger momentarily closed his eyes, savoring the final pull of flavor from his Fatima, then leaned forward, being careful not to aggravate the wound in his shoulder, and adjusted the angle of the shade as the first streaks of sunlight hit the rear window of his RV, a small, nondescript rental not unlike many he had seen on the forty-minute drive north from New York. Satisfied that no one could see into the dark interior, he toggled the switch on his miniscope from NIGHT to DAY and methodically began to scan the neighborhood.

Unlike most American communities, the area had age and character, the street lined with big shade trees and old homes. The lawns were well-kept, the shrubs neatly trimmed, the flowerbeds manicured, the driveways filled with late-model cars. Everything calm and quiet. So quiet he could hear the dew dripping off the side panels of the RV and hitting the pavement. He readjusted his focus, zooming in on the white house at the end of the block, a turn-of-the-century Victorian with a wide porch across the front. Quiet and dark.

Though tempted to go in immediately—he could already feel her skin beneath his fingers—he restrained the impulse. *Patience.* She was only the bait, he reminded himself, a little diversion who would lead him to the courier. *Be the hunter.*

An unfamiliar sound suddenly caught his attention, coming fast from behind. Before he could turn, a young woman in pink running shorts and a white T-shirt swept past the RV, a Sony radio Walkman over her ears, her in-line skates whining over the pavement. He zeroed in on her backside, watching the movement of her tight gluteus muscles as they rippled up and down beneath the thin nylon fabric. *Caspità!* He turned back to the house. *Soon. Very soon.*

The dawn was coming fast now, its crimson aura burning through the fog coming in off the sound, and within minutes the birds were chirping and the bees working their way through the flowerbeds—familiar rhythms laid down by the comings and goings of the sun and sea. At exactly six o'clock two early-morning joggers—one male, one female, both middle-aged—emerged from homes across from each other, met in the street, then set off at a leisurely pace toward Long Island Sound. Five minutes later an upstairs light blinked on in the home of Lara Quinn. Jäger recorded the time in his notebook. Other lights quickly followed.

At 6:45 a van pulled into the driveway, "Long Island Sound Day Camp" printed along its side. The front door to the house opened immediately and two children—a boy, nine or ten, and a girl, not more than eight—stepped onto the porch. Lara Quinn stepped out behind them. Barely able to contain his excitement, Jäger zoomed in with his scope. Dressed in a coppery colored Lycra bodysuit that matched her hair, the woman looked as good as he remembered, maybe better, like a fine bordeaux that improved with age. Just the thought made his taste buds water with anticipation.

She gave the driver a wave, kissed her children, then waited until they were in the van before disappearing back into the house. Jäger marked the time in his notebook. The children, of course, came as no surprise. In fact, he had given their situation considerable thought and had come to the realization that he had no choice but to end their lives. They would soon be without a mother or father—he thought of Leonidovich and smiled to himself—or uncle. No good hunter left behind a nest of babies. Killing them would be an act of kindness. An obligation he must accept.

At 6:50 a teenage boy on a bike came riding down the middle of the street, tossing newspapers from one side to the other and generally missing his target. Almost before the paper landed on her damp lawn, Lara Quinn had the door open. She started to step outside when a stocky young man with broad shoulders suddenly appeared in the door behind her.

She frowned, clearly not liking whatever he said, but retreated back into the house. The man pulled on a sport coat—but not before Jäger caught a glimpse of the 9mm Beretta hanging from a shoulder rig beneath his left arm—and stepped onto the porch. He stretched awkwardly, exposing the fact that he was wearing a Kevlar vest beneath his light summer shirt, then casually glanced around. Though he tried to hide it, there was nothing casual about the intensity of his eyes as they slowly and methodically scrutinized the area. Ex-military, Jäger thought, judging from the man's posture and tight haircut. Apparently satisfied that everything was normal, the man quickly retrieved the paper and disappeared back into the house.

Jäger leaned back in his chair, feeling invisible and surprisingly euphoric. *Professional competition.* This would add some excitement to the game. He could already smell the blood on the trap.

CHAPTER THIRTY

Las Vegas

Thursday, 1 July 11:12:25 GMT –0800

Although most people would have been extremely happy to live and die in one of the country club villas at Steve Wynn's new Las Vegas resort, Simon felt trapped and isolated. The more he understood, or thought he understood, the more unlikely it seemed he would escape the forces aligned against him. They were too big, too powerful, with too many resources. That much was obvious, though he still had no clear understanding of who *they* were.

He pulled the last stack of documents from the printer, still hoping for some clue to that question, and quickly scanned through the pages. More of the same—military and logistical details relating to the overthrow of Kim Jong-il, and political suggestions on how to establish a new democratic republic—but nothing that might indicate who was behind it. Not unless he accepted the obvious—the President—but for some reason that seemed too obvious.

It was also illegal—forbidden by UN charter and agreed to by our government—which would explain the subterfuge, the money, and the GPS tracking devices; but it didn't explain why anyone would want him dead. He didn't really know anything, including the true identity of the people who gave him the documents. For all he knew, *they* had no connection to the government. It could be any one of a thousand mega-conglomerates that stood to benefit by the reunification of Korea. Or some antisocialist eccentric who . . . But as quickly as he considered each possibility, he knew better. It had to be someone inside the Administration, someone with military and political connections. Someone with huge sums of money. Someone powerful enough to get Eth Jäger out of prison. But who? The questions led one into another, into another, with no end in sight.

He leaned back in the plush, ergonomically designed chair and closed his eyes, sure that he had missed or forgotten something. He started at the beginning, the first phone call, replaying the conversation back through his mind—*nothing*—and moved on to the offices of the North Korean Trade Legation. He could see it all—the reception area, the hallway, the boardroom—and could hear the conversations, but could remember nothing he hadn't already considered. Yet he had the feeling it was there, that he was overlooking something. He started back through the memory tape a second time, isolating and dividing the minutes into sensory segments, reviewing each moment from different angles. It wasn't until that point when the men had left the boardroom and he was alone with Jin Pak that he remembered the momentary vibration of his pocket alarm and his assumption that someone had inadvertently jostled his security case. Though it seemed unlikely that anyone could have penetrated the case's security measures and gotten to his laptop without setting off the alarm, he couldn't discount the possibility.

He sat up, waited for his eyes to adjust to the sunlight flooding through the floor-to-ceiling windows, then initiated a selective search of his hard drive, checking for any files that had been added, accessed, or changed since the moment he accepted the assignment. There were only sixteen, fifteen that he recognized and one that he didn't: a voice file that had been added to his CONTACT folder two days *after* the meeting. How was that possible? He double-clicked the file, then sat in stunned silence listening to a man he had never met or talked to, yet whose voice he recognized immediately: *I can't emphasize enough how important this is. Can you help us out?* There was a momentary pause followed by Simon's own voice: *Yessir, of course. Exactly what is it you want me to do, Mr. President?* If he didn't know better, he would have actually believed he had spoken to the man. *Unfucking believable!*

His new cell phone—one of those anonymous off-the-shelf models with prepaid minutes—gave a little chirp and he snatched it up. "You get everything?" Vic asked without preamble.

"Just printed out the last of it," he answered, wanting to hear what she thought before telling her about the recording.

"Pretty damning, wouldn't you say?"

He realized from her tone what she thought, the

question really a statement. "So you think it's the President?"

"Like duh. It's pretty obvious."

"You're wrong, Vic. Someone's set it up to look that way."

"You think that because you've seen the documents," she argued. "They weren't meant for public disclosure."

But he was starting to wonder if that wasn't exactly what they were for. It would explain a lot of those questions still ricocheting around in his head. "The President can't overthrow a foreign government on his own."

"Of course not," she responded dryly, as if certain things didn't need to be explained. "The operation is probably being run by the CIA. But whatever—"

"Wait a minute," he interrupted. "Why the CIA? This stuff looks like it came out of the Pentagon."

"The plan maybe, but not the action. It's not their style. If the President wanted Kim out, the Pentagon would want to do it straight up, a massive bombing campaign followed by an invasion force of two hundred thousand. But either way, CIA or Pentagon, the President gave the order, you can bet on that."

"Save your money, Victoria. I've got evidence that the President is being set up."

Her voice dropped to a confidential whisper. "What evidence? What do you know?"

"Listen to this." He held the phone down close to the laptop and double-clicked the fictitious file. He could only imagine the shock on her face as the President's voice reverberated through the tiny speaker.

She listened silently, waiting for the recording to finish before speaking. "What—" She took a breath, obviously stunned. "What is that?"

"It's pretty obvious," Simon answered, using her own words to make the point. "What do you think it is?"

"Okay," she snapped back, "I get the message. Is it real or not?"

"Of course not. And believe me, I'd remember a conversation with the President."

"So where did it come from?"

Good question. As he thought about it, he watched four young women in sexy little golf outfits maneuver their carts up the eighteenth fairway. They looked good, played bad. "I have no idea. It was installed on my laptop two days after I picked up the documents."

"What's to understand? Someone obviously got to your computer."

But he didn't see how that was possible. "I was over the Pacific Ocean and I had it with me."

"Well, it didn't just materialize out of cyberspace."

Cyberspace. He suddenly realized how it might have been done. He thought back, estimating his time alone with Jin Pak. *Fifteen or twenty minutes*—just long enough for someone to access his security case, boot his computer, and install a program designed to wake up at a later time and carry out its mission. "I think it was done with a Trojan."

"So you—" She paused, thinking about it. "So you

think the file was surreptitiously downloaded while you were online?"

"That would explain it."

"It would also explain why they want you dead."

Back to *they*, he thought, surprised at how quickly she connected the dots. "Exactly. Whoever made this recording doesn't want me around to challenge its veracity. Someone is clearly trying to set up the President."

A good ten seconds ticked by while she considered the possibility. "That doesn't mean he isn't involved."

"What do you mean?"

"Let's say the President ordered the CIA to support this attempt by the KUP to overthrow Kim."

"I'm listening."

"And maybe they don't like it," she continued, the reflective tone of a person thinking out loud. "Maybe they're tired of holding the bag for bad Presidential decisions. The recording might be nothing more than an insurance policy. A way to cover their ass and blame it on the President in case something goes wrong."

Made sense. "And for that to work they would need to kill the messenger?"

"Precisely."

"Interesting theory."

"And that's all it is," she said, making what sounded like a diplomatic retreat. "If you're going to get out of this mess, we need evidence. *Real* evidence."

"Electronic files don't leave fingerprints."

"That's not necessarily true, though I have a feeling that file was thoroughly scrubbed and sanitized. Send me a copy anyway, I'll see if I can find any telltale identifiers."

"As we speak." He right-clicked the file, hit COPY, attached it to an e-mail, and hit SEND. "What about the North Korean Trade Legation? Did you have time to check?"

"I did," she answered. "The offices were vacant and clean. And I mean clean. No hair, fibers, or prints. The information on the rental agreement was bogus."

He wasn't surprised. "How did they pay?" He would have bet the family jewels he knew the answer to that one too.

"Cash," she answered, confirming his suspicions. "And I checked with the other tenants. No one saw anything. Whoever they were, they were in and out in only a couple of days."

Which explained the smell of fresh paint and the magazines without address labels. "Just long enough to hook Simple Simon."

"You got it."

"So how do I get *real* evidence?"

"That's a problem," she answered. "I doubt if you're going to find anything beyond what you already have, and what you have might be as phoney as that recording of you and the President. If I were you, I'd turn everything over to the press. Once it's out there you should be safe."

He knew better. There was no *safe* as long as Eth Jäger was on the hunt. "If I turn it over to the press, all hell is going to break loose. This could be another Watergate."

"Not your problem, Simon."

"I don't want to be the catalyst that brings down a President. Not unless I know he's involved."

"First of all, he probably is. And secondly—" She almost screamed the words: "It's not your problem!"

But it was. He could pretend otherwise, but he would always know better, know that he helped them—whoever *they* were—get away with it. "I can't do it. I need to know first if he's involved."

"Well, good luck with that," she snapped back. "What do you plan to do, call him on the phone for a little one-on-one chat?"

Though she meant to be sarcastic, the words triggered an idea. "Gotta run, Vic, I need to make a call."

"I was joking."

"Understood." But what he had in mind was no joke. "I'll call you tonight." He disconnected before she could ask more.

Fifteen minutes later, Big Jake Rynerson pulled his over-sized and customized air-conditioned golf cart to within a few inches of the veranda door. Dressed in a stonewashed denim shirt and faded blue jeans, he glanced around, as if checking to be sure he wasn't followed, though for a man as large, colorful, and well-known to the public as B.J. Rynerson, he couldn't have been any more conspicuous driving a fire truck down the middle of Las Vegas Boulevard. His canine buddy, who was curled into a ball on the floor of the cart, lurched to his feet and struggled to catch up as Jake pushed open the door and stepped into the villa. Simon gave the old Lab a pat on the head as he lumbered past. "Brownie's moving a little slow, Jake."

"Ain't that a fact. The poor fella's so old he's farting dust and squatting like a bitch just to piss." Jake stopped in the middle of the room and made a slow three-sixty on one heel of his scruffy old cowboy boots. "Not bad. Not bad at all."

Simon motioned toward a couple of oversized chairs overlooking the eighteenth green and a spectacular thirty-five-foot waterfall. "Not exactly what I had in mind when I told you I needed a little place to hide out for a couple of days."

"You said away from the Castle." Jake nodded toward the tan and beige tower rising above the trees that separated the two megaresorts. "This here's away."

Not far enough, Simon thought, knowing Caitlin was working somewhere behind that facade of glass. It was hard enough not to see her—knowing someone might be watching and waiting for him to show up—but even more difficult knowing she was so close. "Dare I ask what all this luxury is costing?" He knew it had to be at least two grand a day.

Big Jake snorted, as if the mention of money gave him a bad taste. "Don't you worry about that, partner, it's all taken care of."

"Jake, I'm not letting you pay for this. I'm not a charity case."

"Hell no, you ain't no charity case." He lowered his huge frame into one of the deep chairs, and Brownie plopped down alongside. "And I sure as hell ain't paying."

Simon grabbed his laptop and took a chair facing the big man. "You want to explain that?"

"This here is what we call a re-cip-ro-cal," Jake answered, stretching out the word as if it amused him. "Just a little accommodation between neighbors."

"I didn't know you and Steve Wynn were such buddies."

"Friendly competitors, you might say. Steve and his wife Elaine are first-class people."

"Even so, I don't feel right about not paying."

"Would it help if I told you he tried to steal your girlfriend?"

"You're kidding." He wondered why Caitlin had never mentioned it. "I thought the guy was happily married."

"He wasn't lookin' for romance. That's not his style. He was lookin' to steal the best damn executive on the Strip."

"Some friend."

Jake shrugged his massive shoulders. "Can't blame a man for trying. 'Course, I woulda slapped that boy into next week if he woulda gone and done it behind my back." He chuckled at the memory. "But old Steve's too smart for that. Way too smart. He made sure I was sitting right there when he made the offer.

Told Caity she ever got tired of cleaning the shit off my boots, she should come see him. Then he looked at me and winked, like he was just making a joke, but we both knew better."

"Sounds like something you'd say, Jake."

"Yup, that's why I like the guy. He's the kind of man that looks you straight in the eye while he's trying to pick your pocket."

"And he knows how to build hotels."

"That too," Jake agreed, glancing around at the palace-like accommodations. "That too." Then his eyes came back, suddenly serious and intense. "Okay, let's cut this horseshit chatter. What's going on? What you got yourself mixed up in this time, Leonidovich?"

A question Simon had been asking himself for three weeks. "Listen to this." He double-clicked the voice file and sat back, watching Jake's expression mutate from curious to cautious. "I'm sure you recognize the voice."

Jake hunched forward, his big arms dangling between his knees. "You're working for the President?"

"Never met the man, never talked to him."

Jake frowned, thinking about that, then he leaned back, stretched his long legs out in front of him, and crossed his boots. "You better start at the beginning."

And that's exactly what Simon did—from the first phone call, to finding the recording on his laptop—everything but Vic's identity. The entire story took nearly an hour. "So what do you think?"

Big Jake whistled tunelessly between his teeth. "Damn! I think you're up to your *cojones* in cow flop, that's what I think."

"That much I know."

"And I think your friend's right, the President's involved."

"Maybe," Simon agreed, "but I need to be certain."

"And just how are you going to do that?"

"I'll need some help." Simon smiled, just enough to let the man know he was looking him straight in the eye. "No question about that."

"Uh-oh." Jake gave Brownie an affectionate pat on the rump. "Hold on, boy, I think we're about to get lassoed into something."

"Sorry, Jake, but you're the only one I know with enough influence to get the President on the phone."

"Shit, I don't even like being in the same room with that polecat."

"So you know him?"

"We've howdied once or twice, nothin' more."

"But he'll take your call?"

Jake snorted. "Well shit, boy, he's a politician and I'm rich as Croesus, of course he'll take my call. Whatchu got in mind?"

"I'd like to get his reaction to these documents."

"That I can tell you. He'll say it's all a bunch of crap, whether he's involved or not."

"Of course. And if he doesn't know anything, he'll go absolutely nuclear. Demand to know where the documents came from, who's involved, etcetera, etcetera."

Jake nodded empathically. "No question."

"But if he *is* involved, he'll know exactly where they came from and who's involved. He'll also realize he's been set up to take a fall. His reaction will be completely different."

A dubious frown creased Jake's forehead and hung there in his tan, leathery skin. "I'm not sure about that. This fella's a politician, he could probably out-act De Niro."

"Maybe, but the minute he's alone he's going to be on the phone. He's going to try and cover up the shit before it starts to spread."

"No doubt," Jake agreed, "that's a beltway tradition. But so what? How's that going to help you?"

"Whoever gets that first call will be the person with the answers. How Jäger got out of prison and how to find him. The one who—"

"The one," Jake interrupted, "with his nuts in a wringer. There's no telling what he'll do. He might run to the press himself. He might just run."

"Either way, it takes the focus off me," Simon answered, though he wanted much more than that. He wanted to know everything—the what and why, and especially the who—and he wanted to see them all in prison alongside Eth Jäger.

"You're forgetting a couple of things, my friend."

Simon had a pretty good idea what Jake was thinking. "Like how will I know who gets that call?"

"That's one."

"My friend in Washington will be able to tell me that." He said it with confidence, though he didn't really know if Vic could or would agree to trace the call. "And two?"

"What if the President *isn't* involved?"

"I'm not certain," Simon admitted. "I guess that depends on what he does."

Jake tapped a finger against his lip, thinking it through, then apparently made up his mind. "Okay, what is it you want me to do?"

"Simple. Call him up, tell him you've been given some documents that are potentially damaging to his administration. Too sensitive to talk about on the phone or to send through the mail."

"He'll ask me to come to Washington."

"Don't do it. If he makes that call from the White House, there's no way my friend can trace it. Make some excuse. Tell him you can't fly right now. Doctor's orders."

Jake bobbed his head agreeably. "I can do that."

"According to the paper, he'll be in California all weekend. A campaign blitz ending with a Fourth of July celebration in Sacramento. That's only a short hop from here. You might suggest he stop on his way back to Washington."

"Should work," Jake agreed. "And what are you going to be doing?"

"I'll be in Washington, waiting to see who gets that call."

CHAPTER THIRTY-ONE

CIA Headquarters, Langley, Virginia

Saturday, 3 July 11:18:27 GMT –0500

The intercom beeped as the line opened, followed by the apologetic voice of Sara, Tucker's weekend secretary. "I'm sorry, Director, I know you didn't want to be disturbed, but Captain Baggett is at Reception and would like a few minutes if that's possible."

"Of course," Tucker answered, being careful to keep the surprise out of his voice. "Have them send him right up." He immediately began clearing his desk so it didn't look like he was purging his files, which was exactly what he was doing.

By the time Sara pushed open the door, Tucker had stuffed two burn-bags of shredded papers into his coat closet and was sitting calmly at his desk reading a report. He stood up, giving Baggett a cordial smile for the benefit of his secretary. "Captain Baggett, this is an unexpected surprise."

Baggett extended his hand across the desk, not a flicker of warmth in his frosty gray eyes. "Mr. Director, thank you for seeing me without an appointment."

"No problem." Tucker motioned toward one of the two chairs facing the desk.

"Coffee?" Sara asked, still holding the door.

They responded together, wordlessly, a negative shake of the head. Baggett waited until the door clicked shut before speaking. "What the hell is going on?"

Tucker leaned forward, letting the man know he wasn't intimidated. "I hope it's the general asking that question, Captain Baggett, otherwise I'm going to have your disrespectful ass tossed out of this building."

Baggett glared back, his face tight with the effort of not saying what he clearly wanted to say. "Yessir, Mr. Director, it's the general that's asking."

Tucker ignored the sarcastic tone. "And what specifically does the general wish to know?"

"Let's start with that damn courier. Where is he?"

Tucker was positive the question had nothing to do with Baggett's unannounced visit. "I'm not sure. I had people waiting for him in Las Vegas, but the plane he was on made an unscheduled stop in San Francisco. He disappeared before I could get someone there."

"He can't evaporate into thin air. What about credit-card activity?"

"Nothing, not since he withdrew forty thousand in cash from his American Express account in Seoul. He's smart enough not to use his cards, but it doesn't matter, we'll have him soon."

Baggett cocked his head slightly, suspicious, as if he didn't believe it. "You know something?"

Tucker typed Jäger's GPS link into his computer and rotated the monitor. "Look for yourself."

Baggett leaned forward, scrutinizing the screen. "Rye, New York. You think Leonidovich is in New York?"

"No, but that's where his sister lives. Jäger will use her as bait."

Baggett nodded slowly, as if considering this new information, but his eyes shifted involuntarily to the right, revealing that he was actually thinking ahead to how he could steer the conversation, to the real purpose of his visit. "Good idea. Very good."

Tucker wanted no part of it, there was nothing *good* about what a maniac like Jäger would do to Lara Quinn, but he only nodded and waited, knowing Baggett was about to reveal himself.

"Very good," Baggett repeated. "That should work."

Tucker nodded again.

"Anything else I should tell the general?"

"Like what?" Tucker asked, growing weary of the cat and mouse.

"Like what you were doing at the White House at seven o'clock this morning."

Tucker almost laughed; Captain Buddy Baggett had about as much subtlety as a combat boot to the crotch. "What's to tell? The President wanted a security briefing before he left on his campaign trip to California."

"A security briefing?"

"That's right," Tucker answered, purposely showing a bit of impatience. "A review of trouble spots around the world." Which *was* the official agenda, though it became instantly clear that all the President wanted to talk about was what documents B.J. Rynerson might have that could embarrass the Administration. Tucker realized instantly what Rynerson had, but was able to hide his surprise behind an expression of feigned bewilderment; the same look he now offered Baggett. "That *is* my job, Captain."

"Did he mention a stop in Las Vegas?"

"He did," Tucker answered, not about to offer anything more before he had some idea how much Baggett knew.

"You don't find that a little suspicious?"

"He's hustling a fat cat for money. That's about as normal as it gets in this town."

"Rynerson's a friend of Leonidovich."

Tucker nodded thoughtfully, not wanting to appear obtuse. "I considered that, but there doesn't seem to be a connection."

Baggett barked a laugh of utter astonishment. "Of course there's a connection. The courier was on his plane. He's probably in Vegas."

"Not likely," Tucker answered, trying to stay as close to the truth as possible. "I've got eyes and ears on both the Wells woman and the Rynerson resort. There's been no sign of him. Not even a phone call."

Baggett frowned, clearly dissatisfied with the answer. "The general thinks otherwise. He believes the courier is behind the meeting."

Tucker was sure of it. He was also sure Leonidovich had accessed the data disc. What he didn't understand was why the man would take the information to Rynerson and not the press; and why Rynerson, a well-known anti–Washington Independent, would take it to the President. "I'm sure the President would have said something if he thought this had anything to do with North Korea."

"And if you're wrong? If Rynerson has the files?"

"That cowboy has no love for the President. He'd turn them over to the press."

"Jesus," Baggett snorted, as if he couldn't believe what he was hearing. "You're missing the obvious. Rynerson could buy himself a real chunk of power with those files. The President would agree to anything to keep that stuff out of the press."

Tucker knew better. Rynerson was too much of a Boy Scout to play the blackmail game. "That's not the way Rynerson works."

"Suppose you're wrong," Baggett argued. "The President would know you set him up."

Tucker now understood the concern, that whatever led to him would lead to the general. "That's not true. The President knows we've been searching for Leonidovich since he disappeared. If Rynerson had the files, the President would naturally assume he got them from Leonidovich, but there's no reason for him to suspect me of anything."

"Except for that bogus telephone recording. If he hears that, he wouldn't need a crystal ball to figure out where it came from."

Maybe, Tucker thought, but without some clue that his laptop had been tampered with, Leonidovich would have no reason to check his files. "Believe me, Rynerson doesn't have that recording."

Baggett pushed himself up from his chair and leaned forward over the desk. "Mr. Director—" He spoke softly, without moving his lips. "—you better be right."

Tucker understood the threat—the message Baggett had been sent to deliver—but he didn't care and he didn't react. By Monday it would all be over. "You tell the general not to worry, Captain, I've planned for every contingency."

CHAPTER THIRTY-TWO

Washington, DC

Monday, 5 July 01:23:19 GMT –0500

"Hold on, Vic." Simon snapped the cellular into the dashboard bracket, where he could easily monitor the signal, then hooked the combination earpiece/microphone over his left ear. He felt a bit like James Bond—admittedly a rather pudgy, low-profile impersonation—with his nondescript black Chevy rental, his all-black jogging outfit, black Nightstalker binoculars, black mini-flashlight, and two black cellular phones, one attached to each ear. "Can you hear me now?"

"You sound just like the commercial. And *don't* use my name."

She was just being paranoid—the signal was scrambled—but he couldn't blame her for being cautious; one mistake and she'd be out of a job, at the very least, and he would probably be swimming with the fishes in the Potomac. "Sorry. From now on I shall call you Moneypenny."

"Very funny."

He lowered his voice to a husky, secretive rasp. "You may call me Bond."

"This is not a game, Bagman."

No, it sure wasn't, but if he didn't do something to relieve the tension, his blood pressure was going to be racing his heart rate into the stratosphere.

"Are you ready?"

"You bet. Got my Walther P99 locked and loaded."

"Please tell me you don't have a weapon."

"Only to the trained eye, Moneypenny. Hidden within my emergency kit is a plethora of superspy weaponry. Zip ties and superglue, a small sewing kit with a needle long enough to strike fear into the heart of the most fearsome opponent. A paperback novel guaranteed to put anyone asleep within—"

"Okay, okay" she interrupted, "cut the shit. Now tell me why you're parked at the Kennedy Center? Wouldn't it be better if you were on the Loop somewhere?"

It was a guess either way, but he knew she was only nervous and doing that female thing—second-guessing his guess—so he indulged her. "From here I can go in any direction, and I'm right next to the Roosevelt Bridge if I need to get into Virginia. Whichever direction you point, I'm ready." The line hummed silently in his ear, and he knew she was checking a map, evaluating his choice.

"Okay," she said, coming back on the line. "You're right, that's a decent enough spot."

"Thank you, Moneypenny. I know how it hurts to admit that."

"Don't abuse me, Bagman, it's after midnight and my fangs are growing longer and sharper by the minute."

Though she said it with a smile in her voice, he felt the warning tap of her fingers along his spine. "I promise to be good."

"Shouldn't the President be there by now? It's almost ten-thirty Vegas time."

"I talked to Caitlin about twenty minutes ago. *Air Force One* was on final approach into Nellis."

"So, he should be at the Sand Castle by . . .?"

Simon pressed the stem of his watch, momentarily illuminating the dial. "Right about now."

Caitlin motioned for Big Jake to lean down, not wanting the two Secret Service agents flanking the elevator to hear. "Now you behave yourself, Jake. Just remember you're doing this for Simon."

He let out a long disgusted sigh, the kind that sounds like an 18-wheeler's air brakes. "Dammit, Caity, Billie warned me about a dozen times already."

"But men never listen to their wives, so I'm warning you again."

"I don't need warning."

"Yes you do. You're standing there huffin' and snortin' under your breath like an old dog that's about to take a bite out of someone's ass."

"Well, I am an old dog, and I don't much like having my territory invaded by some mealymouthed politician."

"It's for Simon," she repeated.

"Now you stop ragging my ass. I'd piss on a spark plug to help that boy, you know that."

The two agents suddenly drew to attention as the

elevator door slid open. Jake offered up a congenial smile and stuck out his hand as the President stepped into the room. "Happy Independence Day, Mr. President. Welcome to the Sand Castle."

The President flashed his perfect snow-white teeth. "Thank you, Big Jake. I appreciate the invitation."

Caitlin gritted her teeth, knowing how much Jake hated the *Big* label, but when he gave her a wink—just to let her know he was being a good soldier—she knew he had taken the warnings seriously. "Mr. President, I'd like you to meet Caitlin Wells, my administrative assistant."

The President took her hand in both of his and held it, his eyes making a quick sightseeing trip over the contours of her body. "Ms. Wells, it's a pleasure. From what I hear, you're the snap in this man's whip."

A line, she suspected, given to him by his advance team, a man and woman who had spent two days at the hotel. "No, sir, I just handle the business end of things." She gently extracted her hand. "Mrs. Rynerson is the only one who would dare touch his whip."

Jake snorted and the President laughed heartily. "That's good, Ms. Wells. Very good." He turned abruptly back to Jake, as if remembering what he needed to say. "Where is Billie?" He spoke as if they were old friends. "I was looking forward to meeting her."

"And she surely did want to meet you," Jake answered smoothly. "But she's got a real mean-ass summer cold and a headache bad enough to kill a mule.

She asked me to apologize for not being here to welcome you into our home."

The President frowned and nodded, the perfect expression of disappointment and understanding. "No apology necessary. The minute she's feeling better I'd like you to visit me at the White House." He turned to Caitlin. "You too, Ms. Wells."

A suggestive look flashed through his eyes, quick as a fire-spark, there and gone, but she had seen it too many times not to know what it meant. "Thank you, sir, that would be a real trip." *A trip through Never-everland!*

"Sure would," Jake added enthusiastically. "Sure would."

The President smiled, obviously thinking he had scored, and turned his attention to the windows overlooking the Strip. "My God, this is where you live?"

"You should have been here an hour ago," Jake answered. "The fireworks are pretty awesome when you're fifty floors up."

"Why don't we go into the Fishbowl?" Caitlin suggested, determined to move things along. "The view's even better from there." That wasn't true, but she knew Simon was sitting and waiting and would pop a carotid if he didn't hear something soon.

"Good idea," Jake answered, turning in that direction. "Follow me."

The President fell in beside Caitlin, his right hand going to the small of her back, as if she needed steering. "The Fishbowl?"

"Jake's office."

"Oh." He gave her another suggestive look, apparently unconcerned with the two Secret Service agents following behind. "I love your dress. The material is so—" his hand slipped an inch lower, testing the waters. "—soft."

For Simon, she told herself. She tilted her head back and peered up at him from under her eyelashes, intimating an interest in his inferred proposition. "Yessir, you can't imagine how soft." Before he had a chance to get any friskier, she stepped aside, ostensibly to let him enter the room first. "Here we are."

He stopped at the oversized teakwood door, admiring the thousand-derrick oil field carved into its surface. "That's some door."

"A little reminder," Jake said, "of where the money came from to build this here little joint."

"I've got some oil property myself," the President responded proudly, as if to establish his membership in the All-boys Petroleum Club, then seemed to regret his words and dismissed the remark with a casual wave of his hand. "Insignificant, really." He glanced back at the two agents, some unspoken signal passing between them, and they immediately stopped and took positions outside the door.

Jake stepped behind the bar. "Can I get you something to drink, Mr. President?" He laid a hand on his copper-topped espresso machine. "Hot, cold, or in between."

"I'm good," the President answered, moving toward the window, which stretched floor-to-ceiling the length of the room. "I don't really have much time, it's almost two o'clock in Washington and I've got an early meeting with the Japanese ambassador."

"Caity?"

"Nothing for me, Jake." She followed the President, being careful to keep some distance between them without making it obvious. "So what do you think?"

He stopped a couple of feet short of the glass, as if approaching a sheer precipice and afraid of being sucked into the neon canyon of hotels and casinos that made up Las Vegas Boulevard. "Spectacular." He looked at her, a lecherous smile coming into his brown eyes. "Truly spectacular."

"Sin City at its finest." She said it without thinking and regretted the words instantly.

He gave her a little wink. "A little sin never hurt anyone, that's what I always say."

Tell it to your wife, Mr. President. "Yessir, that's pretty much our motto here in the desert."

"Speaking of secrets in the desert," Jake said, coming up behind them with a frosted glass of beer. "I'm sure you're anxious to get a peek at those documents, Mr. President."

"Why not?" the President replied casually, as if he wasn't really concerned. "I have to admit, I'm a bit curious."

Caitlin motioned toward the glass conference table. "Then let's have a look. I've got everything right here."

Jake pulled back his custom-made leather chair at

the head of the table. "I'd be honored if you'd take this one, Mr. President."

"Thank you, Big Jake." He lowered himself into the oversized behemoth, which made him look small and insignificant, something Caitlin was sure Jake intended.

She took a chair to the President's left, opposite Jake, offered up a tentative smile, as if she hated to be the bearer of bad tidings, then pulled the documents from a large expansion file and set them on the table. "I think you're going to find these quite interesting, sir."

"Nothing but horseshit," Jake said. "I'm sure of it."

The President gave them a confident smile—the comforting, I'm-in-control-and-there's-nothing-to-worry-about smile that American voters found so appealing—pulled a pair of stylish half-lens readers from the breast pocket of his suit coat and began to read. His eyes widened almost immediately, accompanied by under-the-breath sounds of disbelief. He finished the first page, looked up, shook his head in utter amazement, and went back to reading. After ten minutes, he was skimming through the pages as if reading a boring novel he couldn't wait to finish. He slapped down the last page, expelled a deep breath, and pulled off his glasses. "You said it, Big Jake, horseshit, every bit of it. Horseshit."

Jake nodded vigorously, like he was pounding nails with his massive jaw. "Any fool could see that. It's as plain as a turd in a bowl of milk."

The President smiled, out of relief or amusement, Caitlin couldn't tell which, and though she disliked the man and wanted to believe he was lying, she wasn't sure. He was either a very good actor or completely innocent—neither of which would help Simon. "You'll have to excuse Jake, Mr. President. His language tends to be colorful." Jake grimaced, as if embarrassed, but she knew better. "Though he's obviously right. There's no way you'd be involved in something like this without congressional approval."

"Of course not," the President replied, "that would be insane. But—" He glanced back and forth between them, the pay-attention look he used so frequently with reporters. "—these documents appear to have some legitimacy. As I'm sure you're aware—" Another meaningful look. "—the Pentagon has contingency plans for every possible scenario. Unless I miss my guess, that's exactly what we have here."

"You're saying the documents are real?" Jake asked.

The President nodded in the affirmative, his expression grave. "I believe so."

The man was absolutely innocent, Caitlin decided, or smart enough not to deny what seemed obvious. "Stolen?"

"Either that," the President answered, "or someone's trying to embarrass my administration."

Jake nodded, as if that confirmed his thinking.

The President leaned forward, trying to give Jake the old eye-to-eye, though he looked a bit like a Honda going bumper-to-bumper with a Humvee. "I have to admit, I'm a little surprised you're the one showing me these documents, Big Jake. I know you're not exactly a fan of—"

Jake interrupted with a dismissive wave. "I may not like a lot of what y'all do in Washington, Mr. President, but I'm a patriot and I damn-well know the smell of horseshit when I step in it."

The President flashed his photo-op smile, the one seen by the public whenever he stepped off *Marine One.* "I appreciate that. I sure do." His expression mutated back to serious. "But you know I have to ask where you got these documents?"

"Yessir, I do," Jake answered. "Sure do." He turned and looked across the table. "Caity, honey, this might be a good time to play that recording."

"Oh!" She thunked her forehead, as if it had completely slipped her mind, though realized it would be their last chance to determine if the President was being honest. She pulled a small digital recorder from the bottom of the expansion file, laid it on the table, and pressed the PLAY button. Instantly, the President's voice reverberated from the tiny speaker. *I can't emphasize enough how important this is. Can you help us out?* She tapped the OFF button. "I'm sure you recognize the voice."

The President nodded cautiously, not knowing what to expect, and she pressed the PLAY button a second time. *Yessir, of course. Exactly what is it you want me to do, Mr. President?* She tapped the OFF button. "What about that one, sir?" She kept her tone inquisitive, not wanting it to sound like an interrogation.

A bewildered frown slowly creased the President's forehead. "No, can't say that I do."

She tapped the PLAY button a third time, and then waited for the recording to play out.

"That sounds like me," the President acknowledged without prompting, "but I never had that conversation. I'm sure of it."

"And you don't recognize the other voice?"

He shook his head emphatically. "No, Ms. Wells. I'm sure of that too."

"That's the person who gave me the documents," Jake explained. "Simon Leonidovich—" A spark of recognition flashed through the President's eyes. "You recognize the name?"

The President frowned, his expression a knot of perplexity, but the effort seemed exaggerated and a bit theatrical. "Not that I recall."

So sayeth the lawyer and politician, Caitlin thought, sure now that he was lying. "Mr. Leonidovich was hired by the State Department to deliver the documents to North Korea," she explained, trying to sound helpful, "though it appears someone is trying to make it look like he was working directly for you."

"Obviously," the President snapped defensively. "But I'm telling you I've never talked to the man."

"Don't misunderstand," Jake interjected smoothly, "we know that. In fact, that's exactly what Mr. Leonidovich told us."

Though the President tried to hide his relief, it oozed from his pores like sap from an old maple. "That settles it then. I had nothing to do with this—" He flourished a hand toward the documents. "This . . . this foolishness."

"It ain't quite that simple," Jake continued. "You know how the press is, without Leonidovich around to deny the authenticity of this here little recording, they're likely to believe the worst."

"What do you mean, 'not around'? Where is he?"

"We're not exactly sure," Caitlin answered quickly, instinctively shielding Jake from lying to any federal official. "He's on the run."

Jake bobbed his head, as if to confirm it. "Yup, that's right. There's been a couple of attempts on his life. That's why he gave me a copy of these here documents. It's clear as creek water, someone doesn't want that boy to say anything."

In less than ten seconds the President's relief had dissolved into a look of concern. "This is terrible. A catastrophe."

Caitlin nodded, realizing that when he said *catastrophe*, it wasn't Simon he was thinking about. "Yessir, it is."

"We have to find him. I can offer him protection. I can—"

"I'm not sure that's good enough," Jake interrupted. "He thinks the only way he'll be safe now is for this—" He motioned toward the stack of documents. "—to become public."

"No, no, no," the President said, shaking his head vigorously, as if a bug had just crawled into his ear. "That's not the way to go. It would ruin our relationship with both South Korea and the Chinese."

Jake snorted, a little sardonic hiccup. "I don't think the North Koreans would like it much either."

The President glanced at Caitlin, then back to Jake, searching desperately for an ally. "You have to stop him."

"Not sure I can do that," Jake answered. "As long as he thinks someone is trying to—"

"Don't worry about that," the President cut in. "I can put an end to that." He hesitated, apparently realized he had gone too far, and began to backpedal. "We have tremendous assets. Now that I know what's going on, I'm sure we can find the people behind this."

"I'm sure of it too," Caitlin said, positive the man knew exactly who to call. She reached across the table and gave Jake's forearm a squeeze, as if he needed convincing. "That sounds reasonable, Jake. I'm sure Mr. Leonidovich would cooperate if the President could get him out of this fix."

Jake tapped a finger on the thick glass table, as if struggling to make up his mind, then nodded. "I'll do what I can."

The President expelled a deep breath, almost a sigh. "Thank you, Big Jake. I won't forget this." He turned and flashed a little smile, the effort somewhat strained. "You too, Ms. Wells." He glanced at his watch, making no attempt to hide his impatience. "I should get to work on this immediately."

Simon cut off the ring before it hit a second note. "What happened?"

"I love you too, Leonidovich."

"Sorry, Wells, I'm a little—"

"Understood," she interrupted. "He just left."

"And . . . ?"

"I have to tell you, the guy's smooth. Very smooth. He hardly blinked when we showed him the documents. I have to say he put on a pretty good show of ignorance."

He wanted to scream it again—*So what happened?*—but restrained himself. "From what I've heard, that's not much of a stretch."

"Don't underestimate the man, Leonidovich. He managed to get elected President, and it looks like he's going to be reelected."

Another example of blind stupidity, Simon thought, but decided this was not the time to voice his opinion about the ignorance or the indifference of the American voter. "I'll keep that in mind, Wells."

"It wasn't until I played the recording that he cracked. And barely. But he knows who's behind it, I'm sure of that. Jake agrees."

"So you think he'll make the call?"

"That's my guess."

"Then I need to go. I told Vic I'd give her a heads-up."

"You be careful, Leonidovich. I mean it."

"Not to worry, I just want this to be over. The minute I'm sure who's behind this thing I'm heading straight to the *Washington Post*."

"I just want things back to normal."

Normal, that sounded good, but he had a feeling it wouldn't be so easy.

CHAPTER THIRTY-THREE

Washington, DC

Monday, 5 July 02:32:41 GMT –0500

Tucker rolled over, read the display on the phone console—POTUS . . . 02:32—and knew instantly it was bad news. He sat up, cleared his throat, and snatched up the receiver. "Yes, Mr. President."

"I want you in my office at—" He paused, his voice less sharp as he turned away from the phone. "What time are we due in?" There was an indistinct, garbled response, at least two people speaking at once, then the President was back on the line. "Eight-thirty."

"Yessir, of course. May I ask what this is regarding?"

"No." *CLICK.*

It was the most resounding, most fatalistic sound Tucker had ever heard, like the hammer of a gun being cocked. It was over, he didn't have a single doubt about that, and unless he did something in the next couple of hours he would be unceremoniously thrown from office, possibly arrested, his family name disgraced. Even worse, it meant the President would probably get away with his profiteering and deceit, his rape of the American public, his desecration of the Constitution. It was not the end Tucker envisioned, and not something he intended to let happen.

He snapped on the light, waited for his eyes to adjust, then punched in Baggett's private number.

He answered on the third ring, his voice thick enough to clog a drain. "Baggett here."

"Captain, you know who this is?"

"Yeah." He cleared his throat, a low coughing growl from deep inside. "Jesus Christ, it's two-fucking-thirty in the morning. This better be good."

"It's Armageddon," Tucker answered. "Call me back when you're awake." He clicked off before Baggett could answer, knowing that would get the man's attention.

The phone started to ring even before he put down the receiver. "You awake now, Captain?"

"Yeah, I'm awake. What do you mean, Armageddon?"

"I need to see the general," Tucker answered, ignoring the question. "Now."

Baggett cleared his throat again, his voice suddenly hard and determined. "That's impossible."

"Make it happen."

"Impossible," Baggett repeated. "Once he's down for the night there's no way I can get him out of here without being seen."

"You've done it before."

"From his office. That's different, I can slip him out the back without being noticed, but not from here."

"Don't give me that bullshit, Captain, you're much too smart to put yourself in that kind of a box. You've got a backdoor somewhere."

"Sure," Baggett admitted, "but nobody's watching *me*. You have no idea what it's like living in this goddamned fishbowl."

"Hold on." Tucker grabbed the phone book and flipped it open to a map of the city. "I'll make it easy for you. Take the general out for a little stroll around the grounds. A case of insomnia. I'll be in Normanstone Park. That's right across the street. Just—"

"No way," Baggett broke in. "It's too risky."

Tucker ignored the interruption. "Just head south on the park road. I'll park near the Kahlil Gibran Memorial. You'll see the van. One hour."

"Too risky," Baggett repeated. "The general will never go for it."

"Tell him that when the FBI shows up with handcuffs." He didn't wait for a response. Either the general would come or he wouldn't; either way, Tucker knew what he had to do.

CHAPTER THIRTY-FOUR

Washington, DC

Despite the open windows, the car was a sauna, the air so hot and wet and thick, Simon felt as if he were breathing through a sponge. Though he was trying desperately not to panic, it had been eighteen minutes since Caitlin's call and he was starting to think she had misread the situation, that the President had no idea who might be responsible. *So now what?* How could he find Eth Jäger before that maniac popped out from behind some dark corner? At least Lara and the kids were safe; she had accepted protection without protest—a new high point in their sibling relationship—and actually seemed grateful.

He reached for the ignition, intending to put up the windows and use the AC, when a thunderclap directly over the Kennedy Center nearly sent his heart galloping into the Potomac. *Sweet Jesus!* He took a deep breath, pinched his nose, and blew, trying to equalize the pressure and clear the buzzing from his head when he realized it was the cellular marked VH. He reached out and punched the CON-NECT button. "Talk to me."

Vic's voice reverberated back through the tiny ear-bud. "We may have something."

"I'm listening." He picked up his pen and note-pad, ready to take down the information.

"He made three calls immediately after leaving the Sand Castle. The first went to the White House. It lasted less than a minute."

"Any idea who that went to?" He knew the disclosure of that capability—if the NSA had it—would be classified, but he felt compelled to ask.

"No, I told you that," she replied defensively. "I can only track origination and destination on en-coded calls."

"Sorry, I forgot."

"Bullshit, you never forget anything."

That wasn't entirely true, but he knew better than to argue. "And the second call?"

"To the home of John Paul Estes. That one—"

"His Chief of Staff, right?"

"Right," she answered. "A lot of people think he's the man behind the man. That one lasted six min-utes."

"Okay. And the third?"

"Tucker Stark. At home."

Bingo. "You said this thing smelled like CIA. How long did that one last?"

"Fourteen seconds."

Fourteen seconds, what did that mean? "Maybe he didn't answer. It might have been a recording."

"You don't put a recorder on a secure line. That's a no-no."

Made sense. "So what do you think? Why so short?"

"Hard to say," she answered. "But I don't recall having any friendly chats that lasted fourteen seconds."

"Good point." He dropped the notepad and turned to his laptop, which was open and ready on the seat beside him. "Okay, what's the address?"

As she dictated, he punched the location into his *Streets & Trips* program with its GPS interlink. The house was in Georgetown, almost directly north of the Kennedy Center and not more than ten minutes away. "Thanks, Moneypenny. I'm on my way."

"You be careful, this is the Director of the CIA we're talking about."

"Ten-four." As he turned the key in the ignition, a half dozen drops of rain splattered against the windshield.

"I mean it, Bagman, no weird shit. Just observe. See what's going on."

"That's the plan." He turned onto Rock Creek Freeway, the dark waters of the Potomac on his left, and headed north. The traffic was extremely light, only a few pairs of headlights reflecting off the damp pavement. "Nothing to worry about."

"Just observe," she repeated. "Nothing else."

He had no intention of doing anything else. Once he confirmed the CIA was behind the operation, he intended to turn everything over to the *Washington Post* and let them dig out the details; they did it with Watergate, and he had no doubt they would be more than happy to do it again. "Nag, nag, nag."

"Men call it nagging," she fired back. "Women call it reminding."

"Yeah, yeah, yeah." The few drops of rain had turned into a steady drizzle and he flipped the wipers to intermittent. "It's all semantics."

"Semantics, hell! You think we don't know that men ignore us until we've repeated something at least three times?"

He hit the speed limit and eased off. The last thing he needed was to get pulled over in the middle of the night dressed like a cat burglar. "If I knew what women thought, I'd be a happily married man with two kids."

"Really?" Her hectoring tone instantly softened to a velvety purr. "I didn't know you wanted children."

He didn't either—not until he had spent a few days with Soo-Yun and realized what he was missing—but that was a discussion he needed to have with Caitlin. "Sorry, Moneypenny, but it's starting to rain here and I need to concentrate. I'll call you back as soon as I get there."

"Just—"

He hit the END button before she could pry into his domestic wants and dreams. *Women!* Mention children and they go all soft and gooey on the inside.

He turned left on M Street, then right on Wisconsin Avenue and in less than five minutes found himself in the heart of Georgetown. Everything looked gray—the sky and pavement, the buildings and trees—all the colors washed away by the rain. Leaning forward, he tried to read the street signs through the pulsating wipers as they swept and paused, swept and paused. *Getting close.* He suddenly realized his hands were sweating and his heart thumping like a rabbit. He took a deep breath, forcing his pulse out of the red zone.

It took him only a few minutes to find the right street, located in a tony neighborhood with lots of big trees and stately homes. The block in front of the house was completely empty of cars—a local ordinance, he assumed—every home dark except for that of Director Tucker Stark. Being careful not to slow down, Simon drove past the house—a three-story brick Victorian with a detached garage—and parked around the corner. His plan, to park across the street and observe, was clearly not a viable option. *Now what?* But of course he knew the answer to that. Mentally preparing himself for the argument, he punched Vic's preset number.

She answered even before he heard an audible ring. "Are you there?"

"Around the corner," he answered. "There's no parking on the street. I'd stand out like a black man at a Klan rally."

"So you can't see anything?"

"No, but when I drove past there were lights on upstairs and down. How many people live in the house?"

There was a momentary pause, the rapid tapping of her fingers on a keyboard, then another pause before she came back. "He lives alone. His wife and kids were killed in a car accident two years ago."

That was not the kind of thing Simon wanted to hear; it put a sympathetic face to the man he suspected had turned Eth Jäger loose on the world. "You think he has armed protection living at the house?"

"No, but you can bet he has plenty of electronic security. Including cameras."

"It's dark and raining."

"Forget it, Bagman. He probably has infrared."

"I'll be very careful."

"Don't! It's too dangerous."

Women, they always had to play mother when it came to a little adventure. "There's nothing to worry about. It's not like I'm breaking into the place. I just want to see if he's alone and what he's doing up in the middle of the night. That could tell us a lot."

"Yes, I agree, but—"

"No buts. No one's going to shoot me for being in their yard. I'm not armed, I've got a good story, and—"

"What story?" she demanded.

He hesitated, thinking fast, trying to come up with one. *Why would someone . . . ?* "I'm traveling. I let my dog out of the car to do his thing, there was a lightning flash and he bolted. I've been chasing him for thirty minutes, thought I saw him cut across the yard, blah, blah, blah."

"What kind of dog?"

"A black Lab. Male. Barely a year old. Chews everything. A real scaredy-cat when it comes to thunderstorms."

"That's not bad."

"Thank you."

"You'll be careful? You won't do anything stupid?"

"That's my very first thought every day when I wake up."

"I'm serious, Bagman."

"Me, too.

"If you don't call me back within thirty minutes I'm sending in the Marines."

"I'll count on it. Talk to you soon." He disconnected before she could offer any more motherly advice. He opened the door, momentarily flooding himself in light, and quickly closed it behind him. So much for passing his first test as a secret agent.

The rain was coming down harder now, not pouring, but enough to turn his lightweight jogging outfit into a heavyweight sweatsuit before he reached the alley. At least it was warm. The narrow alley was dark as a cave, but he managed to avoid stumbling over any trash cans without using his penlight and found the house without losing any more spy points. The rain and darkness made it impossible to see if there were cameras, so he kept his head down and began to work his way cautiously down the far side of the garage, toward a sliver of light coming from a window near the front of the house. Reaching the front corner of the garage, he saw that he would need to cross an open area of about fifteen feet to reach the house; and realized this was that moment in the movies when you want to scream at the idiot who ventures into the cellar to check on some obscure noise. *Don't do it!* But they always did. *Had to.*

Shielding his face with one hand and forcing himself to move slow so as not to draw the attention of any motion-sensitive cameras, he edged forward across the open stretch of lawn, one tiny step at a time, not moving any part of his upper body until he could finally flatten out against the dark, wet bricks of the house. He paused, listening, half expecting a phalanx of guards to suddenly materialize out of the darkness, but could hear nothing louder than the beating of his own heart and the gurgle of rainwater rushing through the gutters. *Slow and easy.* He took a deep breath and inched his way toward the window. *One quick peek.* He took another deep breath and moved his head into the narrow beam of light filtering out through a crack in the closed drapes. The room was subdued and masculine, a combination library and office, with a small bar and a large fireplace. Tucker Stark—who Simon recognized from pictures in the paper—was alone and at his desk, writing on a yellow legal pad. His movements appeared to be somewhat frantic, his hand slashing back and forth across the page. Except for the pad and three black clay urns, the desk had been swept clean, everything unceremoniously dumped into a pile on the floor: a mountain of electronic equipment and desk accessories. The man was obviously going somewhere and he wasn't coming back, not if he was taking the wife and kids. Simon ducked back out of sight.

Now what? He knew what Vic would say: *that's enough, the man is guilty of plotting against the Presi-*

dent, now get your ass out of there. That was the right move, he knew it, but didn't like the idea of Stark getting away. What was he writing? Whatever, he suspected it would answer some important questions. *One more little peek.*

Stark was now stuffing what he had written into an envelope. He folded it in half, stood up, slipped the envelope into the back pocket of his khaki slacks, and started toward the bar. Liquid courage, Simon thought, but Stark ignored the bottles and pulled what looked like a raw chicken leg from somewhere beneath a large, glowing aquarium at the back of the bar. He dropped the leg into the water, then while the fish swarmed around it, he used a long-handled skimming net to retrieve two ziplock bags hidden beneath the sand. Each bag contained at least one silver disc. *More answers.*

Stark returned to his desk, carefully wiped the moisture off each bag, dropped them into separate manila envelopes, carefully sealed them with tape, and then wrote something in bold across the front of each with a black magic marker. A tremendous lightning flash suddenly lit up the sky, the thunderclap immense, and Stark glanced toward the window. Simon jerked back, not sure if he was seen or not, not sure if he should run and risk certain exposure, or play possum and hope for the best. Momentarily frozen with indecision, he chose the latter by default, flattening himself out below the window. The sliver of light spilling onto the lawn suddenly widened as Stark pulled open the drapes. Simon buried his face in the wet grass and waited, straining to hear, to get some indication if he'd been discovered, but the rain was too heavy, blocking out any sounds from inside. *Stupid-stupid-stupid!* Now he was really trapped. The seconds ticked by—ten, fifteen, a hundred, maybe two—he had no idea. When he finally dared to look, the light had disappeared, the curtains closed tight. *Thank you, Jesus.* He leaned back against the cool bricks and took a big gulp of moist air, sucking it in like a kind of nourishment, but the relief vanished as a door slapped open behind him. He jerked around, ready to run, when Stark emerged from the house, memorial urns in hand. Wearing a dark jacket and a bucket-style rain hat, he looked neither right nor left, but crossed to the garage and disappeared inside.

Knowing any motion sensors had now been turned off, Simon didn't hesitate, running back the same way he had come. When he reached the far side of the garage he pulled to a halt, momentarily surprised by the spray of yellow light coming through a window about halfway down the side of the garage. Hugging the wall, he crept forward until he could see through the window. A dark-colored van was parked no more than four feet away, the sliding door to the rear compartment directly adjacent to the window. The door was open and Stark was inside, hunched forward below a console of electronics that would have turned Captain James T. Kirk green with envy. Using a hex wrench, Stark quickly removed a small panel of switches, laid it face down, and began to rewire a number of the connections.

What the hell? For every answer there seemed to be another question, and for the first time Simon understood how little he understood. When Stark started to replace the panel, Simon stepped past the window and into the darkness of the alley. By the time he reached his car the rain had subsided to a drizzle, but he was already soaked from head to toe and feeling like a waterlogged buffalo. He started the car, made a quick U-turn without lights, pulled up far enough to see the end of Stark's driveway, shut off the engine, and called Vic.

"Damn you, Bagman, I was about to call 911!"

"No problem," he answered, making a special effort to sound calm. "Everything's cool."

"So what's going on?"

He used his sleeve to clear the window which had started to fog over. "Who said anything was going on?"

"Don't piss me off, Bagboy. I'm very good at hiding bodies."

"I love you too."

"Dammit, you always start with the jokes whenever you're nervous. Now be serious, what's happening?"

"I'm not really sure," he admitted, "but I intend to find out."

"What do you mean by that?"

"He's going somewhere and he's not coming back."

"And how do you know that?"

He quickly ran through what he had seen. "Believe

me, he's not taking the wife and kids on vacation at three o'clock in the morning."

"You're right," she agreed, "but don't even think about trying to follow him. If he's on the run, he's going to be watching his tail. Just get to the *Washington Post* and tell your story."

"And if he gets away, who's going to corroborate it?"

"You've got the papers and the recording."

"Come on, Moneypenny, you know how Washington works. No one's going to admit those papers are real. The President, the CIA, the Pentagon, they'll all deny it. And the recording is bogus. So what's that prove?"

"The Director of Central Intelligence can't just disappear. The media will be all over this thing."

"But what if he does? The guy's in the spy business, he's probably an expert at this sort of thing. I could end up being the biggest chump this side of the planet."

She emitted a sound, a little eruption of amusement. "That's never bothered you before."

"Har-har. Now you be serious. What if you're right and the President *is* behind this thing? That he was calling to tell Stark to get his ass out of Dodge."

"Okay, okay, I get your point, Bagman, but you're *not* James Bond and you're not Wyatt Earp," she replied, mixing her metaphors in a verbal Cuisinart. "You get too close to this guy and you're going to end up dead. Or have you forgotten that's what they've been trying to do?"

No, he hadn't forgotten, not for a second. "He might lead me to Jäger."

"And that would be a good thing?"

"That's when I call the Marines."

"Forget it," she said, "this is way out of your league, Bagman. You need to—"

"Hold on!" He cleared a fresh porthole in the fog as a pair of taillights appeared between houses. "He's on the move."

"Okay, this has gone far enough," she said, her tone a mixture of concern and motherly admonishment. "Don't you even think about following that guy."

"Right." He started the car and turned the fan on high to clear the windows. "I won't think about it."

"You're just going to do it?" She sounded resigned.

"I won't get too close." He waited until Stark was nearly two blocks away before pulling out to follow, without headlights. As he drove past the house, he caught a shadowed movement beyond the downstairs curtains. *Oh shit.* "Moneypenny, you better call the fire department. He torched the house. No telling what kind of evidence he left behind."

"Ten-four. I need to do that from a public phone. I'll call you back."

When Stark reached Wisconsin Avenue, Simon expected the man to turn south, toward one of the major airports, but he turned north, heading deeper into suburbia. There were now a few cars moving along the street, their headlights reflecting like double moons off the wet pavement, and Simon snapped on his lights, staying well back. The drizzle had now turned into a thick mist, reflecting Stark's taillights in a glow of red spray, easy to follow. Near the White-haven Parkway, Stark turned into the parking lot of a closed convenience store and stopped. Simon pulled to the curb, snapped off his lights and grabbed his binoculars. Stark got out of the cab, the two manila envelopes under his arm, went to the row of news-paper racks, stooped down in front of the *New York Times* dispenser—as if checking to make sure it con-tained the latest edition—then inserted his coins, pulled open the door, and slipped one of the en-velopes between two newspapers about halfway down in the stack. He moved to the *Washington Post* dispenser and repeated the process.

What was this, Simon wondered, answers or ob-fuscation? The cover-up or the mea culpa? If the truth, why not drop the stuff in a mailbox? But as quickly as he asked himself the question he realized the answer. The newspaper racks offered a hedge, the opportunity to go back and retrieve the documents if . . . *If what?* He hesitated, trying to decide if he should grab the envelopes or follow. The fact that he had purposely emptied his pockets of change before leaving the hotel provided an easy excuse to follow, a decision he knew Vic would oppose. As if to confirm it, the cellular marked VH began its irritating buzz. He reached down and pressed the MUTE button—*Sorry, Vic*—not wanting to defend his decision.

Stark continued north on Wisconsin, past the Guy Mason Recreation Center, then turned right on

Calvert and left on Observation Circle, which circumnavigated the US Naval Observatory. Where in the hell was this guy going? A brilliant lightning flash suddenly lit up the sky, reflecting stroboscopic patterns of light across the windshield, and the rain suddenly began to fall in earnest, pounding away at the windows as if it wanted in. Stark turned north again when he reached 34th Street, then immediately left into Normanstone Park. Simon snapped off his headlights and dropped back as the trees and darkness closed in, leaving only the red glow of tail lights visible through the gauze curtain of rain.

Stark continued south for nearly half a mile, then turned off the road, the headlights bouncing as he drove over the curb and pulled into a thicket of trees. Simon eased over to the curb, using his emergency brake so as not to illuminate the taillights. The minute he shut off the engine the windows began to fog over. *Shit!* Even with the binoculars, he had trouble locating the dark vehicle until Stark got out of the front and entered the rear compartment. *Now what?* Only two things came to mind: either the man was going to kill himself, which seemed unlikely as he could have done that at home, or he was waiting to meet someone. Either way, Simon realized, he'd never figure it out sitting in a car two hundred yards away with the windows fogged over.

He punched out a quick text message to Vic, who he knew would be tracking his movements and fluctuating between fits of anger and worry.

CAN'T TALK, TOO EXPOSED. WAIT THIRTY MINUTES
THEN SEND MARINES. ON FOOT NEAR KAHLIL
GIBRAN MEMORIAL. BOND

This time he remembered to turn off the interior light before opening the door. He grabbed his emergency kit, pulled it over his shoulder and stepped into the rain, which was now coming down harder than ever, making it impossible to see beyond thirty feet. He worked his way slowly through the trees, staying close to the road so as not to lose orientation. He didn't see the van until it was right in front of him, barely twenty feet away, not a speck of light visible from the interior. Trying to avoid the rain, he snuggled up close to a large tree and settled in to wait. No more than twenty minutes, he promised himself, not wanting to be anywhere around in case Vic panicked and called out the troops early.

It hadn't been more than a minute when he realized someone was coming up behind him: at least two people, moving quickly, their powerful flashlights cutting narrow tunnels through the shroud of driving rain. *Holy Christ!* He edged behind the tree, pressing his face into the damp bark, not daring to look for fear they would see his white face. Within seconds they were on top of him, so close he could feel their hurried tread through the soles of his shoes, so close he was positive they would see him, but they somehow didn't, passing less than three feet from where he was standing.

He silently released his held breath and glanced out cautiously from behind the tree. They were already fading in the downpour, dark silhouettes heading straight for the van: two men, one tall and stocky with a heavy, determined stride; the other lean and muscular with the effortless step of an athlete.

They stopped about six feet from the van and extinguished their flashlights. The thinner man glancing around cautiously, methodically checking the area. There was something about his movements that seemed familiar, something about his posture, the way he balanced his weight, like a wild cat ready to spring in any direction at the first sign of trouble. *Eth Jäger?*

CHAPTER THIRTY-FIVE

Normanstone Park, Washington, DC

Monday, 5 July 03:48:34 GMT –0500

Tucker kept his eyes fixed on the double row of monitors, watching the sweep of their flashlights as they came through the trees. He felt surprisingly calm, all the decisions made, and though he couldn't predict the outcome, there was nothing more he could do. No matter what happened, he would be dead within the hour, and with that he was comfortable. Relieved and ready.

The general rapped his West Point ring against the door, two sharp pings that barely penetrated the soundproof shell, then, without waiting for a response, stepped inside, Captain Buddy Baggett close at his heel. Tucker stood up, wanting now more than ever to demonstrate his respect. "Good evening, General." He nodded to Baggett. "Captain."

The general yanked off his Vietnam-era bush hat, slapped it against his leg to remove the rain, and glared, the look of a bad-tempered rhinoceros looking for someone to attack. "I can't wait to hear what's good about it, Corporal."

Tucker ignored the sarcasm, expecting it. "Yessir, it is a little pissy out there."

"Do you have any idea the risk I'm taking?"

"Yessir, I do." He waited for Baggett to help the general out of his camouflage rain jacket. "I wouldn't have called unless it was critical."

Baggett carefully folded the coat over his arm and stepped back, below the surveillance monitors, not bothering to remove his own hat or coat, as if wanting to let Tucker know this wasn't going to take long. The general lowered himself into the chair facing Tucker. "What's this about the FBI?"

Tucker ignored the question, determined to explain things in his own way. "General, this whole operation has been a cluster-fuck from the start. It's over. The President wants me in his office at eight-thirty. There's no question—"

"Who called?" the general interrupted. "The President or some flunky?"

"The President. Less than two hours ago. He—"

"What did he say? Exactly?"

Tucker took a deep breath, determined not to let the general badger him, to turn their final meeting into a useless shouting match. "Nothing, really. He didn't need to. Rynerson obviously had the documents, and the President somehow knows I'm involved in—"

The general interrupted again. "Deny everything. No matter what he says or thinks. The man's an idiot. All you—"

"Maybe," Tucker broke in, " but by now he's told John Estes the story. And once that bulldog gets his teeth into this—"

"Fuck Estes!" the general snapped. "The man's nothing but a political hack. There's nothing he can do. They can't go public with this thing. It would expose the President's duplicity in the plot to remove Kim."

"Yessir, but—"

"Deny everything," the general repeated. "Offer to resign and assure them you'll never speak of the North Korean operation. Believe me, they'll accept that in a heartbeat. Estes keeps his precious job, the President lives to steal another billion dollars. Everyone's happy."

"It's not that simple, sir."

The general waved his hand dismissively. "Of course it is. You're just upset at the thought of getting fired. How it will look. How it will reflect on your name. Trust me, Corporal, this will work."

Tucker knew better. Even if he wanted to make it work, which he didn't, there were too many cracks in the dam, but the general was now blinded by his ambition, unwilling to stop until he was dead or sitting in the Oval Office. "No, sir, it won't. The documents are in play. Rynerson knows. Leonidovich knows. And—"

"Don't worry about them, Corporal. Your job is done. Captain Baggett will deal with them."

Deal with them! Captain Buddy Baggett had only one method of dealing with problems. "I'm sorry, sir, but I'm afraid there's no way to put this cork back in the bottle. I've prepared a complete dossier on the President and his financial manipulations. Once it hits the papers, the President will probably resign. If he doesn't, there will be an impeachment. He'll be found guilty or he won't. Either way, the country will survive. We need to step back and let the Congress do their job."

"Do their job!" The general snorted. "When did that bunch of political pantywaists ever do their job?"

Tucker opened his mouth, prepared to debate the issue, but realized that would accomplish nothing. "It doesn't matter, sir, it's the right thing to do. We made a mistake. Our intentions may have been honorable, but our methods were wrong. We should have exposed what the President was doing and hoped for the best. We should have relied on the Constitution."

"Hope for the best!" The general uttered a bitter laugh. "Were you hoping for the best crawling through the muck in Nam? Were you relying on the Constitution, Corporal, or the men around you? The Constitution is only as strong as the men who protect it."

With that, Tucker couldn't argue. "Yessir, which we all swore to preserve, protect, and defend. I now realize that I've failed in that responsibility." He glanced at Baggett standing at modified attention near the door, the good and robotic soldier who would never think to question his commander. "Captain Baggett has failed." He turned back to the general. "And you have failed, General. You need to resign your office."

"Resign my office!" the general shouted, spraying Tucker with spittle. "Have you lost your mind!"

Such a small step, Tucker thought, between sanity and insanity, between just and unjust, between hero and traitor. The general had taken that step, and nothing short of a howitzer between the eyes would change his mind. As much as Tucker hated to do it, to actually use extortion against a man he had so long revered, he now realized he would have to use that weapon: the recordings of their meetings, the undeniable proof of their treasonous acts. Faced with such evidence, such betrayal on the part of *his corporal*, the general would have no choice but to resign his position. "I'm sorry, General, but unless you agree to—"

The general leaned forward and clutched Tucker's wrist. "Don't worry about it, Corporal. Your job is done."

Tucker felt a sudden sting, a fire that burned up his arm and spread across his chest. He tried to speak but couldn't move his lips. He tried to stand but couldn't move anything but his eyes. The general stood up, turned over his hand, and removed a tiny spring-loaded syrette that had been taped to his palm. "I hated to do that, but he didn't leave me any choice."

Baggett stepped forward, leaned down, and stared into Tucker's eyes. "You want to hear something amusing, Director? That's Tetrozip. You recognize the name? It came from your very own lab."

Yes, he recognized the name: a hybrid cocktail made with tetrodotoxin—a powerful poison extracted from puffer fish—guaranteed to render a person helpless within seconds, leaving them in a state of paralysis without affecting their mental faculties. *Jesus God.*

Shifting his position for the third time, Simon pressed his ear against the wet shell of the van, but could hear nothing. Either the men weren't talking, or the van was soundproof. Was Jäger in there or not?

Yes, he was almost sure of it. Sure enough that he had to do something. But what? He could call the police and report some outrageous crime, but they probably wouldn't make it in time.

Has to be a way— a way to trap them before calling the police. He circled around the back of the van, just far enough so he could see the door, and gave the handle a quick flash with his penlight. *A zip tie,* that's all it would take, and he had plenty of those in his emergency kit, which he had left in the trees.

Tucker saw the light, a quick flash on one of the monitors, then a dark figure moving down the side of the van. Someone was out there, too heavy for one of Baggett's men, but it didn't matter. Whoever he was, he would be dead in less than a minute.

The general bent down and gave Tucker's knee a pat. "Sorry, Corporal, you were a good soldier."

Fuck you, General.

"I'm afraid this mission was just a little beyond your rank."

And the horse you rode in on.

The general winked and turned to Baggett. "Ready, Captain?"

"Yessir."

"How long do we have?"

"Two minutes, General."

The general slipped into his coat and stepped to the door. "Okay, Captain, do it."

Baggett reached over and flipped the van's self-destruct switch. There was a soft hissing sound followed by Tucker's voice from an overhead speaker: *"General, if you're listening to this I can only assume I'm dead."*

Both Baggett and the general turned and stared at Tucker, who could only smile back at them with his eyes.

"I'm sorry it had to end like this, but unfortunately you've made a bad decision and will have to pay for that mistake."

The general turned and yanked at the door handle. "He's locked us in!"

"Don't be alarmed at the sound, General. What you hear is pure oxygen. Signing off with no hard feelings, Corporal Tucker Stark."

Baggett spun around and toggled the switch back to OFF as a different voice suddenly reverberated from the speaker: THIS VEHICLE WILL SELF-DESTRUCT IN THIRTY SECONDS. PLEASE ENTER PASSWORD TO DEACTIVATE.

Baggett pushed the general aside and rammed the door with his shoulder. "The bastard set us up!"

TWENTY-FIVE SECONDS.

The general turned on Tucker. "What's the password!"

Tucker simply stared back at the man, unable to answer.

TWENTY SECONDS.

"Goddamnit, Corporal, give me that password! That's an order!"

Tucker tried desperately to smile, wanting the general to know how wonderful he felt, but couldn't.

FIFTEEN SECONDS. PLEASE ENTER PASSWORD TO DEACTIVATE.

Baggett yanked a .45 caliber service revolver from his coat. "Cover your ears, General!" He stepped back and discharged four quick rounds into the door handle, the sound like a cannon in the confined space.

TEN SECONDS.

Baggett rammed the door twice more with his shoulder, but failed to budge it.

FIVE SECONDS.

"Do something!" the general screamed.

Baggett shrugged, snapped off a crisp salute, then stuck the barrel of the forty-five in his mouth and fired.

The last sound Tucker heard was his own voice: *"Goodbye."*

Thirty seconds, Simon thought, as he pulled a large zip tie from his emergency kit and started back toward the van, just thirty more seconds and he would have them.

Brrrap—Brrrap—Brrrap—Brrrap.

Though muted, he recognized the distinctive sound of a large-caliber handgun and jerked to a stop. He waited a few seconds, expecting someone to come through the door, then started forward, knowing he had to move fast or miss his chance.

Brrrap.

He stopped again, not more than twenty feet from the door when the van suddenly exploded into a ball of white flame, the concussion knocking him to the ground. Though the heat was intense, the blast was more of an implosion, most of it contained within the shell of the van, and it only scorched his face. *Holy Jesus!* Ten more seconds and he would have been fried—*barbecued Leonidovich.*

He struggled to clear his head and stand, his feet slipping in the wet grass, the sound still echoing in his ears, and tried to move forward, thinking he might be able to pull open the door, but the heat held him back and he realized it was too late. Within seconds the van's skin had melted away, leaving behind a skeleton of struts, spars, and braces; and despite the fire and the rain and the hiss of steam as they mixed together, Simon could hear the pop and crackle of burning flesh. *Much too late.*

What happened? Was that it? Was it over? He knew one thing: he didn't want to be around when the cops started asking those kind of questions. But could he just walk away, forget it, never knowing what it was all about?

No, he still wanted answers, and he had a good idea where to find them. All he needed was a few quarters.

CHAPTER THIRTY-SIX

New York City

Monday, 5 July 07:14:27 GMT −0500

"What exactly is it you do?" the man asked, glancing briefly at the rearview mirror to make eye contact.

Lara forced a smile. Though all of the men with the protection service were very friendly and very professional, and though it was nice having them drive her to work in their big Humvee with the darkened windows, this was another new agent and the fourth time she had been asked that exact same question. It was getting old. It was also costing Simon a fortune, and though he never complained, it was starting to make her feel extremely guilty. Two more days, she decided, the kids would be out of camp and she would go to Vegas. "Frank, right?"

"Yes, ma'am. Frank Costa."

Just hearing the word *ma'am* from a man who looked to be in his mid-sixties made her feel like an old woman. "I manage a small courier service, Frank."

"Oh." He nodded thoughtfully. "You mean those guys you see on bikes darting in and out of traffic?"

Exactly the same follow-up question. "No, we're a

little more specialized than that. We do a lot of international work."

"Oh yeah? So you deal with a lot of valuable stuff, I guess."

"Frequently." She could already guess his next question—*like what?*—but he surprised her.

"So your people have to be bonded? Know some security?"

Now she understood: the man was looking for a new job. By far the oldest of the agents that had been assigned to her, he was going noticeably soft and was probably being forced into retirement by younger warrior types straight out of the military. "That's right. It sounds like you're—" Her phone chirped. "Excuse me." She pulled the cellular from her purse, saw that it was Simon, and pressed the CONNECT button. "Hello, Boris, what's up?"

"I need you in Washington."

He sounded exhausted, obviously too tired to complain about her calling him Boris, so she resisted the impulse to argue. "State or DC?"

"DC As soon as possible, it's important."

It was always important. "For how long? I'll need to make arrangements for the kids."

"Two days, three at the most. I'm at the Willard."

"You're already there?"

"Yes."

"So you heard the news?" she asked. "There was a fire at the home of the CIA Director last night and he's missing."

"Interesting."

Interesting, what kind of comment was that? "And there was a bombing in Rock Creek Park. They think there may be a connection."

"Don't always believe what you hear on the news."

There was something in his voice, some faint whisper of warning, like that first gentle snowflake before a blizzard. "Meaning?"

"It was Normanstone Park."

"And how would you know that?" She wasn't entirely sure she wanted to know.

"Call it a hunch."

Uh oh. "You want to explain that?"

"Better not." he answered.

"Okay." *Message received.* "What about my security?" She noticed Costa glance in the mirror. "It's been a week and there's been no sign of the one-eyed devil. I don't see why—"

"I think he's dead," Simon broke in. "But I'm not sure, so don't get too excited."

Right, don't get too excited, but she could literally feel the tension melt out of her spine. She took a deep, silent breath, working hard not to let the relief bleed into her voice. "And you can't explain that either, I suppose?"

"Not now. I'll tell you everything when you get here. Keep the security people with you until you're on the plane. They can make sure you're the last on and the first off. Then come straight to the hotel. You'll be okay here."

"Okay, see you soon." She dropped the phone into

her purse, then leaned back and closed her eyes, taking a moment to enjoy the thought—*Eth Jäger dead*—it was almost too good to believe. When she opened her eyes, Frank Costa was frowning and looking in the mirror, but not at her. She glanced over her shoulder, through the window. The traffic was heavy—the typical onslaught of morning commuters converging on the city—a motorcycle patrolman about twenty feet back. "Is there a problem, Frank?"

"No, I just don't like having that guy so close on my tail."

A few moments later the trooper pulled alongside, his lights flashing. He gave Costa a stiff-armed, follow-me gesture, then pointed ahead toward an emergency turnout sign. Costa nodded, indicating he understood, and the trooper pulled ahead. Costa glanced in the mirror, making eye contact. "Sorry, ma'am, it's probably just a tail light or something."

"No problem." She wasn't about to let anything ruin her good mood, not even a *ma'am*.

Costa followed the trooper into the turnout—a double-wide strip of pavement, separated from the parkway by a single row of trees—and pulled up close to the guardrail, about six feet behind the big Harley Road King. "This shouldn't take long. These guys are usually pretty good with ex-cops." He leaned forward and pulled his billfold.

"No problem," she repeated, knowing he was embarrassed about being pulled over and worried about the impression he was making.

The trooper dismounted, stabilized the big Harley, then carefully and meticulously straightened his black leather jacket, apparently in no hurry. The ultimate alpha male, Lara thought, who liked to hide behind his sun visor and uniform and strut around playing king-of-the-road in his breeches and black leather English-style riding boots. As he approached the car, he reached back and pulled a summons book and long yellow pencil—which struck her as odd—from a pouch on his belt. Costa extended his arm out the window, clearly wanting the trooper to take note of his credentials before starting to write.

Without so much as a perfunctory "good morning," the trooper took the identification and leaned down, as if to look into the car, and then without warning or hesitation jammed the pencil into Costa's ear, driving it far into his head. The agent let out a guttural shriek and jerked upward, as if he'd been hit with a cattle prod, then slumped sideways onto the seat.

It happened so fast it took Lara a moment to process the information, and another moment to accept it as fact. She grabbed the door handle, twisting and shoving in one motion, but the door hardly moved before it struck the guardrail. *Oh Jesus-God, trapped!* She twisted around, looking for something with which to defend herself, but realized immediately that it was hopeless. The trooper was now leaning through the window, a tiny handgun pointing directly at her head. With his free hand, he reached up and pushed back the visor of his helmet. *"Buongiorno,* Lara

Quinn." Below his single dark eye, his lips curled into a malicious grin, the expression ghoulish.

She could barely hold back the flood of bile that surged into her throat. She took a deep breath, forcing herself not to panic, not to think about Frank Costa and whether he had a family, not to think about some young motorcycle cop who had the misfortune of having the same physique as Eth Jäger, or even to think about her own children and what might happen to them. No, she needed to concentrate, to lead Jäger in the right direction if she hoped to survive. And that meant she would have to put up some resistance, to let him feel the lash of her tongue and the depth of her contempt, or he would never believe anything she said.

He leaned back out of the car, opened the rear door, slid onto the seat beside her and closed the door. He quickly pulled off his helmet and leather jacket, dropped them into the front seat, and ordered her to lie on the floor. "On your back, *rapidamente*."

She did as he ordered and didn't try to resist when he zip-tied her hands to the door handle above her head. He leaned forward and smiled, his dark eye moving slowly over her body, like a lizard anticipating the taste of an unsuspecting fly. "You have missed the hunter, no?"

"Yeah, right," she snapped back, "I think of you every day."

He chuckled softly, taking no offense, as if her sarcastic tone conjured up a pleasant memory. "You know why I am here, eh?"

"Well, gee, let me think. There weren't enough pretty-boys in prison?"

His face paled with controlled anger. "I would very much like to know where I could find the courier."

She realized his fuse was officially lit, but that she needed to keep pushing, showing him resistance. "Sorry, you're not his type. *He* likes girls."

He stared back at her with blank rage, as though the synapses behind that one dark eye had suddenly stopped firing. "You will eventually tell the hunter what he wishes to know."

"Get fucked."

He leaned closer, two tiny beads of sweat glistening at the corners of his nose. "This could be arranged."

"Go to hell, asshole! You're going to kill me anyway."

"I find this language most offensive."

Yeah right, offended by her language five minutes after shoving a pencil up someone's ear canal. But she believed it: the man was an absolute psychopath who functioned beyond the measure of predictable behavior or emotions. "Like I care."

"But you should. You provide me the information and I will let you live."

And if you believe that . . .

He smiled, as if reading her thoughts, and leaned back, making an obvious effort to be less confrontational. "I have no wish to harm you, Lara Quinn. Or your brother." His voice was now soft and reasonable, though a bit patronizing. "I know you don't believe this, but—"

"You're damn right I don't believe it," she cut in, knowing she had to adjust her behavior gradually. "You think I don't know you tried to kill Simon in Korea?"

"Ah, but of course—" He waved a hand as if to dismiss the point. "It may have seemed that way. But this is not true. Not true at all. I could have killed him at any time. But no, I did not. That was not my intent." He suddenly twisted around, looking over his shoulder through the window, then turned back, snatched his gun off the seat, and placed it to her forehead. *"Shhh."*

She could hear it now, over the whine of traffic, the sound of another vehicle as it moved past the dark windows of the Humvee. She never considered screaming, it would only result in the death of more innocent people. The sound gradually receded, then increased for a moment as the driver accelerated back onto the parkway, apparently frightened off by the NYHP motorcycle.

Jäger dropped the small automatic back on the seat. "See, Lara Quinn, when you do the right thing, no one is hurt."

She couldn't resist, it was too perfect. "Right. And *'all that do wickedly, shall be stubble: and the day that cometh shall burn them up.'"*

He gave her a puzzled look. "What is this?"

"It's from the Bible. Malachi, chapter four. You should consider it."

"*Sì*, of course, I have read this book. We must all consider its warnings."

She offered up a little smile, a slight softening of attitude, but was careful not to overdo the thaw. "I'm relieved to hear you say that."

"We all have our enemies, Lara Quinn. That is why I need to find your brother. The same people who wish to kill him are searching for the hunter. This is what I need to know."

"I don't know where he is." She said it quickly, a little too quickly, not wanting him to believe her. "I really don't."

"We need to work together," he said, clearly not believing her. "The hunter will make you a promise. If you—"

"Ha!" She knew the longer she resisted, the more slowly she came around to *her story*, the better chance she had of selling it. "Like I'm going to believe anything you say."

"I am not the monster you believe."

Tell it to Frank Costa, you asshole.

"I have no desire to hurt you."

"You could have fooled me."

He leaned forward and shook his head. "No, that is not the way of the hunter—to leave children alone in the world."

Even though she realized the backhanded threat was meant to scare her, she couldn't stop a cold wave of fear from racing through her body. "I don't know where Simon is. I really don't."

"If you continue in this lie." He spread his hands,

a gesture of helplessness. "Then you leave the hunter no choice."

So that was how he did it: not *he*, but the hunter. "But I don't know. Really I don't."

He expelled a breath, a sigh of resignation. "As you wish. Perhaps your children will not be so—"

"My children know nothing," she interrupted, purposely letting him see a crack in her tough-girl persona. "They're away at camp. They—"

He held up a slender finger, a warning. "Yes, of course. We will have to find some amusement to occupy the time." He smiled and glanced at his watch. "Until five. They always arrive home by five."

Oh Jesus, the thought that he had been watching the house, that he had gotten that close to her children. "But I don't know where he is. I don't know why they're after him."

"I think you do."

"No, really, I don't." She knew this was the moment, that if he took her back to the house, they were all dead. "I thought it might have something to do with that damn briefcase, but that's stupid." She said it very fast, desperately, as if the words had escaped without thought. "Simon doesn't know what's in it. There's no reason for anyone to kill him for something he doesn't know anything about."

Though Jäger tried to hide his interest, there was a still moment, an extra heartbeat that gave it away. "The briefcase?"

"The briefcase he sent back from Korea," she answered quickly, as if trying to cooperate, to please him, to save her children. "The one at the office."

"What is in this briefcase?"

"How would I know? It's a diplomatic pouch." She could see his excitement, the thought that he had found his answer. "Some kind of top secret crap, I guess."

"You are probably right. It is nothing."

Her heart nearly stopped. She nodded, knowing if she tried to convince him otherwise it would only make him suspicious. "I'm sure of it."

"But I would still like to see this briefcase."

"No, that's impossible. It's a sealed diplomatic pouch."

He snorted a laugh of astonishment. "Enough of this nonsense. You will show me the case and you will do nothing—" He leaned down over her face. "—to draw attention." He smiled, as though the thought amused him. "Or the hunter will gut your children like piglets."

She nodded, knowing he would do it. Something that would only make what she intended to do that much easier.

The next forty minutes passed in a fog of images and sounds: the scrape and thud as Frank Costa was pulled out of the car and dropped over the guardrail, the whine of traffic as they drove into the city, the darkness of the underground garage, and the curious looks of strangers as a New York State patrolman escorted her up to the office.

Jäger placed her in front of the desk, zip-tied her hands, and then, exactly as he had done two years earlier, zip-tied her feet to the base of the chair. In her worse nightmare, this was exactly as she dreamed it. But exactly as she had anticipated. *I can do this.*

He seemed to be on some kind of high, pleased with himself as he circled the room, as if taking a pleasant trip down memory lane. "You are most organized, Lara Quinn. This is something the hunter admires. Something we have in common."

Like I care. But she couldn't help smiling to herself, thinking how messy things were about to get. *I can do this.*

He looked over at the under-counter refrigerator, obviously remembering the location of the safe. "Open it."

She pointed with her chin toward the headset lying on the desk. "I'll need my microphone."

He picked up the headset and held the tip of the microphone up close to her mouth. "Computer, wake up."

There was a faint hum as the hard drives came out of hibernation and the three monitors blinked to life, followed a moment later by the computer's response: *Please identify yourself.*

"This is Lara." She purposely waited an extra beat. "Log on, please."

Identification unsuccessful. Please repeat.

Satisfied that she had demonstrated the microphone's sensitivity, she repeated the command. "This is Lara. Log on, please."

Good morning, Lara.

"Lara says—2, 7, I, 7, 2—open sesame." She substituted *I* for *Y* so that the command would fail.

Jäger stared at the unmoving grid beneath the refrigerator. "What's wrong?"

"I don't know." She repeated the command a second time, exactly as before, and again the safe failed to open.

Jäger leaned over her, his face expanding with sudden rage. "You think you can play games—"

"No, I swear. The microphone is very sensitive. If you'll release my hands I'll make sure it's positioned correctly."

He stared hard at her, face to face, as if trying to read her mind, then shook his head. "I will do this." He slipped the adjustable band over her head and positioned the wand directly in front of her mouth.

"It needs to be lower." She could barely control her breathing, her heart beating so hard and fast it felt like it was going to fly out of her chest. "Just below my lips, so it doesn't pick up the sound of my breath."

He did as she instructed and she dictated the command a third time, using the *Y*. As quickly as the words cleared her mouth the reinforced steel grid began to move. Jäger started across the room, then stopped, staring in cold disbelief at the empty cavity. Enraged, he turned back, grabbed her around the throat, and began to squeeze. "You think you can tell the hunter some foolish story and that—"

"No, no, it's there," she choked out. "I put it there myself. A black case. Way at the back."

He released her, stepped quickly to the safe, and bent down, his head right at the opening, and without any hesitation or second thoughts she gave the detonation command. "Malachi four."

She heard the explosion—a muffled *whuuump*—but she had already closed her eyes and turned away to protect herself from the blast. *All that do wickedly, shall be stubble: and the day that cometh shall burn them up.*

CHAPTER THIRTY-SEVEN

Willard Hotel, Washington, DC

Wednesday, 7 July 11:39:15 GMT −0500

Simon jerked around in his chair, startled. "I didn't hear you come in." He had sequestered himself in the suite's smaller bedroom, as far as he could get from the dining room where Victoria and Lara were organizing the documents and chattering excitedly about each new revelation.

Vic patted his shoulder. "Relax, big boy, you haven't taken your nose out of that computer all morning."

"There's a lot of stuff to get through. Stark really did a job on the President."

"I'd say the President *did a job* on the American people."

He couldn't argue with that—the documents were detailed and damning.

Vic cocked her head, her eyes appraising. "You okay?"

He looked up, giving her a full facial. "How do I look?"

She flashed a little grin. "Like the idiot who stuck his head in the oven when he smelled gas."

"I can live with the idiot part, it fits my Simple

Simon persona. It's the not having eyebrows that I don't like."

"They'll grow back."

"Yeah, but until then—"

"You'll look like the idiot who stuck his head in the oven."

"Swell." He glanced toward the door and lowered his voice. "You sure *she's* okay?"

"You've asked me that a dozen times," she whispered back. "She's great. I've never seen her so relaxed."

He couldn't agree more, and he understood her feelings of retribution and relief after two years of emotional strangulation, but she seemed too upbeat—too pumped up. "I think she may be suppressing her feelings."

"Don't start with that psychobabble, Leonidovich. I'm telling you she's fine. Killing that bastard was like getting rid of an undersized sports bra. She can breathe again."

He ignored the bra comment, that was way beyond his need-to-know. "I'm not so sure. She damn near blew the guy's head off. That has to be traumatic."

"Of course it's traumatic, but she's more upset about the bodyguard and motorcycle cop than she is about splattering that maniac's brains all over the office. She's working through it in her own—"

"Hey!" Lara shouted from the other room, "will you two stop whispering. I'm fine." She stepped into the doorway, and though she'd been up for the better part of two days, she looked relaxed and fully charged, almost girlish in a Hello Kitty T-shirt, khaki shorts, and ruby-red sneakers. "I told you I was going to be ready for that sonofabitch, and I was. Mission accomplished!" She raised her hands over her head and did a little Rocky Balboa 360-degree victory dance. "Lara Quinn is back!"

Though he was happy to see his sister back to her former Energizer-bunny personality, he still didn't think it was normal to be so elated about killing someone, even if that someone happened to be Eth Jäger. "I still think you should see a counselor or something. Just so—"

"Just so what?" she interrupted, crossing her arms like a sentry. "Just so I can have some squirrelly-ass idiot with a diploma tell me I'm *suppressing?*"

Vic's dark eyes glinted with amusement. "See, Leonidovich, same old nitroglycerin tongue. I told you she was okay."

He realized he was outnumbered and probably beaten but wasn't quite ready to give up. "Okay, but if—"

"Put a sock in it, Boris." She smiled affectionately, her eyes going back and forth between them. "Are you guys ready for lunch? I'm famished."

Was that a good sign or a bad sign, Simon wondered, she had eaten her way through half the breakfast menu only a few hours earlier. "I think we should wait for Jake."

"Okay." She made a jaunty one-eighty and disappeared from sight. "I'll just order a little snack to tide me over."

Vic glanced at her watch. "By noon, right?"

"That's what he said."

"I can't wait to meet him." She threw up some quotation marks with her fingers. "The *infamous* Big Jake Rynerson." She made a little pirouette, showing off her outfit: a tropical-print sleeveless blouse and a short beige skirt that matched the color of her tan legs and made them look about two miles long. "How do I look?"

A different outfit, Simon realized, from the one she was wearing at breakfast. What was this, some kind of hormonal epidemic? Now they were both acting like girlish teenagers. "He's married, Victoria."

"Well of course he's married." A pink flush spread up each side of her throat. "I'm just excited about meeting the guy, that's all. He's so . . . so—"

"Big?"

"Bigger than life, smartass."

The object of their conversation arrived ten minutes later. Lara yanked open the door without checking the peephole—something she hadn't done in two years—and nearly toppled the big man off the back of his cowboy boots with an exuberant hug. "Jakey!"

Simon could only shake his head in wonderment—*Jakey?*—the woman was either suffering from posttraumatic stress or experiencing some kind of a preadolescent flashback. "Don't pay any attention to her, Jake, she always gets that way after an explosive day at the office."

Jake ignored the witty commentary, never taking his eyes off Lara. "I'm so proud of you, little girl. You gave that junkyard dog just what he deserved."

Lara flashed Simon a triumphant glance. "Boris doesn't think I should be so happy about it."

"What?" Jake turned, a frown of disbelief. "You're not happy that rattlesnake is dead?"

"No," Simon answered. "Of course I'm happy about that. It's just that—" He realized it was useless to explain; Jake was a kick-the-tires, start-the-engine-and-go type of guy, not the kind who got hung up on psychological roadblocks. "Never mind." He extended an arm toward Vic. "Jake, say hello to my friend Victoria Halle. Victoria, I'd like you to meet—"

Before he could finish, Vic stepped forward and stuck out her hand. "Mr. Rynerson, it's an honor. Please call me Vic."

Her tiny hand disappeared into his massive grip. "I won't do any such thing, darlin'." He gave her a smile, a dazzler, bright enough to light up a ballpark. "Victoria's a beautiful name. Now you call me Jake, ya-hear."

Before Vic got too excited basking in the Rynerson magnetism, Simon stepped in, steering the big man toward a grouping of chairs overlooking the Washington Monument. "I appreciate you coming, Jake. I know you're busy."

"It sounded important." Jake let his gaze range appreciatively over the room—the art, the wall coverings, the elaborate window treatments, the antique-quality furnishings—before pausing on a big-screen television. "I assumed it had something to do with that."

Simon glanced at the screen, and though the sound had been muted, the picture spoke for itself—the skeletal remains of Tucker Stark's van—a visual the networks never tired of showing. "I was there."

Jake nodded, exhibiting no surprise. "Kinda figured that when I saw your face."

Simon smiled to himself. Despite Jake's simple, good-ol'-boy persona, the man was quicker than a megacomputer when it came to processing information. "I did get a little close."

Jake smiled, as if to say *no kidding,* then waited for the women to sit before lowering his oversized frame into a delicate-looking Hepplewhite chair. "So you saw what happened?"

"Not really," Simon admitted. "I tried to eavesdrop but the van was soundproof. I couldn't really tell what was going on."

"You think it was some kind of suicide pact?"

Simon shook his head, though he had asked himself the same question a dozen times. "I don't think so. I heard some shots and then—"

Vic snatched up the remote. "Something's happening."

A SPECIAL REPORT banner streamed across the screen, followed by the familiar face of Bill Schneider, reporting from the CNN news desk. "This just in. Dental records have now confirmed the identity of all victims in what is being referred to as the Normanstone tragedy. As suspected, Vice President Thomas McCafferty—" Schneider paused, a long double beat. "His military attaché, Captain Baggett—" Another pause. "And the Director of Central Intelligence, Tucker Stark." Schneider glanced down at his notes, then back at the camera. "The delay of this expected news was caused by the confusion created by the dental fragments of three more individuals, now identified as the previously cremated remains of Director Stark's wife and children, killed two years ago in a tragic auto accident."

Schneider paused again, as if wanting to give his viewers a chance to absorb this new information before continuing. "This revelation seems to confirm the rumors that Director Stark, still anguishing over the deaths of his wife and children, had become increasingly depressed and suicidal over the past few weeks. After gathering the cremated remains of his late wife and children, and then setting fire to his home, Director Stark made one last call—a goodbye gesture or a final cry for help, we'll never know—to his good friend and former Vietnam commander, General Thomas McCafferty. The general, in what appears to have been a desperate effort to console his friend, agreed to meet the Director at Normanstone Park, located directly across the street from the Vice Presidential mansion."

Schneider paused, glanced down at his notes, then back to the camera. "It was during this final intervention by General McCafferty that a bolt of lightning struck the propane tank of Director Stark's recreational vehicle."

Jake gave Simon a sidelong glance. "Lightning?"

Simon shook his head. "Trust me."

Schneider took a meaningful breath before continuing: "This last selfless act so clearly epitomizes the life of General Thomas McCafferty, a man who will be remembered not only as a true American hero, but as a wounded soldier's last friend. A humble man who preferred the title of General to Vice President."

Schneider continued, but they had heard the rest a hundred times—how the general had been tapped by the President to fill the vacancy created by the death of Vice President Williams, who had died two months after being sworn in; how the general was the first and only Vice President who had never held or been elected to public office—and when they started into his war record, Vic muted the sound.

Lara made a sound of disgust and rolled her eyes. "The cover-up is on."

Jake turned to Simon. "Did you know it was the VP?"

"No. Except for Stark, I wasn't really sure who was in the van. It wasn't until later that morning when the Secret Service admitted the Vice President was missing that I figured it out."

Jake nodded thoughtfully. "So if it wasn't suicide and it wasn't lightning . . ." His words trailed away. "So what is it you think happened out there?"

"I'm not really sure," Simon admitted. "But before we start talking about the possibilities, there's some stuff here I'd like you to look at." He gestured toward the dining-room table and the stacks of material Lara and Vic had organized into chronological order, cross-referencing the timing of the President's hidden business investments with pending legislation.

"What is it?"

"Some documents I saw Stark hide before he went to the park."

Jake levered himself up from the chair. "That's a lot of material."

"It was on CD. There's actually more, but I printed out enough to give you a clear picture of what's going on."

"Before you get into that," Lara broke in. "I want to order lunch. Have you eaten, Jake?"

The big man was already halfway to the table and didn't bother to turn. "I'm good, darlin', you-all go ahead."

They ate and waited and let Jake work his way through the documents. Aside from an occasional under-the-breath expletive, he didn't say anything until he had gone through every sheet, a task that took the better part of three hours. Then he stood up, stretched, and shook his head. "I told Caity that peck-erhead was dirty."

"Obviously," Simon said. "The question is, what are we going to do about it?"

Jake hesitated, obviously catching the *we*. "Other than give it to the press, you mean?"

"I'm not sure that would be a good thing," Simon answered. He hooked a thumb toward the television.

"Especially after that. The whole government would grind to a halt while they investigated and pointed fingers."

"You're right about that," Jake agreed, "but we can't let the bastard get away with what he's doing. Another four years of this shit—" He swept his hand over the table. "—and this country could be in real trouble."

Simon exchanged a look with his two female compatriots. "We all agree on that."

Jake cocked his head, giving Simon the eye-to-eye. "You've got something in mind, Leonidovich, I can see that."

Simon smiled to himself, he couldn't help it. "You're going to love this."

CHAPTER THIRTY-EIGHT

The White House

The White House was growing significantly larger and Simon was feeling significantly smaller by the second. *Holy Christ,* how did he ever talk himself into this? The idea—*if it were up to me*—when it first came to him, was only a fantasy, one of those endless little mind games everyone indulged in, but now . . . now that he was actually going to attempt it, to try and turn fantasy into reality, it seemed more than outrageous, it seemed suicidal. To think that he, Simon Leonidovich, could go head-to-head with the President of the United States and—

"You okay?" Jake asked as the limousine rolled slowly toward the West Wing portico. "You're kind of a funny color."

"I'm a little nervous," Simon admitted. He actually felt a little sick, cold and sweaty at the same time. "You've been here before, right?"

"Couple of times," Jake answered. "Just the usual grip and grin kind of stuff."

"Grip and grin?"

"You'll see. Nothing to worry about."

Right, nothing to worry about if you were Big

Jake Rynerson. "Easy for you to say, Rynerson. I've never been in the same room with a President, let alone—" He gestured out the window at a panorama he had seen a thousand times on television but which now looked awesomely large and intimidating. "Let alone—"

"Just bricks and mortar," Jake interrupted. "Bricks and mortar. The power lies in the institution, not the building."

"That's what worries me."

"The institution, not the man. All you gotta do is keep reminding yourself that he's nothing but a dishonest, thieving polecat and you're the American taxpayer. That's a much bigger constituency."

Great, as if he didn't have enough to worry about, he now had the weight of the American taxpayer on his shoulders. "I'll be sure to point that out."

"You won't need to. That's your ace in the hole, Simon boy, he knows it." Jake pushed open the door almost before the wheels stopped turning. "Let's do this here thing. Might be kinda fun."

Kinda fun! Playing tease and tickle with Caitlin was fun. Skiing was fun. White-water rafting was fun. Playing chicken poker with the President of the United States *did not* sound like fun.

Though it might have been the President's house, it was obvious from the moment the two Marine guards snapped open the doors that Big Jake Rynerson was that day's star attraction. Bette Ann Collins, the President's personal secretary, was wait-

ing at the reception desk, ready to escort them to
the Oval Office the moment they signed in. Simon
followed behind, content to hide in the big man's
shadow, but very aware of people lingering in door-
ways and grabbing not-so-casual peeks at the *Vegas
cowboy*. Bette Ann led them down the hall, through
her office, and without announcement directly into
the royal sanctum.

Sitting behind his desk, either working or pretending to, the President leaped to his feet, his lips
stretching back over his gleaming white teeth. "Big
Jake!" He came around the desk in an exuberant
rush, his hand outstretched. "I'm so glad you called."

Though he looked absolutely sincere, Simon knew
better, and realized immediately why the man was so
popular. Lincoln might have been right about not
being able to fool all of the people all of the time, but
that was before the age of media politics, where you
only had to *look good* to be elected.

Jake countered the big smile with one of his own.
"Thank you, Mr. President, I appreciate you making
time for us on such short notice."

"Well of course I'd make time for you," the President scoffed. "I'm sure you're—" He stopped midsen-
tence. "And this must be Mr. Leonidovich." He
engulfed Simon's hand in one of those two-handed,
I'm-your-new-best-buddy handshakes. "It's a real
pleasure. Any friend of Big Jake Rynerson is a friend
of the President."

Simon forced a smile. "Thank you, Mr. President."
He could barely push the words past the nervous

bubble in his throat and they came out a bit strangled. *Way to go, Leonidovich, let the man know you're not intimidated by his title or eggy-shaped office.*

"May I call you Simon?"

Before Simon could clear his throat the President had turned away, back to the person he assumed to have the juice. "It is so great to have you here, Big Jake. We need a picture." He nodded to his secretary who was still standing in the door, clearly anticipating the command. "Bette, please ask Larry to step in here."

In the time it took the photographer to arrive— and it only took seconds—Simon took a visual tour of the world's most famous office. The walls were lined with an impressive collection of early American luminaries, the portraits separated by bookshelves containing a few leatherbound books and many photographs: political dignitaries and corporate moguls. Near the President's desk, which looked more like a museum piece than a place of labor, stood two gigantic globes: one of the earth, and one of the stars. A reminder, Simon supposed, of presidential power and limitations. Interspersed around the room were various objects of art, including a large bust of George Washington and another of Andrew Carnegie, which struck Simon as somewhat prophetic considering the industrialist's predatory reputation and the President's profiteering.

"Here he is," the President announced as the photographer hurried into the room. With regimental precision, the man positioned Jake and the President in front of the grand desk, and *click,* it was over, a routine that was obviously repeated numerous times a day. *Grip and grin,* Simon thought, as he was moved into position and the routine repeated. The President patted him on the back. "A little memento of your visit."

Simon faked another smile. A keepsake that would not be kept.

The President motioned toward a grouping of chairs and two half-moon couches arranged in an oval pattern that matched the shape of the room and encircled a huge Presidential seal embossed into the carpet. "Let's sit over here." But before they had taken a step, as if on cue, John Paul Estes emerged from a side door and the President launched into introductions. "Gentlemen, I'm sure you know my Chief of Staff, Mr. Estes."

Everyone shook hands, all smiling and nodding and showing teeth. The President took the chair at one end of the ellipsis, just beyond his seal of power. Simon took the couch opposite Jake, while Estes settled into a chair on the President's right. Without preamble, prompting, or Presidential permission, and obviously thinking he knew exactly why Jake had called, Estes took over. "Mr. Rynerson, I know you must be concerned about those papers you gave the President Sunday evening, a matter the President has asked me to investigate."

Jake smiled, as if that was exactly why he had called.

"First of all, let me express—" Estes glanced at

Simon before turning his attention back to Big Jake. "—to both of you, how thankful we are that you brought this matter to our attention." He glanced at the President, as if to assure everyone he was speaking on behalf of the Administration, then continued, his tone extremely solemn. "I'm afraid the matter is both sensitive and serious." He paused and took a deep breath, as if it pained him to even discuss it. "Sensitive because it deals not only with our national security, but with the reputation of the CIA and Director Stark." He grimaced. "The late Director."

Estes droned on for another five minutes—his tone reportorial, as if everything he said was a matter of simple truth—blaming the Director for engaging in what he called *an unauthorized and clandestine mission* to overthrow the government of Kim Jong-il, then excusing his conduct as the desperate and misguided action of a good man destabilized by the death of his wife and children. Simon hardly listened—none of it had any impact on *his mission*—and concentrated on trying to calm his nerves.

The second Estes began to run out of gas, the President took over. "Thank you, John." Like Estes, the President directed his attention toward Big Jake. "I think you can understand why I hesitate to do anything. What good would it do?" He frowned and turned up his hands in a gesture of frustration. "This whole affair, combined with the deaths of the Vice President and the Director, is so shocking, so devastating to the nation, I see no compelling justification for exposing this matter to Congress or the press. The American public has suffered enough."

Jake bobbed his head sympathetically. "I couldn't agree with you more, Mr. President."

The President turned to Simon. "And you, Mr. Leonidovich, what do you think?" It was obvious from his tone that he didn't really care, that with Big Jake's support he considered the matter a fait accompli.

Simon nodded, knowing this was his moment. "Yessir, Mr. President, I see no good reason to disparage the reputation of Director Stark." He took a quick breath and silently thanked the gods that his voice hadn't faltered. "It's your reputation that concerns me."

The President blinked, staring at Simon as if he had just popped into existence from another dimension. "*My* reputation?"

"That's what I wanted to see you about," Jake interjected. "Simon finds himself stuck with a whole big slew of documents. Documents which could prove quite embarrassing to your administration, sir."

"I don't understand." He gave them both a puzzled, slightly wary look. "Different documents? What do you mean 'stuck with'?"

"I'm a professional courier," Simon answered. "After the tragedy in Normanstone I was left holding documents that I believe—" It was only a small lie, and who could argue with what he believed? "—were intended for the Vice President."

The President hesitated, the wheels grinding behind his brown eyes. "I'm still . . . What kind of documents are we talking about here?"

"Documents," Simon answered, "relating to your personal business affairs, Mr. President."

"My business affairs!" The President hooted, as if this were some kind of buffoonery, but the sound came out a little choked. "You're joking?"

"No, sir. A complete dossier of transactions."

"Transactions! What kind of transactions? What in the hell are you talking about?"

"I'm talking about high crimes and misdemeanors, Mr. President."

The President leaped to his feet, his jaw flexing, as if someone had slapped his face. "That's preposterous! Utterly preposterous!"

Estes was on his feet too, advancing on Simon like an outraged banty rooster. "How dare you come into the Oval Office and . . ." His words trailed away as the shadow of Big Jake Rynerson suddenly darkened his face.

For a moment—a lifetime that probably lasted less than five seconds—no one moved or uttered a sound, then the President seemed to deflate, collapsing back in his chair with an audible sigh. "What kind of dossier? Who prepared it?"

Estes squared his shoulders and raised his chin, trying to regain control. "I'd advise you not to say anything, Mr. President."

The President looked blankly at his Chief of Staff, almost as if he didn't recognize the man, then he sighed again and turned away. "Mr. Estes, I think it's best if you left the office."

Estes stared at the President in disbelief. "What? I mean, sir . . . you can't—"

"Get out."

Another cold silence followed, no one saying a word as Estes stalked from the room. Simon pulled a two-page list from the pocket of his suit coat—a summarized compilation of offshore corporations, hidden accounts, and foreign depositories the President used to hide his illegal profiteering—and handed it to the President. "This is a summary, sir. I have in my possession over two thousand pages of detailed information."

The President hardly glanced at the list. "Who gave you this information?"

Not about to reveal how he *found* the manila envelopes in two public newspaper racks, whose ownership could be contested in the courts, Simon pretended to misunderstand the question. "Like I said, I believe the information was intended for the VP. It seems to me I now have a legal obligation to turn the documents over to the Attorney General."

Jake leaned forward, his expression sympathetic. "I'll be very candid, sir. Simon was dead set against coming here today. The man's a real Boy Scout, you know what I mean? Stubborn as a mule, but I convinced him coming to you first was the right thing to do. Like you said, 'the American public has suffered enough.'"

The President nodded deliberately, trying desperately to marshal his resources. "Yes. Absolutely. I'm so thankful you did." He looked anything but thankful. "I can guarantee you the documents are nothing more than an attempt to bring down my administration. It's all a bunch of lies and fabrications."

"I would hope so," Big Jake responded. "Any man does that to my country, I'd strangle the bastard myself."

The President attempted a smile, but it congealed in the middle of his face, somewhere between a grimace and an awkward grin. "You have my word. The word of the President."

"I believe you," Jake said. "Sure do. That's what's so darn great about our Constitution, Mr. President, you'll be given a fair opportunity to prove exactly that."

The President's Adam's apple bobbed up and down in an involuntary swallow. "Prove it?"

"Yessir," Jake answered. "In front of Congress and the whole damn world."

"You're talking impeachment?"

"Nothing to worry about. Clinton survived."

"But—" His eyes bounced to Simon, then back to Jake. "But you agreed, another scandal would rip this country apart."

"Oh, yessir, I sure do agree with that," Jake acknowledged. "This couldn't happen at a worse damn time."

"That's right," the President agreed quickly, unable to keep the hope from his voice. "We need to handle this in some other way."

Simon leaned forward, feeling more confident by the second. "Some other way, sir?"

"Well, I mean . . . you know . . . the documents are false. Why should you—"

"I'm sorry," Simon interrupted, not wanting to give the man time to think. "I have a legal responsibility to turn over the documents."

"But there must be some other way. I mean . . . surely . . ."

"Well . . ." Simon hesitated, as if considering the idea for the first time. "You could resign, I suppose."

The man went pale, as if the tan had just run out of his face. "Resign?"

Simon nodded. "It would save the country from another terrible trauma. What's done is done, no reason for the public to ever know."

"And you would get to keep all those nice government perks," Jake added helpfully. "Office. Staff. Secret Service protection."

The President looked back and forth between them, at long last realizing he had no allies in the room and no place to run. "Would that do it?" he asked bitterly. "I resign and no one would ever know—" He flourished the list. "—about this?"

Jake turned to Simon. "What do you think?"

Simon feigned a look of uncertainty. "There's no Vice President, who's next in line?"

The President answered, his voice barely more than a whisper. "The Speaker."

"Well, shit, that's no good," Jake responded. "That guy's nothin' but a damn bureaucrat."

"Jesus Christ," the President snapped, "will you two stop breaking my balls! Everyone in Washington is a bureaucrat."

"Almost," Simon agreed. "Except for the rookies. I guess you'll just have to appoint a new VP before you resign."

The President gave up all pretense of resistance. "Who are you suggesting?"

Simon smiled to himself; it wasn't every day a person got to pick a President. "I like that new senator from New Mexico."

"Jimenez! Are you crazy?"

Jake cocked his head thoughtfully, as if Simon hadn't suggested the name only a couple of hours earlier. "Interesting idea. That sure is someone who knows how to get things done. Former CEO of a Fortune 500 company . . . never a hint of scandal . . . guaranteed quick confirmation. I have to hand it to you, Simon boy, that's a real nice choice."

The President looked as if he had never heard anything quite so preposterous. "But . . . but the senator's an Independent. Not even a member of my own party."

"True enough," Simon agreed. "And you'll go down in history as the man who made it happen. Our first Hispanic president."

"But—" The President took a deep breath, trying one final time to mobilize some resistance. "And if I refuse?"

"Then you'll probably go to jail," Jake snapped back. "Certainly you'll go down in history as the most corrupt sonofabitch to ever sit in this here office."

"And," Simon added, "the government would probably seize your assets."

"I'd make sure of it," Jake added. "You screwed the pooch, Mr. President. Time to pay the piper."

Screwed the pooch! Simon could barely keep a straight face. "It's your choice, Mr. President."

The President looked away, staring out the window at the Rose Garden. "How long do I have?"

Those were the words Simon had been waiting to hear. "No rush, Mr. President, I just want to hear the announcement of Senator Jimenez as your new VP." He glanced at his watch—5:44—aware that this was a historic occasion, despite the fact that no one would ever know about it. "Forty-eight hours, Mr. President, not a second longer."

Las Vegas

Friday, 16 July 16:05:46 GMT –0800

Though he heard the key in the lock, Simon didn't even have time to extract himself from his couch-potato hibernation before Caitlin was inside, the door shut behind her. *"Ooooooweeeeee!* It must be a hundred and twelve degrees out there." She leaned back against the door, reached down and slipped off her shoes, a pair of stylish crossover-tie sandals. "I nearly fried my tootsies getting to the door."

"One hundred and fourteen," Simon said, "if you believe CNN." He pushed himself upright and muted the television. "You're home awfully early for a Friday."

"Nothing going on." She reached down, untied her fabric belt and dropped it next to the mail on the entryway table. "Everyone's hovering in front of a television somewhere. The casino's so quiet you could actually hear the clocks."

"Casinos don't have clocks."

"Precisely." She reached behind her back—a dexterity unique to the female sex—pulled down the zipper of her linen sundress, and in one fluid motion slipped it over her head. "The old-timers say it hasn't been this dead in Vegas since JFK's funeral."

Dead—funeral. He could think of at least two very bad puns but resisted the temptation. "Sorry."

"It's not your fault."

If only she knew. "I like your outfit, Wells." She was now down to a lacy French bra and flesh-colored tanga panties.

She gave him a little no-no finger wave. "Don't you go getting any frisky ideas, Leonidovich. I'm so hot I could—" She suddenly realized what she was saying and stopped herself. "Don't say it. Don't even think it."

Right, as if he could turn off his lustful thoughts with her standing there looking as cool and delicious as a frappuccino crème. "Can I get you anything? A glass of champagne to celebrate the big day?"

She shook her head. "Later." She plopped down on the couch next to him. "I want to take a shower first."

"I volunteer to scrub your back."

She narrowed her eyes, though failed to hide a little grin. "I'll consider the offer." She sank back against the cushions and looked at the television. "You been watching this all day?"

He followed her eyes, the swearing in of Senator Angel Jimenez as the new President. A replay he had seen a least six times. "Pretty much. You?"

She shook her head, the boyish cut of taffy-blond hair, not so much in answer as dismay. "I still don't believe it."

"Which part?"

"All of it," she answered. "Every bit of it. I didn't believe it when the President tapped an Independent for his new VP. I didn't believe it when the Senate confirmed the nomination in less than a week. I didn't believe it when the President suddenly resigned because of a little heart murmur and wanted to spend more time with his wife." She made a little sound of disparagement, like spitting a gnat off the tip of her tongue. "And—" She cocked her chin at the television. "—I sure as hell don't believe that."

Despite his own part in the drama, Simon wasn't sure he believed it himself. "You have to admit, it's pretty compelling stuff."

She gave him a sideways look. "You sure you didn't have anything to do with this, Leonidovich?"

He hated to lie, but they had all agreed: this was one secret no one could share. One tiny whisper and the press would never let go, the Congressional hearings would never stop, and their lives would never be the same. "You've asked me that a dozen times," he answered, avoiding the direct question. "Stark must have done something that forced the President's hand." *True.* "I doubt if we'll ever know the whole story." *Also true.*

"But—"

"But what?" he interrupted, purposely letting a bit of annoyance bleed into his voice. "You'd prefer someone else?"

She looked back at the television and smiled, the proud beaming grin of a schoolgirl who has just discovered that girls too can grow up to become doctors and astronauts and . . . "You know better than that. I can't even say it without smiling."

"Say what?"

"Madam President."

POCKET BOOKS
PROUDLY PRESENTS

The Next Simon Leonidovich Thriller

Coming soon from
Pocket Books

Turn the page for a preview. . . .

CHAPTER ONE

The Pacific Pearl, Macau

"Everything is now better," Quan said, turning over another page of blueprints. He was a slight man in his mid-forties, rather formal in manner, with high cheekbones and saffron-colored skin, dressed in a custom-tailored linen suit and soft leather brogues. "Much better."

Better! Patience was not one of Jake Rynerson's virtues, and it took all his willpower just to remain seated at the table while Li Quan methodically recounted everything that was being done to accelerate the pace of construction. *Better* wasn't good enough, not when a new world order hung in the balance.

As he continued, Quan delicately smoothed down the large dappled sheet of blueprint paper. "Interior work should be back on schedule within two weeks." He spoke with an unusual accent, not quite Chinese, not quite English, a byproduct of his Oxford education. "As you see—" His voice echoed through the cavity of unfinished space: a revolving cocktail lounge two hundred feet above the casino floor. "We have tripled our workforce." He motioned toward the teakwood balustrade, an intricately carved serpentine of dragons.

Though Jake hardly needed anyone to point out the obvious, he realized his attention was expected, and glanced down at the beehive of workers and craftsmen swarming over his magnum opus, and what he now feared would be his albatross. The main tower was a typical John Portman design—huge open atrium with plants hanging off the indoor balconies—except nothing about the Pearl was *typical*. Every suite offered two breathtaking views: outward, over the Pearl River Delta; and inward, over five acres of green felt tables. It was by far the most spectacular of all the new resorts in Macau, exceeding even his own lofty expectations, but he was already late to the party, the last of the large gaming corporations to open in what was predicted to be the new Mecca of gambling. If he hoped to lure the high rollers away from the other resorts, he needed to open with a splash . . . and if he hoped to save the new Pacific Rim Alliance, he needed to open *on time*, something that no longer seemed possible. *Holy mother of Texas!*—he couldn't imagine the ramifications: the hotel booked to capacity . . . Streisand coming out of retirement to open the showroom . . . the collapse of a year-long secret negotiation.

"Three shifts," Quan continued, "working twenty-four hours a day."

Nothing Jake didn't already know. He would have cut the man off, but the Chinese were different from Westerners; they didn't understand his mercurial temperament, and he couldn't afford to offend his general manager four weeks before the scheduled opening. Billie, sitting between the men like a bridge between East and West, dipped her chin, acknowledging her husband's unusual restraint, her subtle way of telling him to keep his big yap shut. He took a deep breath, then let it out long and slow, all the way to the bottom, trying to control his anxiety. How could he have been so confident? The secret was too big, the time too short. All those bigger-than-life headlines must have turned his brain into bullcrap.

BIG JAKE RYNERSON, BUSINESSMAN AND BILLIONAIRE, TAKES ON SOCIALIST CHINA

VEGAS COWBOY RIDES INTO MACAU—CAN HE DELIVER?

Yup, that was it, his balls had finally outgrown his brain. He had clearly succumbed to the myth of his own infallibility. What did he know about Chinese politics? About Chinese superstition? How was a dumb ol' cowboy from west Texas supposed to *appease the Gods, blow away the bad spirits, and soothe the sleeping dragons?* Of all the stupid things he'd done in his life, this had to be the worst—not counting wives two, three, and four—three acts of lunacy he preferred not to think about. At least he'd been smart enough to marry his first wife twice—he gave Billie a little wink—the *best* decision he ever made.

"Of course," Quan went on, "much depends on the weather."

Jake swiveled toward the windows—a 360-degree panorama overlooking the mainland, the islands, and the South China Sea—a spectacular view if not for the onslaught of rain hammering away at the glass, a two-day downpour that showed no signs of letting up.

"It won't last," Billie said, sounding more hopeful than confident. "We're going to make it."

Jake nodded, trying to put on a good face, but he didn't believe it. It was the beginning of typhoon season, the time of black rain, and the onslaught could last for days. *Weeks, maybe,* and if the problems continued . . . they were already $82 million over budget . . . but that was only money, that he could handle . . . it was all the political bullshit . . . the set-in-stone timetable established by some *feng shui* master . . . that's what he couldn't handle.

Li Quan stared at the rivulets of water streaming down the glass, then turned over his hands, a gesture of helplessness. "Very bad joss."

Jake kept his eyes fixed on the gray horizon, barely able to restrain his desire to terminate the man on the spot. Quan was an excellent administrator, but his Chinese mindset—his propensity to blame all problems on *bad joss*—was almost too much. Luck had nothing to do with it. Too many things had gone wrong. *Big things*: a crane buckling under the weight of an air-conditioning unit and crushing two welders; a misplaced wrench tearing out the guts of the hotel's grand escalator, a curving triple-wide mechanical marvel that cost over four million dollars; the sudden collapse of a construction elevator, killing four workers; and two days ago—only hours after the security netting had been removed from the tower—a building inspector had somehow gotten past the retainment barrier and fallen off the roof. Problems that were costing him a fortune to keep out of the press, and far too many to be written off as *bad joss*. "No, Mr. Quan, I don't believe luck has anything to do with it. Someone's behind this."

A wave of confusion rolled across Li Quan's face. "Behind this . . . ?" He turned to the window, obviously wondering how *someone* could control the weather. "I don't—"

Billie, who had an aggravating and somewhat mystic insight into exactly what her husband was thinking, interrupted. "Excuse me, Mr. Quan"—she glanced at her watch, a gold, wafer-thin Gondolo by Patek Philippe with a crocodile strap—"but I think it's time for the uniform review." She nudged Jake's boot with her foot, a reminder that Li Quan knew nothing about the secret negotiations, the proposed alliance, or the true significance of the opening date.

"Right," Jake said, more in answer to Billie's unspoken warning than to what she had said. "Let's get that over with."

"*Hai,*" Quan responded, a relieved lift in his voice. "We should not keep them waiting." He snatched up his two-way radio and began chattering away in rapid-fire Cantonese, the most common dialect within the province. It was that single talent—Li Quan's ability to communicate with the Macanese staff—that kept Jake from making an immediate management change.

Within minutes people began streaming out of

the crystal-domed glass elevators that ascended silently along one side of the atrium, a male and female employee from each department: bellhops and parking valets, hosts and hostesses, janitors and maids, dealers and croupiers, bartenders and cocktail servers, food servers, limousine drivers, and at least a dozen more. As Li Quan began lining everyone up along the front of the balustrade, Billie leaned over and whispered, "You have to be careful, Jake. You can't afford to offend the man. We need him."

He nodded, not about to argue but knowing what he really needed to get the place open was a hard-charging ball-buster like Caitlin Wells.

"And," Billie added, "you can forget about Caitlin. She can't speak the language."

Damn woman, he was starting to think she could read his mind. "Give me a little rope, darlin'. I ain't senile yet."

"Besides, you need her in Vegas. She's got enough to handle with the expansion of the Sand Castle."

As if he needed to be told. "I know that, Billie."

"I know you know, but you look a bit short on patience." She gave him a teasing smile, the kind that could still make his old heart giddyup and gallop. "So I'm *reminding* you."

"Well I don't need *remindin'*," he whispered back, though they both knew that wasn't true. "But if I hear *bad joss* one more time, that boy's gonna be wearing one of my boots up the backside of his fundament."

She chuckled and patted Jake's knee as Li Quan began his fashion parade. Though Jake smiled and nodded to each team as they paraded past the table, nothing registered, his mind struggling to find some way to speed up the construction process. He wanted to pick up a hammer, do something with his own hands, but that would look desperate, and all it would take for the press to unleash their bloodhounds. That's the way it worked: One minute he was that lovable Vegas cowboy, and the next just another dumbass cowpoke from west Texas—but either way, up or down, Big Jake Rynerson made good copy for the tabloids, and their minions were always watching. So he was stuck, hoping Mother Nature would turn her wrath elsewhere, hoping the contractor could finish before anything else went wrong, hoping the press . . .

"What do you think?" Billie asked as a casino hostess in a micro-short dress of shimmering gold stepped forward.

He felt like a lecher just looking at the girl, who couldn't have been more than eighteen, with perfect golden brown skin and pale amber eyes. "About what?"

"The dress. You think it's too flashy?" Billie pointed toward the ceiling and rolled her hand. The girl made a graceful pirouette, her pixie-cut black hair spiking outward as if charged with electricity.

Jake tried to concentrate on the dress but couldn't move his eyes beyond the hemline. "It's awful damn short."

"These girls don't have breasts, Jake. They need to show some leg."

"I got no problem with legs. We just don't want 'em flashing their fannies around, that's all."

Billie tilted her head, looking at him with amusement. "Jake, honey, you're blushing like a schoolboy."

And feeling like one. Embarrassed, he pushed himself back from the table. "It's almost nine o'clock in Vegas. I promised Caity I'd call before breakfast."

"What about the dress?"

"Whatever you think." He grabbed his cellular and started toward the back of the room, but before he could punch in Caitlin's number, the tiny unit began to vibrate. The number on the display, a Macau prefix, was not one he recognized. "Hello."

"Mr. B.J. Rynerson, this I presume?" Despite the awkward syntax, the soft feminine voice was both confident and refined, with only a hint of Cantonese accent.

Jake hesitated, moving deeper into the room. Only three women knew his private number, and this was not one of them. "And who is this?"

"My name Mei-li Cheng. Perhaps you have heard this name?"

"It's possible," he answered cautiously, though he knew the woman by reputation: a well-known power broker, and one of the few Macanese who had managed to maintain influence in the new Special Administrative Region—the SAR—that was formed when Portugal turned the province over to China in '99. "What can I do for you, Madame Cheng?"

"It is more what I can do for you, taipan."

He hated the title—*big boss*—and tried to discourage its use. "Please call me Jake."

"Jake," she repeated, somehow turning his name into something seductive. "I understand you are having problems."

Was she guessing—he knew the Macau grapevine was healthy and well entrenched—or did she know something? "The usual construction delays. Nothing more."

"Not so usual, I am told."

He wanted to know exactly what she had heard and who had said it, but was positive she would never divulge a source or any details of what she knew. That was the crux of her power—*secrets*—and she would know how to use them. "Nothing we can't handle."

"That is most gratifying to hear, taipan. I thought perhaps I could be of some small service—" She paused, her voice a teasing mixture of promise and provocation.

He could already feel her hand in his pocket and knew he was being sucked into a vortex of Chinese graft and corruption. Given a choice, he would have told her to take a flying leap off the Taipa Bridge, but if she did know something, he needed to quash the story before it spread. "Yes, it's true, we've had a few unfortunate accidents." Nothing, he was sure, she didn't already know.

"Accidents," she repeated, as if the word amused her. "I think it is more than that, taipan."

"And you could help?"

"Perhaps. I have some small experience in these matters. There are people I could speak with about these . . . *unfortunate accidents.*"

"And what's this here influence going to cost?"

She made a little sound, a disapproving exhale of breath, offended that he should be so blatant and boorish. "This is not about money, taipan."

He knew better. Once a person acquired that ludicrous title of *businessman and billionaire,* it was always about money. "Please excuse my ignorance, Madame Cheng. I'm just a simple *qai loh,* and a cowboy to boot."

"A foreigner, yes, but we both know you are neither ignorant or simple, taipan. You misunderstood my offer."

"Which was . . . ?"

"To welcome a new friend into the colony. To provide assistance. Your problems are my problems."

He didn't believe a word of it. "That's much appreciated, ma'am. Sure is."

"We should discuss these problems."

Or more accurately, the cost of eliminating them, a situation he could see no way to avoid. If he went to the police—who cared nothing about the problems of a rich *qai loh*—the story would leak out; and if he didn't pay, the *accidents* would continue. The only question was the amount it would take to make the problems go away. "Yes, ma'am. I'm listening."

"These are not matters to be discussed over the phone."

Right, you don't discuss bribes and offshore bank accounts over the airwaves. "What do you suggest?"

"A private meeting."

And you don't discuss such matters in front of witnesses, which was perfectly fine with him. "When and where?"

"I am at your service, taipan."

He glanced at his watch—4:51—and realized the day was rapidly slipping away and the Pacific Rim Alliance was that much closer to dissolving. "Is today convenient?" He tried not to sound as desperate as he felt, but could hear it in his own voice. "Say, nine o'clock?"

"Ten," she answered instantly, obviously aware she had him on the hook and could reel him in at will. "You are familiar with the *Leal Senado*?"

"The old senate building?"

"*Hai*. From there you must walk."

He pressed the RECORD button on his cell phone. "Give me directions, I'll find you."

Billie leaned forward over the white tablecloth, her whispered voice as tight as the strings on a violin. "This isn't like you, Jake. You've never paid a bribe in your life."

He shrugged, trying to keep it casual, nothing he couldn't handle. "I've never done business in China."

"It's too dangerous," she fired back, her words echoing through the dimly lit bistro. "Forget it."

He gave her his best good-ol'-boy smile, trying to dampen the fire in her eyes. "You sure do look spectacular when you're angry."

"Don't you try and sell me with that cowboy bull-shit. Don't even try. I'm too old to buy, and too smart to believe."

"I mean it, Billie." And he did. She might have acquired a few wrinkles around the eyes and mouth, but it was a face, built on a magnificent superstructure of bones, that didn't depend on makeup and perfect skin. "You look as good as the day we got married."

She frowned in mock disgust, though her eyes sparkled with affection. "Like that's a big whoop. We've only been married two years."

"I meant the first time."

"You're so full of bullshit, I'm surprised those baby blues haven't turned brown over the years." She dropped her voice another notch. "What else did he say?"

She assumed it was a man, and he saw no reason to say otherwise: Her thinking he was meeting some Chinese seductress in the backstreets of Macau would only exacerbate the problem. "That was it. The person who called was just a go-between."

"You don't know that."

No, but he believed it. Mei-li Cheng was a political parasite who lived off the misfortune of others; she didn't create the problems. "It doesn't matter."

"It does matter. You're one of the richest men in the world. You can't start paying bribes to everyone who tries to shake you down. For all you know, it's the Triad."

"The Triad hasn't operated in Macau since '98.

These are just some local yahoos trying to score a few bucks from the newest *qai loh* wanting to play in their sandbox."

"I don't think so."

That was the problem with Billie, too damn smart. They both realized the *accidents* were too severe for a bunch of local yahoos. "Why?"

"If this was just about money," she answered, "they would have made a try after the escalator got trashed and before a bunch of innocent people got killed."

He shook his head, but that was exactly his thinking. There was something else going on, something he didn't understand. "There's no reason to worry; they just want to be sure nothing is being recorded. They'll give me an amount and the number of some offshore account, and I'll be back at the hotel in less than an hour. Besides"—he glanced around, making sure no one was eavesdropping on their conversation—"I don't really have a choice. If these accidents continue, we'll never get the place open in time. The Alliance will fail."

"That's not your problem."

"The President made it my problem. I gave my word."

"Don't do it, Jake." She reached out and clutched his hand, the way a person does at 30,000 feet in bad weather. "Please, I've got a very bad feeling about this."

"I've got to, honey. You know I do." He gave her fingers a reassuring squeeze. "I'll be careful."

She cocked her head toward the three-man security team near the door. "At least take one of them."

"Can't do it. The instructions were very specific. Alone. If I don't follow through, there'll be another accident tomorrow. You can bet on it."

She released his hand and slumped back into her chair, resigned.

Ten minutes later he was on the *Avenida de Almeida Ribeiro,* the main thoroughfare dividing the narrow southern peninsula from northern Macau. Despite the late hour and the rain, there was still an abundance of foot traffic, a combination of tourists and locals. Jake pulled the collar of his Gore-Tex jacket up around his neck and hunched over, trying to conceal his massive frame. But it was hopeless, like trying to hide Paul Bunyan in a land of midgets, and he gave up the effort. Guided by street names etched onto *azulejos*—the distinctive blue enameled tiles of Portugal—he turned north on *Rue de Camilo Pessanha,* then west toward the inner harbor, moving deeper into old Macau: a maze of narrow, cobbled streets offering a colorful mixture of shops, churches, and small cafés.

After twenty minutes of back and forth and around, he was thoroughly confused, blindly following Madame Cheng's directions into the hodgepodge of alleyways and backstreets, away from the tourists and pedicabs. From time to time he had the feeling of being watched, eyes following his every move, but he saw nothing and dismissed the apparitions as the products of an overstressed imagination.

Another few turns and he found himself in a dimly lit area of closed shops, the foggy street empty of people. Though the rain had eased to a drizzle, the humidity was thick enough to chew, and his shirt was now soaked through with sweat. He stepped into the covered entryway of a Chinese apothecary, peeled off his jacket, then checked his notes in the reflected glow of his cell phone. *Almost there.* He leaned out into the misty rain, checking the street for any sign of activity. *Nothing,* but he could feel something, or someone, and he didn't like it. The place was too dark and remote, the whole scenario too much like an old Charlie Chan movie the moment before everything went bad. But what choice did he have? If he didn't show up, there would be another accident, more innocent people dead. And that's all it would take—one more accident, and they would miss that magic *feng shui* timetable; and then the dominoes would fall: Taiwan would blame Beijing, Beijing would blame the United States, and the President would have no choice but to blame that dumb ol' west Texas cowboy. *Shit.*

He stepped back into the narrow street, moving cautiously toward the hazy glimmer of a street lamp about a hundred yards ahead. It was like moving underwater, the fog softening the harsh lines of the shops into muted shades of gray, the sound of his own footsteps muffled and distant. At exactly ten o'clock a woman stepped out of the fog and into the yellow cone of light beneath the streetlight. She was dressed in a shapeless silk chemise, as garishly colored as a macaw, a cream-colored shawl draped over one arm. "Good evening, taipan." Her soft, sensual voice dissolved into the heavy air, barely spanning the short distance between them.

"*Nei ho ma?*" he answered, the standard—*Hello, how are you?*—greeting of the province. She was a short woman, not more than five foot, early forties, with black hair tied in a bun at the back of her head, and thick black eyebrows that arched together like bat wings over sharp, black eyes—ugly as a Komoto dragon. "Madame Cheng?"

She smiled coquettishly and dipped her head. "*Hai.*"

He returned the bow and stepped forward into the light. He wanted to get straight to the point, the money—the how much, the when, and the where—but that was not the way of business in China. "It is generous of you to meet me on such a night."

She smiled again, the cryptic grin of a gambler with aces in the hole. "It is my honor to serve the great taipan."

Honor. Great taipan. The bullshit words and exaggerated politeness made his skin crawl. "And it is my—" From the corner of his eye he saw a man step from the shadows, not more than ten yards away, his skin so white it seemed transparent. Dressed in a dark jogging suit and black running shoes, he had the broad shoulders and narrow hips of an athlete, and the steady hand—which held a black machine pistol—of a professional. Before Jake could react, there was another sound, from behind, someone light on their feet, coming fast, emerging out of the fog, arm outstretched, a small chrome-plated automatic waving erratically with each step.

Twisting his body to avoid a direct hit, Jake shoved Madame Cheng out of the way, but he was too slow and too late, a lightning bolt of fire burning through his chest as both guns fired simultaneously. He felt the air leave his lungs, the blood draining from his legs, the earth rising to meet him as he pitched forward onto the wet cobblestones. *You dumb-ass cowboy!*

He landed with a hard, dull thud but felt nothing, his body already numb. He could see the hem of Madame Cheng's dress, her booted feet as they peddled backward out of the light.

"Billie . . . " He gasped her name with his last bit of air, knowing it would be the final word to cross his lips.

Not sure
what to
read next?

Visit Pocket Books online at
www.simonsays.com

Reading suggestions for
you and your reading group
New release news
Author appearances
Online chats with your favorite writers
Special offers
Order books online
And much, much more!

POCKET BOOKS
A Division of Simon & Schuster
A VIACOM COMPANY

**POCKET
STAR BOOKS**
A Division of Simon & Schuster
A VIACOM COMPANY

13456